# LOVING GIA TO DEATH

RENA KOONTZ

Cover Designed by Lisa Conner, Zeto Creative

Book Design by J R Burns Consultancy

Cover Art: 123rf

This book is a work of fiction. The names, characters, places, and incidents are the products of the author's imagination or are used fictitiously. Any resemblance to actual events, business establishments, locales, or persons, living or dead, is entirely coincidental.



Published in the United States of America by

Rena Koontz

1181 S. Sumter Blvd.#143

North Port, FL. 34287

ISBN: 978-1-7322709-7-8

ISBN: 1-7322709-7-X

www.renakoontz.com

## ALSO BY RENA KOONTZ

Other Heels & Handcuffs Novels

Love's Secret Fire

Thief Of The Heart

The Devil She Knew

More From Rena Koontz

Crystal Clear Love

Broken Justice, Blind Love—Award Winner

Off The Grid For Love—Award Winner

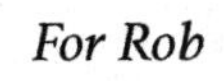

*For Rob*

## ACKNOWLEDGMENTS

My biggest champion—my husband Jed

The nurses in my life—Candy, Sheila, Nora, Helen,
Deb, and Rachael

Debbie Kaszniak—my reader and friend
Jeff O.—for his technical assistance and
the Deep Creek fire station tour
All nurses, police, fire, and law enforcement personnel—thank
you for your service.

# LOVING GIA TO DEATH

RENA KOONTZ

# 1

The 9-1-1 emergency call from his home address sent chills down his back like nails scraping against a chalkboard. Lieutenant Blake Matthews jerked out of his chair so forcefully, it crashed backward with a loud bang.

When on duty, he listened but didn't actually hear the near constant sounds that reverberated through the fire station every day. The radio transmissions faded into the background as white noise until Station Twelve's distinctive two-level tones sounded. Then, just like every man's in the fire station, his ears perked up.

He sat elbow deep in training manuals and spreadsheets, designing a new special ops rescue program for the team when the tones cut through his concentration, and crimped his heart. Before he reached the door to exit the training room, a younger firefighter wrenched it open.

"Go!" he ordered. "I'll call someone in to cover for you ASAP."

Technically, leaving his post without being summoned to the emergency on board the back-up ladder truck or other supplemental fire equipment was a violation of protocol and grounds for suspension. But he wasn't worried. The unwritten rule in Station Twelve, and he presumed any fire department in the country, was that when it involved family, you dropped everything and took off. Your team would have your back, no questions asked.

He lived with these men twenty-four hours a day, every third day, and they were his family too, as much as the daughter he'd created. No one ate, slept, and risked their lives for strangers without forming an impenetrable bond with the man on his right and left side and the squad watching his six. What affected one of them touched all of them.

He raced to his personal truck, barely hearing someone yell from the building to keep them apprised. By now, the ambulance had reached his daughter so he listened to the radio transmissions to decide if he should rush to the house or head to the hospital.

Uncontrolled nausea? How could that be? He'd spent the day with Gia yesterday and she was fine. Laughing that little girl laugh that melted his heart. Sitting on his lap playing a game on his phone. Turning that angel face up to him to cajole him into buying three new frilly headbands instead of two, which was his quantity rule. Hell, she could convince him to buy out the whole store if she tried hard enough. Nothing was too good for his baby girl. And today she was sick enough to require an ambulance? He couldn't fathom it.

He picked up on the paramedics' transmission. They were transporting Gia to Children's Hospital. He'd be waiting.

Paramedic Joe Lystle jumped to his feet when the shrill emergency tone sounded, instinctively listening for the medical details bouncing off every corner of the firehouse. He ran to the ambulance, his half-eaten sandwich forgotten.

"Not again," he snapped. "When is he going to see it? And stop it, for crissake?"

A five-year-old reportedly convulsing, throwing up non-stop

when her panicked mother dialed 9-1-1, the dispatcher relayed. But this wasn't merely any five-year old. This was Argia, the lieutenant's daughter.

Joe and his partner, Rob Yarnell, strapped on their gear with lightning speed while the dispatcher disclosed more specifics about the child's emergency. Uncontrolled nausea. Dehydration. Transport to the hospital STAT.

He cursed and activated the siren.

Rob stomped the gas pedal so hard, the ambulance jerked into motion. "This could be the real thing, Joe. We don't know."

"Dammit, Rob. We know."

Any emergency call automatically spikes a first responder's adrenaline, but when the victim is family, as all members of Deep Creek Fire Station Twelve were to each other, the need to arrive sooner becomes imperative. He mimicked the action when Rob floored the gas.

"We need a sit-down, Joe, that's what I say. It's gonna have to be me. He's gonna be pissed and argue with us. It'll be hard for him to hear but I don't think he'll be mad enough to take a swing at me. If he does, I hope I duck in time. I've seen what he lifts in the weight room."

He nodded and leaned forward in his seat, as if that helped shove the traffic in front of the ambulance out of their way. "Yeah, he'll be mad. He's the classic example of love being blind. But he knows we care about Argia like she was our own. Still, we'll be stepping out of bounds if we tell him what we think."

The ambulance screeched to a halt in front of Blake Matthews' driveway, automatically attracting a crowd of onlookers who spilled out onto their front porches. Joe looked around while he yanked the emergency equipment from the rear ambulance compartment. Why were so many people at home in the middle of the day?

Lynne Matthews burst out of her front door screaming for them to hurry. He braced himself for another irate interaction with the woman. They'd had them before. Just looking at her nauseated him. She splayed her hands against the sides of her face.

"What the hell took you so long?" Her right arm extended toward the house, her finger pointing inside. "My baby's in there choking to death. Can't you move any faster?"

Then she straightened and surveyed the street, assessing which neighbors watched and appeared concerned about her emergency. He rolled his eyes when she tugged on the deep V-neck midriff shirt she wore, purposefully offering an ample display of her assets. She was proud of her gifts. Considering her flare for drama, the woman should've been an actress. Especially since she now spoke as if she were center stage.

"I've never seen a child so sick before. It was all I could do to keep her hydrated. And she just kept clutching to me for dear life." She made this announcement to no one in particular. "If something happens to my darling baby, I don't think I could deal with it."

"Oh, brother," he whispered under his breath as they bypassed her and rushed into the house.

After eight years on the job, Blake knew the staff in the emergency room by their first names and he nodded a silent greeting to each one he passed. Likely they'd been informed already of the incoming transport. He snagged a cup of coffee from the EMT hospitality room and paced at the emergency entrance, barely sipping the brew. In minutes, the ambulance arrived. He ran to the rear and waited for Rob and Joe to open the doors.

Gia sat upright on the cot, an oxygen hose clipped to her nose. Nevertheless, her face erupted into a wide smile. "Daddy!"

Perched beside her, his ex-wife scowled. He stepped out of the way while Rob and Joe rolled the cot out of the ambulance, his anxiety allayed by Gia's pink cheeks and cheerful greeting. They whisked her toward the emergency doors and he turned to follow when Lynne called out to him.

"Really, Blake. Would you at least help me out of this box?"

Her hand stretched toward him in anticipation of his assistance. He fleetingly entertained the urge to leave it hanging there and walk away but his mother raised him better. He respected women and treated them accordingly. Even though his mother wasn't a fan of The Captain, Lynne's self-created position in their life, his mom would expect him to be courteous. He reached for Lynne's hand, eyeing the red high heels and mini skirt. There was a time when an outfit like that would motivate him to crawl into the ambulance with her and lock the doors behind him. But not anymore.

Seductively, she placed both hands on his shoulders and shoved her breasts in his face when she jumped out of the ambulance. Before she could speak, he released himself from her grip and ran double-time toward the emergency doors.

Rob and Joe stood at the counter completing intake paperwork. Joe directed him to the cubicle where they'd rolled Gia's gurney.

The minute he threw back the curtain and reached her bed, Gia jumped to her feet and launched herself into his arms, causing the oxygen line to snap out of her nose and an intravenous pole to roll forward when the line tugged.

"Daddy!" Her arms wrapped around his neck, a feeling he long ago decided he'd never tire of.

Blake hugged her and then, with his hands on her arms, eased her backward. "Hey, peanut. What's up? Are you sick?"

Behind him, Lynne's high-pitched response pierced the air and immediately, Gia's smile disappeared. "Of course she's sick. Why else would I summon an ambulance? She's been puking all over the house. It's been a helluva mess for me to clean up, I'll tell you that. By myself no less."

He ignored her and gazed into his little girl's eyes. "Honey, tell me where it hurts."

Wide-eyed, Gia plopped to the bed, crossing her legs Indian style. Her gaze dropped to a spot on the blanket. "I'm all better now, Daddy. It's okay."

Blake cupped his daughter's chin, the skin beneath his hand as soft as flannel. Was it?

# 2

He'd just dozed off when the baby's mournful cry echoed from a room down the hospital corridor. Blake's eyes shot open in fear that the child's yowl was his daughter's. He rose on his hands and knees off the linoleum floor to peer into the hospital crib. But his sweet Gia slept peacefully, her rosy lips puckered and moving ever so slightly with her measured breaths.

Two weeks ago, he'd rushed to this same hospital after hearing Lynne's emergency call for an ambulance, fear gripping his heart. Lynne claimed Gia had been sick to her stomach non-stop, yet he'd taken her home that same day with more questions than answers cluttering his brain. After administering routine fluids, the doctors discharged her, as bewildered as he.

And yet another emergency tonight.

The neon pink cast encasing Gia's left arm glowed in the shadows of the flickering lights from the machines surrounding her bed. His eyes followed the vines of tubing that connected the equipment to his baby girl's wrist, and the round white patches that attached to her chest, so tiny he could cover it with his open hand. He longed to lay his face on her delicate rib cage and motorboat his lips against the soft, velvety skin of her belly to elicit the squeal of delight the vibrations could draw. No song in the world matched the music of his daughter's laughter.

Somewhere down the hall, the baby's woeful cries persisted, a high-pitched wail that sounded more forlorn than painful. To Blake's ears, it was loud enough to awaken the whole floor.

His ex-wife snorted from the corner of the room, repositioned herself on the hospital cot and resumed her trombone-like snores. Far be it for anything to interrupt The Captain's sleep, including a crying baby a few rooms away. Or their daughter's welfare.

He bristled at the title she'd bestowed on herself barely six months into their marriage, informing him matter-of-factly that marriage was like sailing a ship and she was the captain. Christ, she even referred to herself as Captain Lynne. It was embarrassing.

Lynne Matthews believed it was her world and everyone lived in it to serve on her orders. Pity the ordinary sailor who failed to follow The Captain's dictates. Or the man who'd fallen in love and married her.

Well, he was hardly one to accept anyone's pity or to sit around feeling sorry for a disintegrated marriage. He was ready to sail with Gia toward a new horizon. Without The Captain. It was the right journey for all of them.

Down the hall, the baby still moaned, the octave of its cries rising and falling between gasps for breath.

Blake rose slowly, feeling every football injury and wrestling takedown from his high school and college days in his thirty-year old body. His stiffened joints reminded him he was too old to sleep on the floor. As if he needed reminding. He stretched his neck muscles and massaged his cheek, still cold and numb from being pressed against the linoleum for—how long? He had no idea when he finally fell asleep. The antiseptic odor of the floor cleaner lingered in his nostrils.

Stepping to the side of the crib, he reached to brush Gia's hair off her forehead. The fever was gone, thank goodness. He laid the backs of his fingers along her cheek, as velvety as a puppy's ear. A grateful sigh escaped him with the coolness of her skin. Had his baby girl really had such a high fever she became dizzy and tumbled down the stairs? Was she as accident prone as her mother contended?

Odd that Gia never became sick or injured herself when he had her by his side.

Her long eyelashes fluttered at his touch, but she didn't awaken. Instead, the corners of her mouth turned up in a slight smile, as if she knew he was there. Loving her. Protecting her.

Or was the light tricking his weary eyes?

One last glance at the snoring bear hibernating in the corner and he tiptoed out of the room. Normally bursting in bright lights with colorful murals of rainbows and fairy tale creatures, the corridor was darkened so the children could sleep. All but the baby down the row still taxing his lungs with his screams.

Other nurses were on the floor but only one manned the central station, her head bent over a computer keyboard. She looked up at his approach, her face void of recognition or a smile of welcome. He'd had two run-ins with this woman since arriving at the hospital tonight, panicked by Lynne's message informing him of their daughter's accident. He couldn't have been more irritated by his ex-wife's text message. Any normal person makes a phone call when there is an emergency.

Not The Captain. She might never have called if he hadn't reached out to her first. An odd feeling overcame him while he was at the softball field, almost a sense of panic that he couldn't interpret. And so, he texted Lynne between innings to check on their daughter. If he hadn't initiated the text conversation, would she have let him know Gia broke her wrist? Doubtful. The

Captain enjoyed the role of martyred ex-wife and single mother too much. And she played the part of the poor woman burdened with a sick child whose husband abandoned them both whenever possible.

That was her version of their relationship, one that she told anyone who would listen. Including this nurse on duty, who watched his approach warily.

Lynne's argument that she knew he didn't like being interrupted while at his weekly softball games didn't hold water. Gia was the most important person in the world to him. She knew that. Practically everyone did. Common courtesy dictated a phone call. After all, he was her father.

But The Captain rarely went out of her way for him these days, not that she ever did.

So he'd barreled onto this pediatric floor hours ago, hell-bent on seeing Gia and giving Lynne a piece of his mind and ran smack-dab into Nurse Noreen Jensen. She'd stopped him like a Pittsburgh Steeler offensive guard, demanding identification he didn't have on him. When he played softball, he stashed his wallet and ID in the glove box of his truck and in his haste to reach Gia after reading Lynne's text, he abandoned the game, sped to the hospital, and ran to the entrance, leaving his credentials stowed in the car.

The tenacious nurse hadn't wanted to hear his excuse, had looked down her nose at his dirt-stained uniform, and threatened to call security. In hindsight, the walk back to his vehicle to retrieve his license and badge cooled his temper and cleared his head. Gia had to be his priority.

Nurse Jensen seemed unimpressed to learn that he was a lieutenant with the city's Station Twelve Fire Company. He'd wanted to remind her that they were both dedicated to noble professions and served the public but the stick up her ass hinted she wouldn't bend.

He spent the next hours waiting for his daughter to come

out of surgery, barely speaking to Lynne from across the room once she explained the details of the accident. Complete with crocodile tears about how traumatic it had been for *her*. Never mind that Gia was the one with the wrist broken in three places. Was Lynne's version of what happened the truth? She regularly leaned toward melodrama. Could he question Gia about the events of the day without upsetting her? She was only five. Would she even remember? Maybe once he had her home and settled, tucked into her toddler's bed with Mr. Fox and Mr. Dog, her favorite stuffed animals by her side, he'd attempt it.

Nurse Jensen obviously detected the iceberg between him and The Captain and, of course, sided with Lynne. She offered her snacks and coffee and sympathy. And then the cot.

Cue confrontation number two. Gia's room wasn't big enough to accommodate two cots and Nurse Jensen informed him he'd have to leave for the night. Like hell he'd leave his daughter fresh out of surgery.

The woman stood tall in her defiance, coming to just under his chin but staring him right in the eye. It was a quality he might admire under other circumstances. But he'd be damned if he was leaving his baby's side. When he loudly informed her of that fact, she spat back that the only place to sleep was on the floor, which suited him fine and deflated her argument. She'd pivoted on her heel like a dismissed soldier and exited Gia's room without another word.

Now, their eyes locked as he approached the counter. He was too tired for Round Three.

He tilted his head in the direction of the howls and whispered, "That baby keeps crying. Why don't they pick him up or something?"

The question either surprised or insulted her, he wasn't sure. Her eyebrows lifted and her mouth puckered into a tight oval, as if she'd sucked a lemon. She sat up straighter. "There's no one in the room to pick him up. I've been in twice already but I can't spend all my time in there. I'll go back in when I can."

Her answer dumbfounded him. Perhaps he was more exhausted than he realized.

"What do you mean there's no one in there? Where are his parents?"

Her chest rose with a deep inhale that she loudly released. "Not everyone has the luxury of staying here with their child, spending the night here. Some parents have jobs to go to or other children to care for."

Did she think sleeping on the hospital floor was a luxury? He let that slide.

"Do you mind if I go in?"

She catapulted out of her seat, her hands fisted as if she prepared to fight him. "For what purpose?"

What the hell was the matter with this woman? What did she think he'd do?

He ran his hands through his hair, aware that he must look like a disheveled lunatic in a sweaty ball uniform. He couldn't stand one more minute of the baby's sobs.

"Maybe I can comfort him. Hold him. Let him know he's not alone."

The nurse's head shot back in surprise. "Why would you want to do that?"

Poor woman. Her heart must've frosted over years ago. It was the only explanation for such a frigid human being. Didn't she understand the love for a child? Any child? Until he became a parent, he hadn't fully understood the depth of a father's love. Certainly, his parents loved him, he'd known that growing up.

But when the baby was a part of you, like Gia was his own flesh and blood, the love was different. Deeper. Unconditional. Limitless. He'd die for his daughter. Or kill for her.

The baby crying in the other room wasn't his but he understood how to love a child. The day Gia was born was the day his heart blossomed. And like a wild shrub that's never been pruned, that love knew no constraints.

Hearing this crying baby gutted him. He had to do something. The nurse glared at him, waiting for an answer.

"Listening to him breaks my heart." He threw his thumb over his shoulder to indicate Gia's room. "My daughter's sleeping soundly. She doesn't need me right now." And then he shrugged. "I'd like to try to reassure him he's okay."

Slowly, she nodded and stepped around her chair to leave the horseshoe-shaped station. She motioned for him to follow her into the darkened room identical to his daughter's. Similar machines cast a dim light over the bed. The baby's fisted hands flailed in the air, his feet kicked and his perfectly round face shone beet red. He couldn't have been more than one-year old.

Blake began a soft conversation as he reached for the baby, mindful of the wires and tubes that monitored this child's progress. He touched the baby's hand and he grasped it immediately, five fragile bones wrapping around his index finger.

"Hey buddy, shh, you're okay." He rubbed the silky top side of the baby's hand. It was no bigger than a quarter and his thumb dwarfed it.

The crying lowered a decibel, but he still whispered. "It's all right, little guy. I know you're scared but the folks who work here will take good care of you."

The shuffling sound behind alerted him that Nurse Jensen stood sentry in the doorway monitoring him. Without letting go of the fragile hand, he asked over his shoulder. "What's his name?"

"William."

"What's wrong with him?"

"By law, I'm not permitted to divulge that information."

Of course not. That would be an empathetic thing to do and Nurse Noreen Jensen was anything but warm and fuzzy.

Figuring it was better to suffer the consequences rather than ask for permission, he lowered the safety rail on the bed and eased his hands beneath the baby, intent on cradling him.

The nurse was by his side in an instant. She reminded him of a mother bear protecting every baby cub on this hospital floor. He admired that. Sort of.

"What are you doing?" she snapped.

Once in his arms, William's cries softened to a whimper. With the baby tucked safely in one arm, Blake rolled the intravenous stand and second monitor away from the bed and moved to the rocking chair in the room. Gia's room had a rocker too but Lynne had loaded it up with her purse, sweater and designer shoulder bag that likely brimmed with cosmetics. He'd never understood the need for all the stuff she hauled around. She was a beautiful woman.

"I'm going to rock him for a while. Maybe he'll go to sleep."

William already was quiet, his blue eyes wide and focused on Blake. He started to rock the chair in slow movements, all the while speaking to the baby. "Relax, Willy, you'll be fine. I know you're frightened. My little girl is scared too. But there's nothing to worry about. It's gonna be okay."

Nurse Jensen watched with her hand pressed to her chest. He'd wager there was a rock beneath the fabric of her shirt instead of a beating heart. And then miracle of miracles, she smiled.

"You're a natural," she whispered. "Look."

Willy slept soundly in his arms. Still, he rocked the baby, using his free hand to caress the boy's cheek and pudgy body. "Gia likes to be rocked. I try to read to her every night before bedtime and she always crawls into the rocker."

Well, that every night ritual had been suspended when he moved out but this nurse didn't need to know that.

The brief smile disappeared while she studied him. "I thought you didn't live with your wife and daughter."

His stomach knotted. Lynne hadn't wasted any time sharing

her tale of abandonment. No wonder Nurse Jensen didn't trust him. Lynne had already brainwashed her. He'd never make this nurse understand that leaving his daughter was the only way he could save her. It'd been the hardest decision he ever made and yet, the clearest. But this stranger in giraffe-printed hospital scrubs didn't need to know any of that.

Willy released an audible sigh, his pint-sized chest rising and falling against Blake's stomach, prompting them both to refocus on the baby.

He eased out of the rocker and returned Willy to his crib. "Poor little thing must've exhausted himself with his tantrum. Maybe he'll sleep through the night now."

He'd no sooner raised the side rail and clicked it into place when an alarm sounded from the nurse's station. The intermittent beep increased in volume and repetition the longer it rang, emphasizing its urgency. Nurse Jensen ran to the counter and peered over the edge, then shot a wild-eyed look at him.

In that second, he understood the alert came from Gia's monitors. Nurse Jensen broke into a run down the hallway but his legs were longer and he beat her to the doorway. Lynne leaned over the guardrail, blocking the view of his daughter. He shot to the bed, grabbed her shoulders, and shoved her aside. The nurse was right behind him.

"What happened?" she asked, rushing to the machines.

Gia lay motionless, all color drained from her apple cheeks.

Lynne screamed. "I think it was a seizure. Her systolic BP soared." She fell to her knees, clinging to the bedrail. "Oh, my poor girl. A thrombosis might have caused it, I'm not sure. She'll be brain damaged, I know it."

He whirled on her. "Shut the fuck up. You don't know what you're talking about. You're not a goddamn doctor." And then he returned his attention to his baby girl.

"Gia? Honey, it's Daddy. Gia, wake up."

Her petite puckered lips parted, slowly spreading into a smile that lifted the weight of the world off his shoulders. Her eyes fluttered open, deep brown and focused. They were his very own Hershey's kisses on his darling daughter's buttercream face.

"Daddy, I'm still sleepy."

He choked on his tears as he reached for her, scooping her into an embrace so tight, she squirmed. "Daddy, ouchy."

"I'm sorry, sweetheart. Daddy doesn't mean to crush you." She wound her free arm around his neck, the casted one falling with a thud onto his chest and dropped her head onto his shoulder. "Still sleepy, Daddy."

Cradling her, he began a slow swing from side to side, rocking her in his arms while he turned to see the women behind him. "Daddy's got you now, Gia. Go back to sleep."

Lynne still squatted on the floor, glowering at them. For all the hysterics she'd displayed minutes earlier, her cheeks were dry of tears. And the glare she leveled on him wasn't one of fear for her child. It felt more like hatred for his interference.

Standing beside the now-silent hospital equipment, Noreen Jensen stared at Lynne, raised her eyes to him and then reached to lift Lynne off the floor. "Get up, hon, the floor is no place for you."

He stifled his retort. Nurse Noreen didn't seem to mind him sleeping on the floor but it wasn't good enough for Captain Lynne. These women were two of a kind.

"Lynne, can you tell me what happened? There's no indication that the machines malfunctioned yet something set off the alarms. By all appearances, your daughter seems fine. I don't understand."

Neither did he. What set off the emergency alert signal?

Lynne raised a trembling hand to her brow. He scowled, recognizing the gesture. She was about to perform a one-woman show for her captive audience.

"I-I don't know. Her vitals were all within the normal range. And then suddenly—" She clutched her chest and fell back against the bed as if she might faint. Noreen took the bait and grabbed for her.

"Here, here. Lie down on the cot. I'll pour you some water." Lynne stepped toward the bed as if she were feeble, unable to move without Noreen's assistance. He backed out of their way.

"You can return her to her bed, Mr. Matthews. She seems to have fallen back to sleep."

Armed Marines with orders to shoot on sight couldn't pry Gia out of his arms. "We're fine, thanks."

Noreen eyed him as she settled Lynne onto the rollaway bed and filled a glass with ice water from the pitcher on Gia's night table. He rolled his eyes after Lynne breathlessly thanked her, reached for the glass with two trembling hands, and whispered, "I'll be all right in a minute. I was just so frightened."

So typical. It always had to be about *her*.

Noreen straightened and focused on the rocker loaded with Lynne's paraphernalia. "You can't stand all night while your daughter sleeps."

If that's what it took to keep her safe he could.

She began uncluttering the rocking chair. "At least sit here." In a matter of seconds, she'd relocated Lynne's junk to the foot of Gia's bed despite Lynne's protests that her designer tote contained breakables. Noreen moved to the IV stand next to him. "I'll follow you with this."

Odd that the other monitor connections were no longer attached to Gia. He hadn't noticed the nurse disconnecting them but he didn't pay attention to either woman in his haste to reach her. Noreen didn't seem bothered by it so maybe she detached them.

Lynne sprang off the cot, her finger pointing in the air. "Shouldn't you check her out? She had an attack. You can't simply let him sit there and rock her. Aren't there tests you can run to make sure there's not internal trauma?"

Jesus. She always wanted tests run on Gia. In her short five years of life, his baby girl had endured more medical tests than any child he knew. Tests for seizures. Tests for muscular dystrophy and multiple sclerosis and conditions with initials he'd never heard of. The results always came back negative. And The Captain always discovered something else wrong.

Noreen shook her head. "She seems fine. I'll get her settled and check her vitals. At this time of night, there isn't anyone in the labs to run tests anyway."

Thank God at least one of them was sensible. Just as he'd done with Willy, he cradled his daughter and began to rock slowly, whispering his love to her. To his surprise, Nurse Noreen displayed smile number two.

"You're crimping her neck," Lynne barked. "You should return her to the bed. She's going to wake with a headache if you keep her in that position."

Hers was the neck he wanted to bend. More like break.

The Captain wasn't giving up. "Argia suffers from migraines, Noreen. He's going to increase the probability of her suffering a debilitating headache."

Endearing herself to the medical staff had always been important to Lynne. He was convinced she fantasized she was one of them. Too bad she wasn't smart enough. It didn't surprise him that Lynne was on a first-name basis with the nurse.

However, the instant change in Noreen's manner did astonish him. Any warmth he thought he detected disappeared and her stare turned cold, literally sending a chill down his spine.

Once again, he locked eyes with his current nemesis. His temper was frayed and his words, low and guttural, hinted he'd had enough of both women for tonight. "Gia doesn't have migraines. She's never had a headache. She's resting now and you're not going to move her." He glared first at Noreen and then Lynne.

"You're not home to see it. You're gallivanting who knows where every other day."

He studied Lynne's face, barely recognizing her. He'd loved her once with his whole being. Wanted her by his side for their lifetime. He'd been thrilled that they were having a child together. And now, being with her was tiresome. Draining. Slowly killing every heartfelt emotion he'd ever felt for her like an invasive weed takes over healthy grass and suffocates the life out of it.

"I'm at work, Lynne. Twenty-four hours on and forty-eight off. You know that." Twenty-four hours that he lived in fear for his daughter's safety.

Nurse Noreen stepped forward, her arms outstretched. "Mr. Matthews, perhaps—"

"No!" He snapped at her louder than he intended but Gia only snuggled closer to his chest.

Lynne snatched her cell phone from beneath the pillow on the cot. "Should I call hospital security? Or dial 9-1-1? See, I told you. He's becoming belligerent."

He shook his head in disbelief and stared at his ex-wife. It wouldn't be the first time she filed a false police report against him. But Noreen was a witness this time and she could attest he'd done nothing wrong. Refusing to return your daughter to a hospital bed wasn't illegal.

Noreen raised her hand to run interference. "There's no need to call anyone, Lynne. Mr. Matthews, if you'll—"

"Gia is fine, nurse. She's in my arms and nothing more is going to happen to her tonight. I suggest you return to your station and do whatever it is you're tasked with in the middle of the night. We'll just be one big happy family here in this room until morning."

Lynne caught her breath in dramatic fashion. "Don't leave us here with him. I'm in fear of my life. Of the welfare of my child."

The rocking halted and he leaned as far forward as he could without crushing Gia. His words dripped with the venom that flowed through his veins. "She's my child too, Lynne. And you're the one she's afraid of. Not me."

# 3

Noreen studied the couple, half expecting them to hiss like snakes. They despised each other. It was obvious. How did a man and woman who vowed to love one another until parted by death end up like this? Hating. Glaring at each other. Their body language revealing their repulsion. It made her sad. And equally angry because the little girl was caught in the middle.

He was the worst. Since Blake Matthews walked into the building, he hadn't offered his wife an ounce of comfort nor displayed the common courtesy strangers might share in an emergency.

Yet his actions toward his daughter and the sheer devotion in his gaze indicated he wasn't the cold bastard Lynne Matthews described. His conduct, both toward his daughter and Little Willy, were quite touching. She didn't doubt for one second his ability to love.

Situations like this, when a child was ill or, in this case injured, strained a tenuous marital relationship. She knew that. Had seen it enough times to be turned off by the idea of a lifetime commitment to one man. And she'd been a nurse long enough to know people presented their rawest side in these situations. But there was something more going on with these two.

Lynne shook her fist at her husband. "How dare you make that accusation? Argia loves me. She cries for me."

The woman didn't hide her anger nor was she shy about sharing details about her crumbled marriage with anyone who took the time to listen. Noreen had been an unwilling listener while she completed Argia's pre-surgical assessment, wondering why a mother would drag a child's father through the mud while the poor kid writhed in pain from a broken left arm. Instead of calming the little girl, Lynne seemed intent on painting the child as careless and making sure Argia knew how distraught her mother was because of the accident.

And then Blake Matthews came barreling onto the floor, acting like the brute of a man Lynne had described. She feared he might forcefully thrust her aside when she stopped him in his tracks demanding identification. Without offering specifics, Lynne intimated Blake had been physically abusive toward her in the past.

The odd thing though, the moment that made her question Lynne Matthews' account of her life situation, occurred when she finally allowed Blake access to his daughter. She'd followed him into the room as a precaution and witnessed the spike in Argia's heart rate and, despite the sedative starting to kick in, the smile that spread across the girl's cherub face.

Lynne exploded in a tirade when he charged into the room but Blake turned a deaf ear to her, instead rushing to Argia's bedside, calling her name, and reaching for her. Despite whatever pain she endured, Argia responded with a look of joy. "I'm here, Gia. I'm here for you," he'd whispered and Argia beamed. Turning to the monitors, Noreen noticed the higher blood pressure and pulse rates dropping, as if hearing her father's voice calmed her more effectively than any sedative. Within seconds, the girl was asleep, her right-hand clinging in her drug-induced respite to her father's calloused hand. Only after the orderly rolled Argia out of the room did he turn to Lynne and demand to know what happened. Argia had been his sole focus.

Fearful of leaving the two of them alone she'd fussed with the monitors, pretending not to eavesdrop. Lynne described a raging fever that caused Argia to plummet down the stairs. Yet her temperature registered normal by the time the ambulance transported the girl to the hospital. Blake challenged Lynne's account of Argia's mysterious illness, saying she was fine the day before, which launched Lynne into a litany of insults aimed at him. She faulted him for not being there to care for his daughter or witness her fall.

That's when Noreen interrupted and relocated them both to the surgical waiting room, effectively ending the verbal battle. In the hours it took to insert the pin and reset Argia's wrist, Noreen checked on the Matthews three times, noting that Blake's mood had swung like a pendulum to brooding silence. Lynne's brutality accusations might be on target.

But she'd seen only a doting father once Argia returned to her room, one who opted to sleep on the floor rather than leave his daughter's side. A man so moved by an unknown baby's cries, he comforted the boy. Was theirs a real-life beauty and the beast tale and Blake Matthews a man with a hidden violent side? Was he the abuser Lynne hinted at?

Noreen was good at reading people and he didn't read that way.

She studied Blake as he sat back in the rocking chair. Dark circles ringed his bloodshot eyes. The man had had a difficult night.

Lynne turned her malice on her. "Are you going to simply stand there and let him contort my daughter like that? He's probably causing spinal compression. Do something."

Blake leveled fatigued eyes on her. Challenging. Defying. Pleading for her understanding. Argia's angelic face nestled against his bulging bicep.

Taking a deep breath, she addressed Lynne. "She seems content, Lynne, and what she needs most is sleep. I think you all do. Why don't you relax on the cot and get some rest? I'm sure Argia will be fine and Mr. Matthews, if she becomes a burden feel free to lay her in bed." Both adults stared at her so she moved to the bed to tighten the sheets and avert their lines of vision.

Blake's shoulders relaxed and his head dropped to the rocker's headrest. Slowly, his eyes closed.

Lynne didn't intend to follow suit. "I can't rest here, not with him holding my child hostage. This is absurd."

Blake's lids opened in slow motion, like the curtain rising on stage, and he stared at her, waiting for a response. His muscles flexed ever so slightly when he tightened his grip on Argia. She suspected he'd protect his daughter to his last breath. Did the girl need his protection?

As flabbergasted as Lynne acted, Blake was the polar opposite. Sitting. Watching. Waiting for Noreen's counter-move. His eyes held her gaze as tightly as his arms embraced his little girl. She forced herself to look away.

"Let's not disturb Argia any more tonight. She's sleeping soundly and I doubt you're in any danger with your husband in the room. You should rest now."

"He doesn't care anymore. I told you he divorced us," Lynne spat.

Involuntarily, Noreen braced for a counter rebuke from Blake. She didn't want to witness another verbal skirmish between these two. But he ignored the comment intended to poke him and instead, nodded his head toward her in thanks and closed his eyes again. His head dropped to the back of the chair and his breathing evened, but his grip on his daughter remained firm. Even in the throes of slumber, he'd guard her life.

Lynne began to speak but she hushed her with a raised hand. "Please, Lynne, get some rest and allow your daughter to sleep. I'll be right down the hall if you need me."

The smile that spread across Lynne's face puzzled her. The woman seemed happier when she was the center of attention. Taking that as a cue, she tightened the bottom sheet on the cot and held the top sheet away, inviting Lynne to crawl in between. Dutifully, she slipped into bed and allowed herself to be tucked in.

"I probably won't sleep much with him so close," she whispered, "but I'm comforted knowing you're not far away." And then, as if the sedatives administered to Argia earlier had been pumped into Lynne's veins, her eyes clamped shut and she began to snore.

Noreen returned to the nurse's station, satisfied that the Matthews family was settled for the night, even though it was closer to morning and her shift almost over. But not before peeking in on Little Willy. He slept soundly since being comforted by Blake Matthews. Just like Argia.

The adage "drunks and small children always tell the truth" flashed through her mind. Was that the saying? Were these children trying to tell her something?

Sitting in front of her computer she clicked on the open tab for Argia and reviewed her medical chart. It read like a familiar script. A child falls down the steps and breaks a bone. She'd seen countless similar accidents. Her eyes scanned the boxes in which Argia's pulse, heart rate, breathing and temperature were recorded. Temperature—normal.

Lynne Matthews claimed her daughter's fever raged and caused her to dive head first from the second floor to the first on carpeted stairs. Yet no other abrasions or contusions were noted. There was no record of the paramedics administering any medication to bring that fever down in the twenty-minute ride from the Matthews' home to this hospital. She searched the boxes for the paramedics' names. She knew this crew. Next time she saw them, she'd ask about that.

# 4

Noreen's shift ended without further drama. All three Matthews slept soundly when she poked her head in their room on the way to the elevator.

Last night had seemed more grueling than usual. A hot shower and straight to bed was her plan. Unlike other days when errands needed run or chores required her attention before she returned to work, she could sleep later today and veg out until heading back to the hospital for her seven-to-seven shift tonight.

But her mind wasn't cooperating. She lay in bed with her sleep mask in place recalling the scene in Argia Matthews' hospital room. The little girl clung to her father in slumber and Blake Matthews hugged his daughter to his chest. Off to the side as if out of the picture, Lynne Matthews slept, the child's mother whom one would expect a little girl to normally seek comfort from. The bond between father and daughter was evident. Where was the mother-daughter connection?

When sleep eluded Noreen, she shoved the slumber mask up on her forehead and reached for her cell phone. The paramedics who transported Argia to the hospital were out of Fire Station Twelve. Rob Yarnell and Joe Lystle were conscientious veterans, among the best at their jobs. Noreen called up the emergency directory in her contact list and tapped the phone to call the station. The men might not be back on duty yet, but they'd return a message when they could. She selected Joe's voicemail and asked him to contact her. And then, she slept.

It didn't surprise her to find Argia had been discharged by the time she returned to work that evening. Once the drugs were out of the little girl's system and she could take fluids and keep them down, there'd be no need for medical oversight. Only parental care. What kind of environment did the child return home to? Hopefully not one as hostile as what she'd witnessed within these hospital walls.

Halfway through her shift, her text message tone sounded. Joe and Rob were in the ER and, if it was convenient, they'd stop at her station per her request before going back out on the road. She met them at the elevator and directed them to a vacant patient room.

"I'm not certain the question I'm going to ask you is ethical and if you ask why I want to know, I don't know that I have a valid reason. It's more a nagging in my mind." How could she explain the gut feeling that *something* was wrong in the Matthews' home? She stood before them wringing her hands and, upon realizing it, dropped her arms to her sides. "You transported a broken arm patient yesterday, Argia Matthews. Do you recall that run?"

Rob smiled. "You mean Lewey's daughter? She's a cutie, isn't she? Calls me Uncle Rob."

Noreen hadn't considered that Rob and Joe might be friends with Blake Matthews, but the minute Rob spoke, she remembered that he worked out of Fire Station Twelve. This might not have been a good idea.

She nodded in response to his remark. "Are you friendly with Lieutenant Matthews?"

Rob's head bobbed. "I was best man in his wedding. Known him, oh, I don't know, about seven years. He's careful not to mix business and personal though. The man has ripped into me more than once for a minor oversight when we've been called to an accident. I swear he knows everyone's job to the letter, including his own. He's a taskmaster."

She waited for Joe's reply. He shrugged. "Rob's right. Lewey demands perfection from himself and everyone around him. I'm not as close to him as Rob. My girlfriend babysits for him sometimes. On duty, the man scares me, but I'd follow him into hell. I suppose I'm as friendly as anyone can be. The lieutenant keeps to himself, pretty much. He'll admit he's not much of a people person. But yeah, we get along with him okay. Why do you ask?"

Did that mean Blake Matthews was anti-social and Lynne's rants were correct? If he demanded perfection and someone, even a five-year-old fell short of the mark, did he react violently? Was Lynne right to fear the man?

If these two were Lieutenant Matthews' comrades, they weren't the right ones to share her concerns with. She'd need another source for an unbiased opinion of Blake Matthews. But she could still ease her worries about Argia.

"I'm not so much asking about him. I'm curious about yesterday's transport. Specifically, the little girl's condition. Was she out of her mind with fever? Had she fainted? I didn't see any fever-reducing meds on the chart and I thought, maybe, in the urgency, you might not have noted it." She held her hands up when both their eyes widened. "Not that I'm accusing you of anything. I'm simply asking about Argia's fever."

The paramedics stared at her, their eyebrows knitted in confusion. Rob rubbed the back of his neck. "I don't recall a fever, Noreen, and I was the one checking her. She was crying, maybe a little hysterical so all her readings were elevated. But having me there, her Uncle Rob, helped I think. It was obvious she was in pain and she's such a tiny thing to begin with. I bet she's at least fifteen pounds underweight. She was flushed but I think that was distress, not fever. Why do you think she had a fever?"

Caution bells sounded in her head, warning to choose her words carefully. The relationship these men shared with their lieutenant was unknown. Would they tell Blake she was asking questions? And her doubts were murky, even in her mind. This was more feeling than fact.

"The mother seemed to think Argia had a fever but she was as frazzled as her daughter so ... I don't know. I wanted to check with you two for my own satisfaction. It's nothing official, nothing for the medical records. Maybe I'm confused."

But she wasn't. Lynne told her and Blake that Argia became dizzy and fell due to an elevated temperature. Those were practically the exact words the woman used.

Joe and Rob looked at each other, wordlessly collaborating. Did they know about Blake Matthews' unstable personality? Were they good old boys bound to stick together? Or were her instincts totally off base? She'd worked eight straight days, four of them sixteen-hour shifts due to her colleague's illness and an unplanned staff shortage. The extra money was wonderful but, admittedly, she was exhausted. Physically and mentally except when it came to her patients' care. Then, somehow, her energy revamped.

The next three-days were much-needed time off. She could simply be reading too much into a normal accident and a little girl caught in the middle of an unpleasant divorce.

Rob nodded. "The woman doesn't handle a crisis very well. Yesterday was the second time in a couple weeks we were there. She hits the panic button real fast, maybe too often. Kids are bound to have runny noses and bumps and bruises, but Gia's mom overreacts. We've made several runs there and, I'll tell you, the kid handles an emergency better than the mother."

Her attention spiked. “The second time? What happened the first time?”

Rob shook his head slowly. “She said her daughter wouldn’t stop throwing up.”

She hoped her stone face masked her surprise. “Was it some sort of stomach virus?”

Rob locked his lips tight but Joe spoke up. “When we got there, the little imp was running around the living room like nothing was wrong. Her mother insisted that the girl had thrown up non-stop but, if you ask me, she didn’t even appear dehydrated. But to appease the mother, we pushed fluids and transported her to the ER. Waste of money and our time in my opinion.”

“Did you come here? To this hospital?”

Their radios squawked in unison, indicating they had another run to make and both men rushed to the door. Joe gave her a quick affirmative and they were gone.

An hour later when everyone on the floor seemed settled for the night, Noreen searched Argia Matthews’ medical history. If she’d been treated at any of the five hospitals within their healthcare network, her information would be logged in the system.

A few mouse clicks and an entire page filled the monitor screen, presenting an itemized list of described ailments for Argia Matthews. Noreen found the file for the reported nausea. Joe’s assessment was correct. The emergency room staff conducted a routine check of Argia’s vital signs and released the patient shortly after her arrival. No signs of distress.

Before Noreen could open the other files, a child’s monitor signaled for her attention. An investigation into the Matthews’ family medical history would have to wait.

Blake wrestled with his decision to return home with Lynne and

Gia. He didn't want to leave his b
Lynne in their former home toge
for mother and daughter. Gia ha
quickly than Lynne, who still live
their marriage. The concept of lo
unacceptable to The Captain.

The day after he presented Lynn
ago, he moved out. He'd hoped for a
a public scene, attracting the attentio nosy neighbors. He rolled up in his truck with Joe and Rob behind in a rented moving van and directed them to remove the furniture, television, sound system equipment and other items enumerated on a clipboard from the basement. He'd cordoned off a portion of the underground area and converted it to his man cave. Everything down there was his. He'd planned to toss his clothes and other personal items in a couple of moving boxes and haul it all to a two-story house he rented across town in Plum Borough, in the same housing development that his mother lived in. Lynne likely was unfamiliar with the gated community since she'd never visited her mother-in-law and rarely ventured beyond her comfort zone of familiar destinations, but if she asked, he'd share the address. She never did.

When he provided the address to Gia's schoolteachers, none of them seemed surprised that the marriage wasn't working. In hindsight, that should've been a clue. Nevertheless, he explained the rental was temporary and should not be considered Gia's primary residence as it was outside their school district. Once he had full custody of Gia, he planned to build or buy a house on a couple of acres where a dog could run, with a fenced backyard for her to play in, large enough for an in-ground pool. That would entail changing schools and he didn't want to add that challenge to an already tumultuous year for her.

Lynne hadn't taken him seriously when he asked for a divorce and didn't believe it until he began packing his things. Then, like

Captain offered to help, grabbed a pile of his ssed them into the yard, shrieking about abuse, nt, and adultery. He was never sure where that last on came from and suspected she added it for the neigh- s' gossip pool. Thank goodness Gia was in school and missed the vicious performance.

Gia was accustomed to him sleeping away when he was on duty but she was also smart for her age. Smart enough to realize too many "nite nites" in a row had kept him out of the house. When she asked where he was and why he wasn't in his bed, he avoided using the word divorce and instead, explained that he and mommy were making changes but none of them would change how much he loved her. He said he was living near Grammy for a little while to see how he liked it and she'd have more opportunities to see her grandmother.

That temporarily satisfied his daughter's curiosity. Gia loved her grandmother and expressed delight when he added that they could have sleepovers at Grammy's. His mother welcomed the time shared with her granddaughter. Carole Matthews hadn't liked Lynne from the minute they met and her feelings had never changed. They only hardened in the face of Lynne's attempts to keep her and Gia apart.

His little girl studied him while he painted the picture of the new living arrangements, leveling that soulful stare of hers on his face and he swore she understood exactly what was happening. She'd laid her small palm against his heart and he covered it with his big, rough hand. "You're always there, Gia," he'd whispered. And he knew she knew.

The rental worked nicely for now and Gia liked the new living quarters. Every time he packed her blue puppy backpack, she created an adventure for her and her beloved stuffed animals, Mr. Fox and Mr. Dog, to embark on. She hadn't yet tired of the game.

But today, Blake saw that the surgery took its toll on her. The sunlight that usually beamed from her round chocolate eyes was absent as he wheeled her out the hospital entrance. And the energy that effervesced from her like the bubbles she loved to blow was weak. He conceded she would rest easier in her own room, surrounded by the myriad of items she collected.

Lynne's glee shone when he buckled Gia into the car seat and informed her he'd follow the SUV back to the house. He managed to switch shifts with one of his co-workers so instead of going to work this morning, he had a three-day window to devote to Gia. It wasn't his intent to stay with Lynne all three days.

After he moved out, Lynne had manufactured endless reasons for him to return to the house on his days off. A power outage that required a simple flip of the breaker. But she swore she tried that and it hadn't worked.

A malfunctioning front door lock. It looked tampered with. Her flat tire on a school day. He'd been tempted to tell her to call the auto club but that would've made Gia late for class. She already had too many tardy marks on her record, all occurring on mornings when it fell to Lynne to drive the little girl to school.

He finally stopped the emergency house visits by calling and paying for servicemen to respond to The Captain's crises. Funny, after a week of that, the catastrophes ended.

Upon their arrival at the house, he tucked Gia in bed and she immediately fell asleep. Likewise, Lynne declared she was exhausted and needed to rest. Standing in front of him, she unbuttoned her shirt and dropped it to the floor, taking a deep breath to exaggerate the effect her push-up bra already had on her voluptuous breasts. "You could use some relaxation too, Blake." Her words were whispered, seductive.

When they were first together, he could happily get lost in her cleavage. She was still one of the sexiest women he'd ever known. His desire for her hadn't diminished, as evidenced by the tightening in his jeans. But the last time he reached for her, thinking he could make love to her and mend the growing rift between them, she laughed in his face and threatened to charge him with rape if he touched her. It had been the final straw for him.

Lynne's attempt at seduction fell on blind eyes. Without bothering to respond to her invitation, he turned his back and strolled into his daughter's room, stretching out on the toddler bed, his feet dangling over the edge, and drawing his beautiful bundle from God closer. Gia was all the love he needed.

Hours later, he awoke when Gia stirred. Her light brown hair spread out on the pillow in a tangled mass. He gathered it in his hand and dropped a kiss on the base of her neck. "Hey, sleepyhead. How do you feel today?"

She turned awkwardly, the cast jabbing into his stomach as she rolled, and gifted him with a bright smile. The light was back in her eyes, shining into his heart.

She giggled. "Daddy, you're too big for my bed."

Her laugh was contagious and he grinned. "Am not. It's the bed that's too small for me." She erupted in a fit of laughter.

He brushed the hair off her forehead and leveled his gaze on her. Ever since she was an infant, he could look in her eyes, almost into her soul, and communicate with her. She turned equally as serious and returned the stare, the two of them silently sharing their feelings, unspoken devotion passing between them. He dissolved into her and she into him when their eyes locked like this, their love flowing like a river between them. It never failed. From the very first time he looked at his daughter, he felt a tug on his heart, as if a chain stretched from his chest to her tiny torso, linking them together. The bond grew stronger, tighter, more unbreakable every time they shared this moment.

He leaned in to kiss her forehead. "I love you, Gia."

A slow smile creased her face. "Twofers, Daddy."

It felt as if his heart burst in his chest. Their special ritual. His sustenance. He dropped a kiss on her right cheek. "One." And then her left cheek. "Two." Her forehead next. "One." And last, her mouth. "Two."

Her laughter filled the room as he sat up and lifted her into a sitting position. He gathered her hair into his hands and began weaving a braid down her back, his fingers working nimbly through the steps. More often than not he'd been the parent who awakened her in the mornings, helped her dress and coaxed some semblance of breakfast into her.

"You hungry, peanut?" She was a terrible eater but he could sometimes cajole her into a decent meal. As a baby, she had nutritional issues, which he blamed on her mother. Lynne hadn't wanted to gain too much weight while she carried their child and Gia was born small and premature. Lynne refused to breast feed and they struggled with formulas to sustain the baby, ultimately resulting in the diagnosis that Gia was a failure-to-thrive child. Blake fought for every ounce his daughter gained, despite the odds stacked against her developing normally.

He'd diligently added a tablespoon of olive oil to every feeding, and slowly, ounce-by-ounce, she'd gained weight. She still fell below the normal level on the growth chart but, like him, she was a fighter. And she survived.

To this day, Gia ate very little at mealtime and she was quite picky when she was hungry. He expected she'd grow out of that.

The braid complete, he spoke softly in her ear.

"How about some Mickey Mouse pancakes?"

Gia shook her head. "I'm not hungry, Daddy."

"What about peanut butter and jelly?" Again, she declined.

"Your favorite cereal?"

That at least had her thinking. She wasn't a fan of cereal but she loved the chocolate bits mixed with the corn flakes. She raised her head to look at him. "Maybe a bite of cereal."

He smiled. "Only a bite? How about two bites just for me?"

Her shoulders raised an inch when she shrugged. "Okay, two bites."

"What about three bites?"

She giggled and knocked into his chest. “Daaaddddy. Two bites.”

Blake smiled and rose from the bed. “All right. We’ll count your bites together.” He reached for his daughter. “First the bathroom and let’s brush those teeth.” The arm that disappeared inside the cast looked like a toothpick. He braced it for her while he walked her to the bathroom and settled her on the toilet seat. “Don’t move until I come back.”

Gia needed a sling. The cast weighted her arm. He wanted something bright, a wrap that would make her happy. Lynne had an assortment of linens for the dining table. She insisted on a theme for every occasion and required tablecloths, linen napkins with matching plates and other paraphernalia to complete an event. Like everything else, he’d indulged her wishes.

One year’s Fourth of July festivities included oversized linen napkins with colorful fireworks exploding on the cloth. Gia had loved them. He rifled through the drawer until he found the napkin, spying the Easter bunny set and the Thanksgiving turkeys. Those delighted her too and he snatched them up. An array of fun slings might counter the fact that she needed one to begin with.

As he approached the bathroom, Gia’s sweet voice drifted from the room. He tiptoed to the door and peeked around the frame. Perched on the toilet, her feet swinging back and forth, she carried on a conversation with one of her imaginary friends, explaining how she “bwoke” her arm. “It weally hort,” she said, rubbing her hand along the bright cast. Then she knocked on it. “But I can’t even feel it now. The bweak is under here but,” she tapped the cast again, “no more hort.” Then she moved to her fingers, still swollen and stiff. “My fingers weally hort too. Bad enough to make me cwy. But Mother says only babies cwy so I can’t.”

His temper shot through the roof. Leave it to Lynne to forbid the little girl to shed tears to ease her pain. It was bad enough she insisted on being called mother. She was a mother all right.

He stepped into the bathroom and the dialogue ceased. Dropping to his knees, he grasped her sides with both hands. "Gia, honey, if your hand hurts bad enough to cry, you have to tell me."

Her lips puckered and the bottom lip protruded slightly. Tears rimmed her eyes, but she shook her head. "It's okay, Daddy. I'm not gonna cwy."

Maybe now was the right time to ask the question that gnawed at him all night. "Gia, do you remember falling down the steps? Do you remember what happened?"

One lone tear escaped and slid down her cheek. His thumb looked huge when he raised his hand to her face and swiped it away. "Honey, you know you can tell me anything, anything at all."

The lower lip receded inward and she clenched her teeth, as if imprisoning words inside her mouth to keep them there. Slowly, she shook her head. Her soulful look betrayed her five years and pierced his heart.

"It's all right, baby. We can talk about this later." He held up the napkin. "Look what I have. This is going to make your arm weigh less and make that cast easier to manage." All signs of distress disappeared as he positioned her arm across her stomach and folded the cloth into a triangle. He knotted it behind her neck and spread his hands wide, palms up. "Perfect. You look like a holiday."

She rewarded him with a burst of giggles. He yanked the other two napkins from his back pocket. "We can use these too so you'll be a festival of colors."

Once the bathroom duties were complete, he chose a pale green sleeveless dress for her to slip into. Although Argia wasn't a girlie-girl and rarely played with dolls, she favored dresses and skirts over shorts or pants. That was the one thing he credited Lynne with. From the day she was born, Lynne dressed Gia in frilly dresses and lacy socks, her sparse hair always ribboned or bowed. His daughter would grow up with a honed fashion sense and conscientious about her appearance. And likely as beautiful as her mother.

His large fingers had become quite adept at mastering the miniature buttons and snaps on her clothes. Hand in hand, they made their way to the kitchen.

The Captain was still asleep and likely would log several more hours in the sack. He didn't understand her insistence on having ten or twelve hours of sleep every day, especially with a child to care for, but he relished the quiet time with Gia. Lifting her into a chair at the breakfast bar, he opened the fridge. "Juice?"

"Water and ice, Daddy. Please."

Lynne insisted Gia was lactose intolerant and avoided dairy products, which early on contributed to the failure-to-thrive diagnosis. It was one of the reasons his mother detested Lynne. When Carole Matthews was in charge, she served chocolate milk by the cupful. And ice cream. But Gia quickly learned to drink only water when her mother was nearby. And she never outed her grandmother for breaking the rules. Somewhere along the line, she'd flipped the words "ice water." The way she said it was so cute, he never corrected her.

Lynne emerged from the bedroom just as he placed the bowl of cereal in front of Gia, dutifully using the milk substitute Lynne stocked. He stifled a smile when he saw Gia's nose crinkle. He didn't blame her. The stuff tasted like watered down wallpaper paste.

"What's going on here?" No good afternoon, no hug and kiss for her daughter, and no warmth in her voice.

He scowled and noted that Gia ignored her mother. "Just having a little breakfast." With her good hand, Gia picked the chocolate bits from the bowl.

"Breakfast? It's almost three o'clock in the afternoon. You're going to spoil her dinner."

She marched past him to the coffee pot.

"She's hungry, Lynne. It's fine."

That's when Lynne closed the lid on the coffee brewer and finally looked at Gia. The shriek that followed scared them both.

"What is she wearing? That's my good linen napkin. It'll be ruined. Take that off immediately. The hospital sent a suitable sling home for her."

He didn't like arguing with Lynne, especially in front of Gia. One of his biggest fears was that his daughter watched the interaction between her parents and would grow up believing that it was acceptable for a married couple to argue, yell and generally disrespect each other. Children are a product of their environment. Sadly, the atmosphere here lately was toxic. He strived to maintain a level tone in his voice.

"I was unaware there was another sling and the cast is heavy for her arm." He winked at Gia. "Besides, I think she looks like the little firecracker she is. She won't ruin the napkin. She's very careful with her things."

"Well, you should take it off. It's probably not the correct elevation for her arm and is impeding the circulation. And the knot in the back will likely compress her atlas."

"Her what?"

Lynne raised her chin in the air with her inferred superior knowledge. "The atlas. It's the top bone in the vertebrae. Don't you know anything?"

He knew enough to get out of this marriage. And as soon as he could, he'd get his daughter out of this house.

# 5

Noreen stretched, yawned, and lay still, listening to the muted sounds in her apartment. The purr of the refrigerator. Her grandfather clock in the living room, its ticks echoing a soothing rhythm through the rooms. After her brain finally shut down, she'd slept soundly. But reaching that state, wrestling with questions that swirled through her head about Argia Matthews, had taken some time.

But today was a day off and for sanity's sake, she needed to forget the hospital and its issues. When she returned, she'd look further into the Matthews' file if her curiosity about Argia's well-being persisted. Maybe by the time she reported back to the floor she'd forget the whole family.

She retrieved the newspaper from the hall and set the coffee to brew. After a quick shower, she slipped into jeans and a Penguins hockey sweatshirt and stepped out onto her balcony with an oversized mug and the paper. It was mid-morning and her neighbors already had departed for their respective jobs or day's errands. The quiet mimicked a soft sweater wrapped around her shoulders and she relaxed into the lounge chair.

Feet up, she began reading, enjoying the luxury of solitude. And then there he was. In a color picture on the front page of the local news section. Blake Matthews invaded her privacy like a missile launched from the page. He stood beside another man, both in uniform, a certificate between them. The headline hailed him as a hero. For a second time.

Her eyes dropped to the accompanying story. According to the news account, Lieutenant Blake Matthews rushed into a burning building, carried an unresponsive woman and a boxer puppy from the flames and revived the woman on the front lawn. The article also recounted a rescue earlier in the year when he saved two teens from a car sinking into the local reservoir.

She studied the picture. His gray eyes didn't show up on the page but she recalled them vividly. Piercing. Intense enough to make her heart skip. Again. Those eyes jolted her when she first stared him down, toe-to-toe in the hospital hallway while she insisted he leave. Her heart raced then, but the tense encounter between them accounted for the rush.

Not so now. Her heart skipped staring at the page. She swallowed a large gulp and looked up to casually survey the park area behind her building. *Find something else to look at.* But the picture drew her back. Dark hair. His blue shirt tucked into a trim waist. The uniform fit as if it was tailored to his bulges. The photo caption identified the man beside him as the chief and he smiled broadly. Not Blake. He stared tight-lipped at the camera as if he counted the seconds until he could move out of the spotlight. Was that the anger Lynne Matthews described? The defiance she'd encountered? Or something else, more deep-seeded, and dangerous?

She scanned the rest of the news section but her attention returned to the front-page story. Finally, chastising herself even as she went through the motions, she awakened her laptop and typed his name into the Internet search bar. Her eyes widened when the computer screen filled with links to various news stories and information on Blake Matthews. Unable to stop herself, she clicked through the sites.

His job performance was outstanding, earning him numerous citations and meritorious awards. His community service was laudable. One picture showed him ringing the bell beside the Salvation Army kettle in a swirl of snowflakes, and in another he stood beside a child's bed in full firefighting gear wearing a canted Santa hat, fulfilling a young girl's wish. In another link, he raised a softball trophy with teammates and there he was taking his oath of service on his first day at Deep Creek Fire Station Twelve. The more she read, the wider the smile on her face spread.

She spotted Argia in a group of children touring the firehouse, grinning happily as she clung to her father's hand. Another photo caught the breath in her throat. This one depicted him shirtless on a rooftop joining forces with men repairing a house for a homeless family. Yowser! Even his muscles had muscles.

Noreen wedged her lip between her teeth over an article about a fallen firefighter and the accompanying picture of Blake as one of the pallbearers, unashamed of the streaming tears on his face.

Where was the monster Lynne Matthews claimed she lived with? Certainly not on any of these webpages. The man described on all of these sites was a saint.

Finally, she closed her computer and tackled the small task list for the day. Thinking about Blake Matthews confused her. He was a conundrum, and not one she was prepared to deal with today. If ever. He wasn't her type anyway, all macho and self-confident. His job was dangerous and he likely lived life that way, never knowing what the next fire siren might bring. Taking risks. Living at top speed. She didn't need that kind of man in her life again.

Tom had lived like that and destroyed himself right before her eyes. And her heart with it. He'd teased her incessantly, mocking her conservatism and daily caution, comparing them as a couple to the tortoise and the hare. She'd been afraid to love like he loved. In hindsight, maybe he knew his life would be cut short and that's why he lived balls to the wall. But life in the fast lane wasn't for her, the tortoise who made it to the finish line alone. She preferred her reclusive lifestyle, finding satisfaction in caring for children who returned affection without expectation. She had no desire for a permanent attachment to those kids or anyone else. Her niece and nephew quenched any maternal yearnings she occasionally felt. And then, happily, she returned them to her sister's care.

Today was one of those days she'd enjoy a dose of their love.

Days off from the hospital usually guaranteed family time, whether it was one-on-one sister time or, like tonight, a dinner invitation and a welcomed niece and nephew fix. She spent as much time with those kids as she could, often grateful that at the end of a full day at the zoo or after a movie marathon night she could return them and enjoy the peace and quiet of her own life. Julie and Justin were eight and six and she loved them as if they were her own. Thinking about their antics while she drove to her sister's home already had her smiling.

The traffic jam she encountered on the way was unexpected, especially because it was too early for rush hour. From the driver's seat, she saw a crowd gathering and heard raised voices. Mostly borderline hysteria. Mechanically, she shifted her car into park, grabbed her cell phone and dashed toward the commotion. The odor of gasoline permeated the air when she drew closer. People shouted and off to the side, a woman sobbed. Shattered pieces of glass crunched beneath her feet as she neared the accident site, dodging strips of fiberglass that peppered the street. Abruptly she stopped when, amid the frenzy she spotted Blake Matthews pointing and barking orders to several men, apparently orchestrating the removal of someone from a car crinkled like an accordion. Threatening plumes of dark smoke rose from beneath the hood and her nose immediately began to leak.

He wasn't in uniform. Blue jeans and a T-shirt, both already smudged with dirt. But an air of authority surrounded him as he directed the rescue. No one questioned his commands.

Dragging her eyes away from him, she rushed to two people off to the side of the road, a man doubled over on his hands and knees vomiting and a woman prone on the ground. She dropped to her knees beside the unconscious woman and, finding a weak pulse, began checking for obvious injuries. "Did anyone call 9-1-1?" she asked out loud to the gawking spectators. A voice behind her affirmed that help was on the way. The man crawled toward them, blubbering as he called the woman's name. "Millie! Millie! Please tell me she's okay."

And then three of the men who'd surrounded the tangled mess of metal, rubber and fiberglass deposited a young boy close by, his face contorted in pain and his femur protruding through his ripped jeans. She looked up long enough to see Blake Matthews waving wildly at the other onlookers, signaling to them "One more," he yelled. "One more in the back seat." The trio and some new recruits ran toward the vehicle and she returned her attention to the woman, grateful for the wail of sirens that grew closer and louder. She hadn't discovered any clear injuries but the woman remained unresponsive.

A man's voice pierced the air in a scream of panic. "Fire! The car's on fire!"

Noreen looked up the moment the hood shot sky high from an explosion that shook the ground beneath her knees and rocketed the handful of would-be rescuers into the air as well, dumping them on their backs with loud thuds. The sight mesmerized her. As if in slow motion, Blake rolled over, coughed, and arched his back. Then he began a slow crawl on all fours to the rear door, yanking it open and thrusting his upper body inside. She watched, afraid to look away, her heart thudding like she'd run toward the car with them. Her eyes watered as the pungent engine smoke drifted toward the onlookers.

Was Blake crazy? Bright orange flames danced in long fingers from the front of the vehicle toward the rear. Toward him!

Another man shook his head like a dog shakes off rainwater and crawled toward the burning car. A third rose tentatively and stumbled over to them, his arms flailing for balance. He dropped to his knees beside the second man and both of them reached inside the cloud of dark smoke. The commotion of sirens, screams and panic deafened her. She squinted to hone in on the blackened interior, trying to make out what was happening.

Four arms stretched into the back seat, accompanied by grunts and groans and incoherent orders. They tugged on Blake while they leaned back, trying to extract him. *Dear Lord. Hurry.*

Like a magician pulls a rabbit from a hat, Blake glided backward, clinging to a bloody young girl, dragging her from the seat as he withdrew and dropping her on top of his chest when he collapsed onto the asphalt. The crowd applauded and several onlookers ran to assist, carefully lifting the girl off Blake and carrying her to safety.

He rolled over on all fours gasping, looked over his shoulders at the now fully engulfed burning vehicle, and belly crawled away from the heat and flames.

Firefighters surrounded the burning heap and began dousing it with water. Two teams of paramedics tended the injured and, after providing information from what little assessment she'd made regarding the unconscious woman, Noreen stepped out of their way. She scanned the crowd for Blake and saw him well off to the edge of the chaos, hunched over, hands on his thighs, coughing with each deep breath he inhaled. The troops already had forgotten their leader, more curious about the injured and the wreckage than the man who crept off to the curb, away from the throng. As her feet propelled her toward him she rationalized that she was a nurse and he might need help.

Tentatively, she touched his shoulder. "Are you all right, Mr. Matthews? Do you need the paramedics?"

Still winded, he didn't look up and barely shook his head. "No. I'm fine." The rawness of his voice sent a small thrill through her.

Dirt covered his shirt and the backs of his jeans. Soot smeared his face like a sweaty football player wearing greasy eye black. "Are you sure? That was quite a spill you took."

When he answered a second time with a headshake, light reflected from it like a disco ball. "Hold still, Mr. Matthews. You have pieces of glass in your hair." She reached toward his head intent on picking it out and, for the first time, he raised his face toward her.

"S'okay," he croaked, swatting her hand away. He struggled for a clean breath. "Don't bother." He coughed to clear his throat. "I can get it."

Noreen recognized his stubbornness. "Don't be silly. Let me." She reached for a particularly big piece and eased it from his dark hair. The bits of glass were easy to spot in his military style haircut.

He didn't like the attention and in seconds he grunted and straightened. "It's fine, ma'am. I'll take care of it."

She smiled at the creases around the corners of his eyes, emphasized by the soot smudges. Little pointers directing her to those striking gray eyes, arousing her, like they could see right through her. The dirt only served to enhance his sharp features. High cheekbones and the shadow of a beard. His eyes shone through the dirt but not with any sense of familiarity.

"It'll only take a minute, Mr. Matthews. But now I can't reach you so bend over please. Then I promise I'll quit bothering you and let you get back to your daughter. How's she doing?"

His eyebrows shot up and she watched him search her face, trying to place her. Well, she couldn't blame him. At the hospital, she fashioned her hair in a tight knot at the base of her neck, wore minimal make-up, no jewelry and those hospital scrubs hardly alluded to the fact that she had a figure. She exercised regularly at the gym, even on the days when she was dead tired, to preserve it.

Even though they'd stood toe-to-toe that night in the hospital when she challenged him to leave, they were in a different element and in her blue jeans, peep-toe pumps, with her hair curled and falling in soft waves below her shoulders, he likely wouldn't add two and two to get four. Eye make-up and round gold hoops swinging from her earlobes further complicated the picture. At least she hoped so. She laughed at the confused look on his face.

"I'm flattered that you don't recognize me. I try hard not to look like a nurse when I'm off duty. I tended to Argia's broken wrist after her surgery. Noreen Jensen."

You could've knocked him over with a feather, even if he wasn't weak from smoke inhalation. This was stick-up-her-ass Nurse Noreen standing in front of him? Laughing? Her blue eyes twinkling? Blond hair floating in the breeze around her face like some mystical aura? His head must have hit the concrete when he dropped like a rock and now, most certainly, he was delusional. Although why his brain would summon *her* up at this moment confounded him.

"Ma'am?" It was the only word his addled brain could manage.

Her smile grew wider. Yep. He'd lost his mind.

"Noreen Jensen," she repeated, as if he'd gone deaf too. "The nurse at Children's Hospital. I took care of your daughter. Are you all right? You look a little dazed."

She didn't know the half of it. He shook his head to clear it. "I-I'm sorry. I didn't recognize you." Jesus, she continued to smile. His eyes had to be playing tricks on him. Maybe he'd gone blind too.

"As I said, thank you. Please, lean forward and allow me to remove the glass from your hair."

Automatically, he raised his hand and brushed it across his head sending bits of glass flying toward her. The smile disappeared when she jerked backward. But she laughed and the lilt in her voice thrilled him. Imagine. Noreen the No-Heart nurse had an enticing laugh.

"That wasn't helpful, Mr. Matthews. Now you've covered me with glass." She brushed the front of her shirt, flicking windshield pieces off breasts he tried not to notice. She raised her hand toward him. "Will you let me?" This time, her words were more insistent.

"Blake. My name is Blake." Spoken like the robot he'd morphed into. What the hell was going on here?

"Lean forward." She ordered and he obeyed. His gaze dropped to the ground and he spied the navy stilettos. He blinked to focus. Holy hell, he wasn't blind. He saw the high heels as plain as day. Two dark red toes peeked out at him from each shoe. It was crazy but, in his mind, a woman who cared for her feet paid extra attention to the key details of life.

High heels and tight blue jeans. A combination every man conjured up in his fantasies. "This isn't necessary, ma'am."

"Be still." Ah, there it was. The dictatorial tone in her voice.

"I don't like people fussing over me."

"Well, then stop moving, let me finish and I'll leave you alone." Air nipped the back of his neck. "Wow. You've got bits along your collar and down your shirt." Warm fingers brushed the nape of his neck, shooting a wave of heat along his back. He jerked upright.

"It's okay, ma'am. I can get it. Thank you."

She stared at him and then shrugged. "Fine. Have it your way." She started to turn and he touched her arm. He couldn't think of a thing to say but damn if he didn't want her to stay.

"I'm sorry. I don't mean to sound rude. Thanks for your concern, nurse."

There was that smile again. Different from that night in the hospital. More spontaneous. Infectious. And directed at him. The jolt that surged to his crotch surprised him.

"Noreen."

"Ma'am?"

"Noreen Jensen. You didn't answer my earlier question. How's Argia feeling?"

The mere mention of his daughter's name grounded him. His head cleared and the circumstances of his acquaintance with this woman resurfaced. She wasn't his friend, nor could she ever be. She'd seen the cracks in his life as if under a microscope, thanks to The Captain. Nurse Noreen knew too much about his personal circumstances and not all of it accurately.

"She's feeling better, thank you." The formality in his tone didn't escape her notice. Disappointment shadowed her face and he felt like an ungrateful jackass. The smile disappeared and her shoulders straightened. All that was missing was the hospital garb.

"Good to hear." Her words were as cool as her posture. Now he recognized her. "Take care, Lieutenant Matthews." Abruptly she pivoted and strode away, the sway of her hips catching his attention. Quite curvy in those skinny jeans.

"Nurse. Wait." He stretched but his hand caught only air. He'd opted not to engage in a casual conversation with her but hell, he didn't want her to leave. From behind, someone called his name.

"Blake. Hey, Blake. You okay, man?" Joe Lystle approached carrying the station's portable oxygen apparatus.

When he looked back, Noreen was gone. Evaporated into the growing crowd of rubber-neckers.

Joe touched his arm. "Lieutenant? You with me?"

He closed his eyes and shook his head. "I think I need oxygen, Joe. Lots of oxygen. I'm hallucinating."

# 6

He'd been on his way to the market after tucking Gia into her sleigh bed at his rental home. Her vibrancy shined again but her energy hadn't returned. And she'd grown quieter. Barely speaking most of the time when her mother was around. When she did say something, she whispered. And only to him. Lynne exploded in a tirade of accusations about secrecy and deliberate efforts to alienate her child from her so he packed Gia's bag, carried her to the truck, and drove to his house.

His mother waited for them, insisting she'd see for herself how her granddaughter was dealing with her first broken bone. Gia remained silent during the ride over and, despite Carole's outstretched arms and welcoming words, his daughter hadn't offered her usual greeting to her grandmother. Usually she skipped up the walkway hollering for her Grammy, sometimes so loud he had to quiet her. How he wished that were the case now.

Gia nodded affirmatively to the few questions he asked including if she wanted to rest. Certain that this mood would pass, he tucked her into bed and took advantage of the window his mother's visit opened to run for groceries, since he hadn't planned on having Gia until the weekend.

Fresh milk and a few of her favorites were on the grocery list still laying on the passenger's seat. He hadn't witnessed the accident, only heard it. But his training kicked in and he'd run to help. Now, other shoppers stared at him as if he'd spent the day digging ditches and didn't have the sense to clean up before shopping. It didn't bother him. He didn't much care what anyone thought of him beyond his team at the fire station. He needed the respect of those men and he'd do practically anything for it. But these strangers gaping at him were of no consequence. Five people were still alive to have dinner tonight and he'd helped accomplish that. That was worth the stares.

His filthy appearance hadn't stopped Noreen from approaching him. He grunted. The only time she ever saw him, he was grimy. First a grass and dirt-stained ball uniform and less than two hours earlier, smelly street clothes. *Way to impress the lady, Matthews.* Not that he wanted to impress her. Miss Hard Ass was too friendly with The Captain. Still, her conduct today was a pleasant surprise. Like him, she'd jumped into action to aid injured strangers. Never mind liability concerns. He liked that about her. She'd faced him down at the hospital in a move to protect her patient and today she ran into an unknown situation with no other motive except to help. He glimpsed a different person this afternoon. One he apparently couldn't erase from his mind. Not that it mattered. He'd never see her again.

Joe loaded the breakfast dishes in the dishwasher in the firehouse kitchen. Today was the day they planned to confront Lewey, at his urging. He'd tried hard not to eavesdrop on the conversation between Blake and his ex-wife but when the lieutenant raised his voice, it was hard not to hear. Christ, Blake practically single-handedly saved five lives and all his ex could do was accuse him of neglecting his daughter.

His girlfriend, Brittni, had watched Gia a couple days before she broke her arm while the lieutenant and other officers attended a mandated budget meeting with the city council. She'd told him Gia ate a serving of tater tots casserole the size of the toast plate he slid into the bottom dishwasher rack. And an hour later, a peanut butter and jelly sandwich. That's why his ears had perked up when Lewey asked, "What do you mean she's not eating?"

The kid ate for Brittni like there was no tomorrow. Or maybe, there was no food at her mother's house. He hated the thought. Sure, her appetite might be affected by the broken arm, the drugs and the overall trauma. But wasn't that when you spoiled a kid with ice cream and popsicles and whatever the hell she wanted to eat? He wasn't a father but sure as shit, that's what he'd do if Gia were his.

Blake's mood was sour after that phone call. That crazy woman was mentally torturing him, using his sweet little girl as the weapon. Sometimes, people needed to hear the ugly truth before they could admit it. Lewey was like that. Show him the facts and he was on board with the plan. The facts were that whenever Gia was with her mother, an emergency occurred. She was a good little girl. She listened well, said please and thank you and caused no trouble. Gia wasn't the problem.

The other men agreed. It was time for a sit down.

The men in his unit wanted a pow-wow. He was deep in concentration, mapping out a new rescue operation in the event of a water emergency when Rob knocked on the door and interrupted him. Here in Pittsburgh, where three rivers snaked through the city and spilled in all directions, the possibility was real and he was eager to draft the final scenarios and test the new techniques.

But the falter in Rob's voice and his nervous demeanor hinted that delaying the unit meeting until later wasn't an option. In talking with the other shift commanders, he knew that the latest memo regarding budget cuts had a lot of men grumbling.

He'd listen to his squad's concerns but bucking the bureaucracy was a David and Goliath task.

Rob joined the five men at the Table of Trust, their nickname for the large oval table in the kitchen quarters. This was where the men shared their problems about the job, their home lives and whatever else was on their minds, knowing that the discussions went no further than these walls. Some heated arguments had flared up and been resolved here and healthy venting about innumerable concerns occurred. This room was better than any therapist's couch.

The spots at either end of the table were deliberately left without chairs. There was no head honcho at this table. Everyone was equal.

Blake sat in a vacant seat on the left side and waited.

Rob cleared his throat. "Lewey, we want to talk to you about something personal that pertains to you."

He sensed his eyebrows knit together. If this wasn't about the budget, was there a problem he was unaware of? He spread his hands wide. "Shoot."

Only Rob and Joe maintained eye contact with him. The others stared at the table surface or off in the distance.

Rob took a deep breath. "It's about Argia."

His heart skipped at the mere mention of her name. The shining sun in his day. He'd hated taking her back to Lynne's last night.

"We think something is going on, Lewey. Something bad."

Now, twelve eyeballs stared at him expectantly.

Blake shrugged, clueless to what Rob's reference meant. "I don't know what you're talking about. What's bad?"

"She's only five and yet she seems sick all the time. In that little girl's life, there have been more emergencies and crises than a full classroom of kids her age." Rob rested his open hand flat against his chest. "We've been involved with several of the transports and observed it firsthand. And we've listened to you talk about a few of the other events and you leave us scratching our heads. Something is wrong, Lewey."

All around the table, heads nodded. His comfort level wavered. "I appreciate your concern, all of you. Gia is a little on the frail side, I'll admit. And I think her resistance might be lower than other kids her age so she's more susceptible to illness, but she had a tentative start when she was born. You all know that. As she gets older, she'll grow stronger."

Rob inhaled deeply. "Lower resistance doesn't equate to broken bones, Blake."

They knew. Or at least suspected. The looks on their faces told him so. He'd never discussed his fears with anyone, always managing to convince himself he was off in left field thinking that Lynne might....

But these men, whom he trusted with his life, saw it too. "Why don't you say what you mean?"

Beside him, Joe slapped his hand on the table, drawing everyone's attention. "Don't you see it, Blake? It's too much. It happens too often. It's not Argia we're talking about. It's...." His words faded, leaving the sentence unspoken.

He sensed his body temperature rising and a flush engulf his face. He twisted in his chair and planted his feet more firmly on the floor. "It's what, Joe?"

The silence lay like a heavy tarp over the room. Once more, all gazes lowered to the tabletop, except Joe's. He required another fortifying breath before he spoke. "It's Lynne."

He hadn't revealed many details about his disappointing marriage, even though if anyone could be considered a confidante, every man around this table qualified. Some of these guys spilled every personal detail about their lives in this room. But for him, a failed marriage and ultimate divorce was his personal challenge to work through. These men knew only the barest details about what led up to the split.

And they had only his best interests at heart. His and Gia's. "I understand your affection for my daughter and I thank you. She endears everyone who meets her, I know. It's part of some special energy she possesses, I guess. As for her mother, she's never been a strong woman and she's had a tough time with the divorce. She's on her own now and when her child falls ill, naturally, she overreacts."

All heads lifted and shock etched his friends' faces. They were smart, these men he trusted and knew as well as he knew himself. They expected more from him. He was their leader and he was failing to act.

Joe huffed. "It's more than overreaction, Lewey. Why can't you see it?"

"I do see it, Joe, and I've asked myself the same questions. But proving Gia's maladies are invented or created is damn near impossible. Don't think for one minute I haven't tried."

"Let us help. You know we'd do anything for you. And for Gia." To a man, they all agreed.

His heart lifted. In this room, he could express the ugly thoughts about his ex-wife and share his fears for his daughter without judgement. Here was support and help just waiting for a green light. But he wasn't ready to identify the problem, to hang a verbal tag on the horror.

He smiled and stood. "I know that, Joe. I'm filing for full custody soon. My attorney thinks I have a strong case and can win and Gia will be under my roof. If I need any of you for character witnesses or anything else, I won't hesitate to ask."

"How long will that take?" his colleague Shaemus asked.

He shrugged. "I don't know."

Joe exhaled loudly. "Jesus, Lewey, what if you don't have that kind of time?"

Blake rose. A strong army makes its commander better. That's what they were doing, bringing up the rear in a battle yet to be waged.

"If it becomes an emergency, gentlemen, we do what we always do. We strategize, we mount up and we advance. For now, you all stand down."

# 7

Damn Blake Matthews. He haunted her thoughts for days. As she recounted the accident and her efforts to assist at her sister's dinner table, she mentioned him often. Too often. Her sister immediately sensed her fascination and grilled her about the man.

"He interests you," her sister exclaimed, clapping her hands like one of the children.

"No. He arouses my curiosity."

"You call it curious, I say interested. No matter. Tell me about him." She leaned in conspiratorially.

And as Noreen answered her sister's incessant questions, she realized she knew little about the man. Tall. She guessed six-foot-one. Handsome. In a brutish sort of way. Commanding. A leader, especially in an emergency like the car accident, but she envisioned him stepping up in any situation. He wasn't one to stand in the back of the room.

"He has a knack with children, his or a stranger's." Willy's angelic repose popped in her mind.

Her sister's flying eyebrows registered concern. "He's married?"

"Recently divorced so," she paused to doodle on the placemat with her finger, "he's damaged goods."

A slow smile spread across her sister's face. "How so?"

"He probably has commitment issues or, I don't know, baggage." Like a life-sized suitcase named Lynne Matthews. The room grew warmer. She should just shut up and end her sister's inquiries. If her finger had been a brush she'd have painted a mural on the placemat by now. "He's someone else's mistake. I'm not interested." She'd added the caveat to counteract the way her heart pumped when she talked about the man. Double time. He was dangerous. And tempting.

A twisted smile contorted her sister's mouth. "Oh. Someone else's mistake. Is that what I was?"

It was difficult to remember her sister had been a divorcee when she met the love of her life. They were perfect for each other. Anyone who met them saw it immediately. She almost envied her sister's fairytale life. When Noreen dated Tom, they'd come so close to the whole marriage gig but, looking on it as a memory, they weren't in sync like her sister and brother-in-law were. They didn't finish each other's sentences or literally light up when the other entered the room. She would have been happy married to Tom but she recognized now it would be more contentment to live with him than exhilarated to spend every day together. No matter. Happy-ever-after hadn't been in the cards for them.

Her sister still smiled at her, waiting for an answer. "I didn't mean that to come out the way it did. You weren't anyone's baggage. Your circumstances were different."

"Ah, I see. But divorced is divorced, isn't it? Do you know what his circumstances are?"

Possibly but only because Lynne Matthews had more than hinted about domestic violence. But she didn't want to divulge any of that. And her sister was oblivious to the cruelty of real life. Or death and how it had no regard for love or marriage or happy endings. There was no point in commitment and planning for the future because when the Grim Reaper decided it was your time that was it. She'd seen him shatter lives one too many times, including hers.

"I don't. But it's not worth my time to find out. I'm not interested. This subject is closed."

Noreen returned to work determined to dismiss Blake Matthews from her mind. Too bad her concern about Argia sidetracked those intentions.

The hospital floor was like a different world after her three days off. Only a handful of patients remained and the staff was back to a normal schedule so her workload lightened. It allowed time to read Argia's other medical reports.

The child had a history in all five hospitals within this health care system. Every visit was for a different complaint so she rarely saw the same physician twice. When there was a repeat, weeks or even months had passed. A doctor could hardly be expected to remember treating the child previously, even though Argia was a memorable child. But the number of trips to the emergency room was alarming, and the list as varied as a restaurant menu—high fever, uncontrolled vomiting, abdominal pains.

Each time, the admitting parent was Lynne Matthews. Noreen searched for a pattern but found none. The days of admission, even the times, varied. Much like a firefighter's schedule might.

She sat back in her chair holding her chin in her hand, stunned by her thoughts. And the nagging questions. Were those days when Blake Matthews was on duty? Or at home taking care of his daughter and possibly hurting her? Leaving his wife to clean up his mess?

As if they had a mind of their own, her fingers typed Lynne Matthews' name into the search field. Network records older than five years were archived so the incidents that surfaced regarding her appeared as two-line summations from the General Hospital adjacent and connecting to Children's. Second-degree burns on her left arm. Stitches required in her right hand. A concussion diagnosis. A sprained ankle. Like her daughter, the woman was no stranger to the hospital. But all of her emergencies occurred before Argia was born. At least the ones recorded in this hospital network. Who knew where else she might have received treatment. But the dates she read made it apparent that Lynne's medical emergencies ceased once Argia was born. Since then, only the little girl required treatment.

Noreen searched Blake Matthews' name and found three admission reports from next door. Treatment for smoke inhalation occurring in the line of duty. A sprained ankle for him as well, listed as a softball injury. Bet that made him mad. And five stitches in his left thigh, the gash unintentionally caused by his spouse, per the notes. Her brow furrowed. How does one accidentally slit someone's thigh unless they are wielding a knife? She studied the screen. They could have been horsing around in the kitchen, preparing dinner together, maybe a little drunk, or a little too eager to remove each other's clothes. With a knife in hand? That scenario didn't play out.

Were they fighting? Had Blake attacked her and Lynne Matthews was forced to defend herself? Were the police called? The report said the patient was self-admitted so he hadn't arrived at the ER in a squad car. She tried to read between the lines but other than the sinking feeling that something was wrong in that household, there was nothing.

Noreen dialed the Matthews' home number. It wasn't unusual for her to make follow-up calls to her patients to inquire about their well-being after being discharged, especially children who spent a chunk of time in her care. She wanted to check on Argia.

Her heart crashed against her chest while she waited for someone to answer the ringing phone. What if Blake Matthews picked up? No, his wife said he'd moved out. But where was she?

~

For two more days, Noreen tried to reach Lynne Matthews by phone. Never an answer. Yesterday, after her shift ended, she drove out of her way to ride by the Matthews address listed on Argia's medical records. The house was closed and dark. She shouldn't obsess about the kid but the lingering feeling that an ugly secret lived behind the walls of their two-story brick home pestered her.

Even several days away from the hospital failed to allay her concerns. Finally, more than two weeks later, she ran into paramedics Rob Yarnell and Joe Lystle as she left the hospital one morning. After exchanging the usual social greetings, she posed to Rob what she hoped was a nonchalant question.

"How's your niece been?"

He frowned.

"You know, Argia Matthews? How's she doing with her broken wrist?"

At the mention of her name, Joe muttered something unintelligible and stepped away. Rob's eyes darkened. "She's not really my niece, but I gladly claim her. Her arm is healing fine. I saw her last weekend and she's regained movement of those fingers. As for the rest of her...." His words trailed off and he shook his head.

Noreen's stomach twisted. "What do you mean by that? Did something else happen to her?"

Was that why the Matthews' home seemed uninhabited? Were they spending their days in another hospital? Was Blake Matthews the reason?

"I'm not sure what happened, no one is. All of a sudden, she's not talking. To anyone."

The screws twisting her stomach tightened. "I don't understand. You mean like keeping a secret not talking? Playing a game? Who isn't she talking to?"

"To no one. Not her mother, not Blake, not even her toys or stuffed animals and she was a chatterbox when she played with them. She simply stopped talking."

"Did something happen to cause that? Something traumatic?"

Joe wandered back to them and grunted. "Isn't that the million-dollar question?"

"What does that mean?"

Rob tapped Joe's arm as if to signal that he shouldn't say any more. But she wasn't letting this go. She couldn't. Should she have been more aggressive in her attempts to check on Argia's welfare? Could she have averted further injury by interceding? If that were the case, if Blake Matthews lost his temper and took it out on that poor child, she'd never forgive herself.

"Did someone hurt her? Did her father cause it? What'd he do? What happened?"

Both men looked at her with disbelief, their brows furrowed. "Her father?" Joe shook his head vehemently. "Lady, you're way off base if you think Blake would harm a hair on that kid's head. Every breath he takes is for his daughter. He's as stumped as the doctors."

"So she's seen a doctor? Was there a diagnosis?"

Rob studied her, his eyes narrowed now, suddenly less communicative. "What's your interest, Noreen? Argia was your patient weeks ago. And this is the second time you've asked us about her."

She shrugged, ignoring the sour acid releasing in her stomach. "I tried to make a welfare check after the hospital discharged her. I was never able to reach anyone at the Matthews home and I don't like loose ends. She was such a sweet child. I'd like to know she's doing okay."

He stared at her as if he didn't believe her. "Did you try calling Blake or just the house?"

She recalled the blank lines on Argia's chart and the mother's insistence that she was the primary caretaker and the only contact of record. Lynne Matthews clutched her cell phone in her hand even as she'd insisted the landline was the only phone number to reach her.

"The only information listed is a home number for the mother and, even though I called several different times, there was never an answer."

"Probably at the spa," Joe said under his breath.

Rob shot him another silencing glance.

"Do you want Blake's number? I'd feel more comfortable if you asked him your questions." He reached for the cell phone in his back pocket.

"No. No, that's not necessary. I don't want to bother him. I'll try the house a few more times and if I can't reach anyone, I'll let it pass. I simply thought you might know how Argia's doing." She was saying too much, speaking too fast. The men noticed.

Rob raised his head in question. "How about if I have him call you? He's not easy to find to begin with so that's probably a better option."

Her hasty reaction betrayed her words. "No. No, it's fine. Really. I must run. Nice seeing both of you. Stay safe." Turning on her heel she rushed toward her car in the parking lot. The last thing she needed was Blake Matthews calling her. Asking her questions about why she was asking questions. What would she say? She couldn't erase him from her thoughts. Or his daughter.

It looked like the little girl needed help. Saved. But from whom? The monster Lynne Matthews described? She'd seen no evidence that Blake Matthews was anything other than a devoted father, a dedicated firefighter, and a selfless public servant. Easy on the eyes, too. That thought was the final surge for her stomach, which shot a wave of acid up her esophagus. She grimaced at the bitterness in the back of her throat.

Her mind cleared after she slept a few hours, showered, and dressed. But that sickening sensation returned the minute her cell phone rang with an unrecognizable phone number. It was him. She knew it.

"This is Noreen Jensen."

"Blake Matthews."

Her heart shot to the ceiling and she jumped up from the sofa as if propelled by the sensation. Worse. She lost the ability to respond.

Silence stretched between them. Was he calling from the fire station, dressed in his blue uniform, sitting at a desk strewn with papers and reports? She pictured it. Or was he at home in the blue jeans she'd seen him in, his hair tousled, maybe shoeless in white sweat socks, his feet propped up on a coffee table in front of a sofa. Dear Lord, her mind was imagining his home décor.

He cleared his throat. "Did you want to speak to me?"

No. Yes. What the hell? She did want to talk to him. About Argia. That was all.

"I'm sorry to bother you, Mr. Matthews. I tried to complete a welfare check on your daughter and I've been unable to reach you or your wife. I just happened to ask Rob Yarnell about her when I ran into him because I know that he's close to her. Or rather to you. But it was unnecessary for him to contact you. I didn't ask him to do that."

Jabbering. She was jabbering. For the second time today. She recognized panic when she heard it and it spewed from her like hot lava from an active volcano.

"It's not a bother, Miss Jensen. How can I help you?"

"How is Argia?"

"She's fine."

Was that all he was going to offer? Two words?

"Ah, good to hear. Is she able to use those fingers at all? Has she adjusted to having her arm in a cast?"

"The swelling subsided after a few days. She's using her thumb and fingers as best she can. The cast comes off pretty soon."

And? She waited. Apparently, he was a man of minimal words. The quiet deafened her.

"I'm glad to hear that. You and your wife must be taking good care of her." What in the world made her say that?

"Ex-wife."

"Excuse me?"

"Ex-wife. Our divorce was final some time ago. Gia's mother refuses to accept it. But she's my ex."

Her heart thudded. "Oh. I'm sorry."

"Don't be."

No remorse. No feelings whatsoever. Lynne Matthews had called him a heartless bastard. The cold from his tone flowed through the phone to her ear, chilling it.

"I meant, it's always sad when a divorce involves children. I hope Argia wasn't too upset."

"It's sadder when a child is forced to live in an atmosphere of hate and disrespect, don't you think?"

That certainly was the demeanor she'd witnessed between husband and wife. "I'm sorry Mr. Matthews, I'm overstepping my bounds."

"Yes, I think you are."

The gaping divide between the phone connection widened. Why didn't he simply hang up? She heard him inhale. "I appreciate your concern for Gia, Miss Jensen. It's easy to fall in love with her. She manages to entice everyone she meets. I assure you, she's fine."

Noreen gripped the phone tighter. If she didn't press him on what she knew, she'd never let it go. She had to ask.

"Rob Yarnell mentioned that she stopped talking." Might as well float the assumption that she suspected something was wrong and see how he handled it.

"She's only five, I'm sure it's a phase. I'm not too worried about it."

"On the contrary, Mr. Matthews. A five-year-old normally talks non-stop. They ask endless questions and speculate about everything from the family pet to the moon. For a child to go completely silent is a concern, don't you think?"

"How many children do you have, Miss Jensen?"

His question stunned her. Whether or not she had children wasn't the issue. "That's of no matter, sir. I'm a pediatric nurse and children are my specialty. I care for hundreds of children a year. More than I can count. Your question insults me and avoids answering mine.

"Have you taken Argia to see someone?" She knew the answer so his response would be telling. But he was truthful.

"She's met with several specialists. Her mother made sure of that."

"Do you mind my asking their conclusions?"

Did he mind? Blake wasn't sure. Something about this woman wouldn't leave him alone. Part of him wanted to scream, "butt out of my life, lady," yet another part sensed she might enhance it. He remained wary. "Do you mind if I ask what concern it is of yours?"

Through the phone, she gasped. "Argia was a patient of mine, no matter for how short a time. And it disturbs me to think of that sweet child refusing to speak for, for whatever reason. The fact that you circumvent answering my questions is highly suspicious."

The mere tone of her voice made him laugh. He imagined her standing in her nurse's animal-print scrubs, all prim and proper, her toe tapping the floor and hand on her hip. She had balls, he'd give her that.

"This is no laughing matter, Mr. Matthews." She'd been on the defensive when this conversation began, practically apologizing for his call. Now, the offense had the ball.

"I'm not laughing, Miss Jensen." Despite his words, he chuckled again. "Forgive me. It's simply that your tactics amuse me. Why don't you come right out and say what's on your mind?

You strike me as a woman who expects and can handle forthright honesty."

He'd given Noreen Jensen—the woman—considerable thought, wondering what made her go into nursing, specializing in pediatrics, and further narrowing that field to surgery and concentrated care. If a splinter found its way into Gia's finger, he shared the pain. How could someone endure seeing suffering children day in and day out and, in some cases, witness an unhappy conclusion? It likely required a cold heart, which had been his first impression.

But she'd displayed the opposite at the accident scene. She'd thrown herself into the action without concern for self-preservation. Somewhere beneath the ice, she cared. And the image of her in those heels and tight jeans left a lasting impression, one that, to his surprise, affected him now. This conversation was exciting physically and emotionally. He enjoyed talking to this woman, despite her unspoken accusations.

He'd bet right now, she debated how best to find out what she really wanted to know.

She inhaled, mustering her courage he suspected. "All right, sir. Did you do something to cause Argia to stop talking?"

"No, ma'am. I did not."

"Then how do you explain it? What did the doctors say?"

"They have no explanation. She's scheduled for a battery of tests over the next few weeks, procedures I'd rather not put her through but I have no choice. Not with the threat of a child abuse claim hanging over my head. That's what you're beating around the bush about, isn't it Miss Jensen? That I'm somehow mistreating my daughter? Isn't that the seed her mother planted? And without knowing a thing about me, you choose to believe that and perhaps prove it yourself. Am I correct?"

Nothing but silence in his ear. "Who's avoiding a reply now, Miss Jensen?"

Her voice was one decibel lower when she responded. But her

courage sustained. "You're right. That's what I might think. Without a solid foundation, I admit."

God, he loved this woman's backbone. He'd bet she straightened to her full height before she responded. Just under his chin. He remembered.

"Would you like to build that foundation? Do you want to see for yourself?"

"Sir?"

Even as he spoke, he felt his eyebrows come together. Where had this idea come from?

"I asked if you'd like to see Gia. You said the reason you tried to contact her mother was to complete a welfare check. I'm giving you the opportunity to do that. In person. If we can coordinate our schedules, we'll meet you for lunch. Or a cup of coffee or ice cream. Gia loves ice cream. That will allow you to personally assess my daughter and my ability to care for her. You'll see first-hand how she's treated. Does that suit you?"

*What the hell? Are you really asking the Frost Queen out for coffee? Have you lost your mind?*

While the voice in his head berated him, his heart raced. He wanted her to say yes, but she hadn't answered. Probably just as stunned by the invitation as he was. He persisted.

"When is your next day off, Miss Jensen?"

The attitude disappeared from her voice. She sounded apprehensive. He could easily check the hospital schedule and find out for himself. "I, um, I finished my shift this morning. I'm not scheduled back for three days."

"Well, as it happens, I'm off today as well. We've already missed lunch. How about a late afternoon ice cream? Say four-thirty. Gia favors the Scoops ice cream shop on the Boulevard. Do you know it? I can text you the address."

"No, that's not necessary. I know where it is. But—"

"Good. We'll see you there." He ended the call without letting her say another word, smiling at his cleverness.

This wasn't about proving to a nurse that he was a good father. This was about seeing the woman again.

His mother frowned when Blake and Gia stopped at her house.

"Yes, we're still planning to have dinner with you, Mum, but we're taking a little adventure first. We won't be long."

Gia hadn't been eating well to begin with. Even Carole Matthews' special mac-and-cheese hadn't interested her.

His mother shook her head. "But it's almost dinnertime now. And I'm making one of Gia's favorites. Beans and wienies." She dropped to her knees, eye-level with his daughter. "How does that sound, sweetheart?"

Gia only nodded. She stood beside him holding his hand and he squeezed it. "We're gonna try something a little different tonight and eat dessert first. We're going for ice cream."

Gia's face split into a wide grin and she looked at her grandmother and nodded vigorously. How could you not smile at that face? His mother laughed. "Well, I guess one time won't hurt. But save room for dinner. Come here and give Grammy a kiss goodbye."

She stood. "Don't be too long. Have fun you two." He'd omitted the fact that Noreen Jensen would also be there.

In the car on the way, he asked if Gia remembered the nurse from the hospital. She wrinkled her nose in thought and then shook her head. He explained "her" nurse wanted to see her again, which was why they were going to meet her. The old Gia would have inundated him with questions about the woman and launched a ten-minute debate with some imaginary friend about what flavor ice cream she might choose. Today, his daughter simply shrugged and his heart splintered a little more.

They arrived ten minutes early, a norm for him. Anyone who knew Blake Matthews knew punctuality was important to him.

Yet, at four-forty when Noreen still hadn't arrived, he was more concerned than irritated. What if she didn't show?

He'd be disappointed. For some unclear reason, he truly wanted to see her.

His heart leapt when the gold bell above the door jingled and she appeared. She hesitated, despite spotting them immediately. Only two booths in the place were occupied. He rose when she approached with slow, measured steps as if she contemplated turning to flee.

Blake extended his hand and hers slid into his, firm, warm, and titillating. "Miss Jensen, glad you could make it." Gia looked up from the drawing she'd been coloring and smiled.

Nurse Noreen appeared flustered. "I-I misjudged the traffic. I'm sorry for being late. I'm usually rather punctual."

"It's fine. I wondered if you were standing us up." They stood awkwardly, facing each other, their hands clasped. She eased hers out of his grasp and settled onto the seat across from them, turning her attention to his daughter.

"Hi, Argia, do you remember me? How're you feeling?"

Noreen plopped her purse and sweater beside her on the bench seat and folded her hands in front of her on the table. Gia smiled, observing every move. But she didn't speak.

He resumed his seat and wrapped his arm around Gia's shoulders. He leaned to whisper to her. "Gia, you didn't answer Miss Jensen. That's not polite. She asked if you remember her from the hospital."

She studied Noreen as if trying to recall their meeting, and then slowly shook her head. Noreen smiled and his stomach tightened.

"Well, it doesn't matter if you remember me. That was a difficult night. What's important is that I remember you. I hope you don't mind that I wanted to see you again."

Gia's round, chocolate eyes appeared to twinkle when she

gifted Noreen with a wide smile. Noreen refocused her gaze on him and his heart skipped. "Please call me Noreen."

Christ, he acted like a teenager, allowing a giant grin to crease his face. "Okay. If you'll call me Blake. What's your favorite flavor?"

"Excuse me?"

"Ice cream. We waited for you to order. What flavor would you like? I'm a mint chocolate chip man. Gia favors chocolate." He turned to his daughter and whisked her hair over her shoulders. Earlier today he brushed it to a high chestnut gloss and held it back with a frilly headband but allowed it to fall freely in soft waves to her shoulders. Gia loved her headbands. She rewarded his attention with a toothy grin.

Noreen tsked at him like a mother hen. "What kind of example are you setting, allowing ice cream so close to dinner?"

Her smile indicated she teased and he relaxed against the seat back. He wanted to impress upon this woman that he loved his daughter and would never hurt her. Besides that, he wanted to impress *her* for reasons he didn't care to examine.

His smile matched his daughter's. "You sound like my mother, Noreen. Haven't you ever allowed the sweet things in life to come first? If not, you should try it sometime. There's nothing wrong with dessert before dinner, once in a while. What flavor would you like?"

She scanned the menu on the wall and requested one scoop of mint chocolate chip also. It was a small victory, finding common ground in a mutual love for the same ice cream flavor, but it felt like a giant step toward progress.

He winked at her. "That's taking one for the team. Gia, sit here with Miss Noreen until I come back, all right?" She nodded as he slid from the booth. While he waited for three small cups of ice cream he kept an eye on them. Rarely did he ever have Gia out of eyesight if they weren't at home. Even then, he always knew where she was.

Noreen engaged her in conversation, apparently asking yes or no questions. Gia's head bobbed her responses. Amazing. Without uttering a single word, Gia still managed to communicate her feelings.

"I brought extra napkins because one of us usually ends up wearing our ice cream, don't we peanut?" Gia giggled. Noreen watched her attack the treat. In turn, he studied Noreen, wondering about the woman's true agenda and whether she was friend or foe. He wanted her to be a friend. Or maybe more. That left him with an unsettled feeling, almost queasy.

Admittedly, it was shallow but he was a man who first noticed a woman for her rearview or shapely legs. Lynne's mini skirt and black leather boots hit him like a wrecking ball the first time he saw her. He hadn't seen either with Noreen. The shapeless hospital scrubs did little to show off her figure. So why the attraction?

In spite of the unknown baseline factors he usually relied on when it came to the opposite sex, Noreen socked him right in the crotch from the get-go. In the midst of their first hospital confrontation, a small voice in his head alerted him that he liked this woman and her dedication to her patients. It had been arousing.

The front doorbell chimed and Gia's casted hand thumped his thigh. She moved to crawl onto his lap and he lifted her into place, missing The Captain's grand entrance. Lynne stormed the table and Gia shrunk closer to his chest.

"What's going on here?" Her shrill question startled Noreen, who sat with her back to the door. He hadn't had time to warn her.

Blake recognized that tone. Batten down the hatches. The Captain had the throttle wide open and she was haulin' ass through the waters of her world. "Hello Lynne. What are you doing here?"

Lynne stared at Noreen, seemingly not recognizing her in a

setting outside the hospital. He understood that. Out in public, Noreen looked much different, soft, and sexy. At the hospital, with her hair tied back, she was all business.

This was a good sign. Maybe they weren't conspirators.

"What is all this?" Lynne's hand swept the air. "Who are—" She stopped mid-sentence, her eyes narrowing. "Noreen? What are you doing here?" Amazingly, Lynne's voice lost its piercing pitch with that last question. She had an audience now and an act to perform.

Noreen remained silent, more focused on Gia than her mother.

In a public setting like this, among strangers except for Noreen, Lynne was unlikely to make a scene. Nevertheless, he wanted control of the situation.

"Lynne, you remember Nurse Jensen, don't you? She's completing a welfare check for the hospital and agreed to meet us here. She just began her eval—"

Lynne's head swiveled like a loose bar stool. "At an ice cream shop?" Her tone was incredulous. "A welfare check on my child in an ice cream store where Argia is not only exposed to harmful bright lights but also loud noises? You have no business bringing her here, knowing she has lactose issues and her palette is sensitive to hot and cold. I suppose this was your idea?"

Against his chest, Gia nestled tighter. "The only loud noise is your raised voice, Lynne. Don't make a spectacle of yourself."

Lynne turned her attention to Noreen. "You should have notified me. I'm the primary medical contact. I would've brought her to the hospital for tests and a full and proper evaluation. This isn't even a sanitary setting for her and her resistance is so low, she's susceptible to bacteria. Argia also has sensory issues and this environment could be harmful to her. You're a nurse, you should know that. You're the professional, or at least I thought you were."

Leave it to The Captain to take a cheap shot. Noreen had either lost her ability to respond or been stunned into silence.

But he wasn't. "You don't have to insult her, Lynne. This was the most convenient meeting location that accommodated our schedules. And it's my understanding the hospital did try to reach you, but you weren't home. Where have you been? Another spa getaway for your mental stability?"

God knows, he'd paid for enough of those. He learned early on that any crisis that arose, be it the decision to move from an apartment to a house or whether or not to save their marriage, required a weekend at the spa for Lynne to "meditate and find her true self."

She turned on him with vengeance in her eyes. "How dare you? First you take my daughter out of my house against my wishes and then you imply that I escape the emptiness within those walls with a frivolous excursion. For your information, I've been meeting with specialists about her condition. I've arranged for an expert in the field of autism to assess her. That's why I'm here. The appointment is tomorrow so I need to take her home. Your mother told me where to find you."

Across the table, Noreen's jaw dropped.

He chose his words carefully, needing to repress his rising anger. "She's not autistic, Lynne. And she doesn't have a condition. I'm not going to allow you to torture Gia with needless tests."

"It's not for you to decide. Come, Argia." She stretched for Gia with long, red, perfectly manicured fingernails coming through the air like a hawk's claw reaching for prey. Instinctively, he lifted Gia from his lap and placed her by his side, shielding her from her mother's grasp.

"I won't let you take her."

"Then I'll have you arrested." Her head pivoted toward Noreen. "Again. It wouldn't be the first time the police were called to play referee between this brute and my well-intentioned plans. Did you know that?"

Poor Noreen. She wore that deer-in-the-headlights look.

"Come, Argia. You're not allowed to have dairy, your father knows that. He's deliberately trying to make you ill."

Blake swatted Lynne's arm away and jumped out of the booth. "Back off, Lynne. You can't storm in here and snatch her from me like this. I'll break your arm if you try that again."

He regretted the threat immediately. Lynne screamed and stepped away from the booth. "Did you hear that? He threatened me." She pointed to Noreen. "You're my witness. My God, he threatened me with physical harm." She spun toward the counter where the employees and every customer in the shop stared at her. Cue the centerstage spotlights.

"Help me. Call the police. My life has been threatened."

He pressed his hand over his mouth to keep from snapping at her then raised both open palms in the air. "It's all right, folks," he said to everyone in the store. "There's no need to call the police. This is just a minor disagreement."

"Minor disagreement?" Lynne's high-pitched squeal filled the room and somewhere, a child burst into tears. "You call threatening to break my arm a minor disagreement?" She locked her hands in prayer mode. "I beg you, please," she beseeched the two stunned teenagers behind the counter, "call the police before he kills me."

He didn't blame the pimple-faced girl when she reached for the phone. The exhibition was frightening. His shoulders slumped knowing this couldn't end well. He turned to reassure his daughter that it would all work out and his breath caught at the sight of her empty spot.

His eyes darted to Noreen who cuddled Gia against her side. A look of terror etched both of their faces.

He sat down slowly and eased Gia's ice cream cup toward her. "It's okay, peanut. Finish your ice cream. Me and your mom only need to work some things out. It'll be fine." He raised his eyes to Noreen. Oddly, it was comforting to see her protecting his baby girl. Gia must have crawled under the table to sit by her. Had she done that of her own volition? Or had Noreen encouraged her to safety?

He wanted to plead for Noreen to take his side and yet she needed to see why he ended his marriage to this maniacal woman. And why, no matter how long it took, he had to wrest his daughter away from her mother.

# 8

Beside her, Argia trembled. She didn't hesitate when Noreen motioned for her to drop beneath the table and sit beside her. And it felt like the most normal action in the world to wrap her arm around the child and draw her closer.

Together, they watched the disagreement unfold between Blake and Lynne Matthews. Lynne wailed her fear for her safety at the counter while Blake sat silently across from them, his shoulders drooping, his eyes cast downward. Scoops of ice cream slowly melted in their cups while everyone waited.

When the bell above the door chimed, Blake looked up and then toward her. "I apologize for all of this. I'd like the chance to talk to you alone sometime if you're willing to keep an open mind about the situation. It's not what you think. *I'm* not what you think."

Over his words, Lynne directed the police toward the table. "There. My husband threatened my life."

Two uniforms stopped at the table, blocking the view of the shop and buffering Lynne's accusations. The male officer spoke first.

"Blake? I think it's best if we step outside."

The personal greeting sounded as if the police knew Blake, which could be good. Maybe they'd go easy on him. He stood as the female officer addressed her.

"Ma'am? I wonder if I could take a statement from you about what happened here." Her focus redirected to Argia. Cops are trained observers and she likely noticed the white pallor of the child's face. And possibly her own. "Is she okay?"

Before Noreen could respond, Lynne shrieked from behind the police woman's back. "You should be asking me that question." She emphasized the word 'me' and Noreen immediately visualized all capital letters in a text message. "She's my daughter and she's likely not okay. I'm certain she's terrified. I came here to take her home and her bully of a father threatened me. That would terrify any child."

Argia's grip tightened on her pant leg and she dropped her hand on top of it and squeezed. Blake's sad gray eyes rolled from her face to Argia's. "I love you, peanut. I'll call you soon." Then he voluntarily walked away with the cop.

"Come Argia, it's time to go home." The long red nails on Lynne's outstretched hand beckoned and suddenly, she understood Blake's impulse to slap it away. She wanted to as well. Instead, she dropped a light kiss on Argia's forehead. "Go with your mom, honey. I'll see you again and we'll finish this ice cream, okay?"

The child's deep brown, expressive eyes stared at her, silently communicating a plea for help. Noreen knew it. Felt it in her bones. Was helpless to do anything about it. For now.

Lynne's words cut through her heartache. "I already told you, Noreen, she's lactose intolerant. Don't fill my daughter's head with promises of treats she can't have. Argia, come!"

Dutifully, Argia crawled over her legs, took her mother's hand, and walked away, looking back over her shoulder only once with wide eyes and that beseeching expression. Noreen's heart sank.

The police officer slid into the seat across from her and flipped open a pocket notebook. Noreen responded to the basic questions with confidence, providing her name, her position at the hospital, explaining how she knew the Matthews and the circumstances around today's meeting. Only when the police officer asked whether she'd heard Blake threaten Lynne did she stammer.

In the middle of Lynne's tirade, she'd resisted an overwhelming urge to pick up her cup of ice cream and smash it into Lynne's face. The woman deliberately antagonized Blake in public and terrified her daughter.

"No, officer, I didn't hear Mr. Matthews threaten her. He moved her hand away from his face. If he hadn't, it looked like she might've jabbed him in the eye. But that was a defensive reaction, not an aggressive one. Beyond that, there was no threat."

The women stared at each other. "You didn't hear Mr. Matthews threaten to break his wife's arm?"

"No, no I didn't. I was trying to console Argia. The poor thing was so frightened. If he made a statement like that, I missed it."

Blake uttered those words under duress without meaning what they implied. She was certain of that. No different than someone casually saying, "I'll kill you if you don't show up or I'll kill you if you play that song one more time." They don't mean it literally and neither did he.

The slightest smile lifted the corners of the officer's mouth. "Thank you for that. Without a corroborating account, we can classify this as a simple domestic spat. Both parties will receive a warning and we won't press charges against Blake."

Relief flooded her body, a reaction she didn't understand. At that moment, she realized Lynne and Argia were no longer inside the ice cream shop. She swiveled in her seat for a better look but they were nowhere to be seen. Didn't the police need to interview Lynne too? She returned her attention to the police officer, suppressing the urge to laugh at the sight on the table. Pools of flavored ice cream rimmed three Styrofoam cups, a replication of the meltdown that had occurred. This entire incident was ridiculously overblown.

The officer rose, shook her hand, and walked away, speaking into a microphone clipped on her shoulder as she did. This afternoon's meeting had been intended to clear up Noreen's suspicions about Blake Matthews, not leave her with conflicted feelings. Its purpose was to allay her fears for Argia, not heighten them. She'd expected a normal conversation, not an interrogation by police and never in her wildest dreams did she anticipate that she'd provide an alibi to keep Blake Matthews from going to jail.

The ice cream shop employees stared when she stood to leave. Had they heard the entire conversation or did they speculate something more salacious, like a love triangle and she the other woman? At this point, she didn't care. She tugged on the glass door, involuntarily shuttering when the bell chimed, and stepped outside.

It stayed lighter longer every day as spring edged toward summer but the daylight already had started to fade. She walked toward her car lost in thought. She didn't see Blake in the shadows, leaning against the side of the building three doors down with one foot propped against the wall until she was within reach of him. He stepped out and she gasped, her steps halting inches from his body. Reflexively, she stepped backward.

"I didn't mean to scare you. I'm sorry." His voice was deep, his words low—capable of melting ice cream in a cup—or barriers around a heart. "I owe you an apology, Noreen. And, according to the police, I should thank you as well." In the dim light, he looked tired. Defeated. Normally, he stood at least a head taller than her. But not tonight.

A thousand questions puddled in her mind yet the only one she voiced surprised him. "Would you like to buy me a drink? I think we both could use one."

A thin flicker of white teeth appeared. "Yes, I could use a

drink. That sounds like a good idea." He pivoted and moved in beside her when she stepped. "There's an out-of-the-way bar right around the corner. We can walk."

Noreen drew her sweater tighter across her chest. It wasn't chilly this evening. The impulse confused her. And Blake noticed.

He cupped her elbow with his hand. "Are you afraid of me?"

She was nervous, that was certain. And despite what she told police, he did threaten Lynne. Was she afraid of him?

"I'm not sure, to be honest. I might be."

He exhaled. "That's a refreshingly truthful answer. But I already knew that about you. I'm not a violent man, regardless of what Lynne alleges or my words tonight." He pointed down the street to a grocery store, liquor store and a handful of offices still well lit. "There's a lot of activity around us and the bar is close. You're safe."

She felt childish. And rude. "I didn't mean to insult you."

"You didn't."

He maintained a light hold on her elbow while he directed her to the corner and across the street. They strode in silence toward a green neon sign that blinked: "No Problems." Inside, he maneuvered her to a rear booth. He ordered a scotch on the rocks and she requested a vodka soda in a tall glass.

Blake picked up the drink coaster the waitress placed on the table and began rotating it in his hands like a steering wheel. He didn't look at her when he spoke.

"I have to start by saying thank you. Quentin told me that you told his partner you didn't hear me threaten to break Lynne's arm. I appreciate that since I know that's exactly what you heard."

"Who's Quentin?" He still hadn't looked at her, instead focusing on the coaster that he now let slide through his fingers to the tabletop, lifted and let fall again.

"He was one of the uniforms that showed up."

"So, he's a friend of yours?"

Blake shrugged. "We know each other from work. We've been

on a few emergencies together and drank beers at a couple of events, you know, bachelor parties and retirements. I'd say we're friendly acquaintances." Now he leveled those dark gray eyes on her. "But he's good at his job. A professional. And he would've arrested me if he had to. I don't want you to think he cut me a break or anything."

Their drinks arrived and they stared over the rims of their glasses as each sipped. She positioned hers on the coaster but Blake continued to fiddle with the square cardboard, rolling it through the fingers on his right hand like an extra-large coin.

"I have to confess I did some Internet research on you."

If that surprised him, he hid it well. "Why?"

Her heart flipped because she'd asked herself the same question. Why did this man fascinate her? He was like the hot iron your mother warned would burn if you touched it and yet, you are compelled to touch simply to see how hot it really is. Blake was hot enough to burn her. She already knew that.

"I'm not sure why. But I was impressed with what I read. You've certainly received a lot of professional accolades. You should be very proud."

His head tilted slightly. "I shred those."

He what? As easily as he concealed any surprise, his comment raised her eyebrows and opened her eyes wider. "You shred them? But why? They signify recognition by your peers and superiors of your accomplishments."

He looked directly into her eyes, sending a warm quiver through her. "I do my job the same way every day. Some days, things don't go the way I want. Others, I get lucky. Why should I be lauded for saving someone's life one day when, maybe the day before, I lost someone? They were no less important to a husband or wife or family. To give me a certificate for saving one person diminishes the value of the man or woman I didn't save. I'm not penalized for one, why should I be applauded for the other?"

"That's an odd way to look at it, don't you think?"

"No. It's reality."

An awkward silence settled over them. Blake worked the coaster like a stress ball.

"Did you find what you were looking for when you read all those articles about me?"

She wanted answers and they hadn't been on those web pages. "No."

He raised those piercing gray eyes to hers again. "So, what do you want to know?"

If she could lay to rest her concerns about Argia, maybe she could kick this man out of her head.

"Have you been arrested before?"

The look on his face was that of a little boy's when asked by his mother if he broke the window with the baseball. "Yes, twice. Both times, the charges were dropped."

"What were the charges?"

Long eyelashes shaded his eyes but he took a deep breath and raised his chin to meet her again eye to eye. "Domestic violence." He stared at her, forcing her to ask the next question.

"May I ask?"

The corners of his mouth dropped down as if he clenched his teeth. "Sure, Noreen. What do you want to know?"

He didn't plan to hand her the information outright. She'd have to work for it. All right. A nurse sometimes must ask several questions before learning a patient's specific complaint. For a patient to say, "My stomach hurts" is not enough.

"What were you accused of?"

"Which time?"

She smiled. He was good at being coy. "The first time."

"My ex-wife claimed I struck her."

"So, it was after your divorce?" That would make the infraction recent.

"No, we were married at the time."

"Struck her where? How?"

He pointed to his face. "Black eye. With my fist."

"Did you?"

"No ma'am."

"How'd she end up with a black eye?"

He shrugged. "I don't know." And then he grinned. "It was a doozy, though, a real shiner. If it was self-inflicted, it had to hurt."

Was he kidding? "Do you think she hit herself?"

The smile disappeared. "I don't know." He folded the coaster in half, and then in half again. Next, he thumbed the sides, slowly separating the cardboard layers.

"Is she capable of hurting herself?"

Blake threw his head back and laughed. "You'd be surprised what that woman is capable of."

She leaned into the table. "I'd hoped we could sit down and talk like two adults who share a mutual concern for Argia. Instead of playing this cat-and-mouse game with me, why don't you tell me what's going on? Talk to me, Blake. Otherwise we're wasting our time."

Although sitting across from him was hardly a waste. It afforded her a better look at his handsome face, those sensuous lips and eyes that opened a door to his soul. If she hadn't heard Lynne's stories and implied accusations, she'd describe Blake Matthews as an amazing man. But he was someone else's mistake. She had to remember that.

His eyes narrowed and he mimicked her movement, leaning in until their faces were inches apart. His voice resembled a growl.

"Why do you want to know, Noreen? What reason do you have to delve into my life? To stop co-workers and ask about me? Oh, it's a good ruse, claiming you want to check on Gia but you barely treated her." He sat back and his index finger tapped the table to emphasize his words. "I'll answer any question you ask with the truth. But first I have to know the reason for your so-called concern."

That insulted her and she squared her shoulders. "My concern is genuine, sir. Do you think I'm some sort of spy for your ex-wife? Why so mistrusting unless you have something to hide? I just lied to the police for you. Don't sit here and challenge me, you self-righteous bastard. I have questions and I want answers."

He nodded slowly and raised his glass to her in a toast. "Touché."

An uncomfortable silence permeated the space between them, despite the bar's activity around them. She sipped her drink. The alcohol warmed her as it eased down her throat. She hadn't eaten much today and she already felt its effects.

Blake concentrated on peeling apart the cardboard coaster layers one by one. Finally, he sliced through the quiet. "It seems we want to talk to each other but neither one trusts the other." He laid shredded pieces of the coaster in a pile. "I'm not interested in continuing this dance but I doubt we can discuss the weather or spring training or any other topic until we settle the matter of my daughter's welfare." He drained his glass and signaled the waitress for another round.

He ran his fingers through his hair. "So, here's the deal. My daughter is the most important thing in my life. I plan to do everything I can to take her away from her mother and gain full custody. If you are here as Lynne's mole, that's the message you can take back. You can make all the accusations you want against me, parroting the claims my ex-wife makes." He pointed at her. "I assure you, I'll fight every charge and I'll do whatever it takes to win."

The fire in his eyes was a turn-on. The man was devoted to Argia. A woman he fell in love with would likely enjoy the same commitment. What would make a woman walk away from a man like Blake Matthews?

"I'm not here as Lynne's spy."

His right eyebrow arched. "Then why'd you ask me to buy you a drink?"

She straightened her shoulders. "Why'd you wait for me?"

They stared at each other defiantly and simultaneously smiled and then laughed. Blake's shoulders relaxed when he spoke.

"I think we could give Gia's little friends a run for their money." Laughter lightened his voice. "Next thing you know, we'll be in a did-too-did-not showdown."

She agreed. "Honest, Blake, I'm not your enemy." His name rolled off her lips so easily. "If anything, I'm an advocate for Argia, which makes me your ally. I can't explain why." She clutched her stomach. "It's a gut feeling I have that something is wrong. Argia's eyes are so expressive and when she looks at me, I see a plea for help. I hear it in my head."

Her father's eyes were equally as communicative, and they bore into her as if she stood naked before him. She stuttered but continued.

"I-I sense something is going on in your house that is harmful to Argia. Do I suspect you? Maybe. Based on statements your wife made, if I believed them, yes, I'd think you were the problem. But there are events that don't add up. Tonight, I saw a different Lynne Matthews than the mother I dealt with in the hospital. What's more, I've watched you care for your daughter. You adore her. It's obvious. And I saw the terror in Argia's eyes when that whole debacle unfolded. So now, I don't know what I think. I'm inclined to pound on your front door with Child Services standing behind me and take Argia away from both of you."

He tensed immediately and she reached across the table and touched his forearm. "I would never do something like that. Never. That would only hurt Argia and that's the last thing I want to do." Electricity charged through each finger and up her arm from his skin. His gaze fell to her hand, as if surprised that she touched him. She eased her hand back and dropped it in her lap, aware of the heat pooling below her waist.

"More like I'd pound on the door, whisk her away to my home

and hide her from both of you to protect her. I think she needs protection. I'm not certain from what. Or who."

He'd annihilated the coaster and flicked the pea-sized pieces with his finger, staring at her. His gaze dropped deep into her heart. She gulped from her second drink. "I'm sorry to be so blunt. Alcohol usually loosens my tongue."

As if a mood light glided over his face, Blake's features softened and he smiled. "Let's order some food. I'll tell you a little bit about the nightmare that was my marriage."

# 9

They went through the motions of reading the menu and ordering dinner. Noreen tried to reconcile this meeting with a man she barely knew, partially feared, and found so damned attractive. He was obstinate, a tad intimidating and too self-assured. With each sip of vodka, her defenses weakened whereas the alcohol seemed to fortify him.

The waiter scooped away the remnants of the coaster and disappeared. What would his nervous energy target next? He couldn't sit idly without something to divert his attention. But he tried. He folded his hands on the table and leveled a bright smile on her.

"So. The weather. What do you think of the winter we had?"

It was the perfect statement to ease the awkwardness that had settled between them again. She chuckled and relaxed against the seatback. "I'm happy that we had so little snow this year. And I'm excited that spring training has started. I'm a Pirates fan, in case you planned to discuss baseball next."

He laughed lightly and reached for a sugar packet. "You have a nice smile. You know, when we first met I thought you were a heartless witch. I was wrong."

That statement stung and she gulped. "What makes you say that?"

Starting at the edge, he rolled the yellow packet into a tiny tube. "You were determined to protect Gia. I know that now. But that night, knowing my daughter was injured and suspecting what I suspect, all you were to me was a roadblock to my baby girl. And an ally to Lynne. Or so I thought."

She narrowed her eyes at him. "Please, Blake. Tell me what's going on."

He nodded, dropped the damaged sugar packet that now seeped granules, and began curling the edge of his napkin.

"I didn't see it at first. Even when my friends and my mother tried to point out what was so obvious to them, I gaffed it off. From the first minute I laid eyes on Lynne, I was captivated." He flattened his hand against his chest. "I loved her deeply and when you're that enthralled by someone, you're blind to their faults. So, I wrote it all off as clumsiness or carelessness."

"Wrote what off?"

He spread his hands wide, the napkin waving like a flag. "All the complaints. The ailments. She was always sick. And accident prone, especially in the kitchen. Lynne hates to cook and she's terrible at it. I was the cook in the family. But I thought it was sweet that my girlfriend tried to cook romantic dinners to surprise and please me. Unfortunately, every attempted meal ended in an injury or an accident. She'd burn her hand or cut her finger. The quart of milk or canister of flour would somehow tumble over, making it impossible for her to finish whatever recipe she attempted. And of course, it was the end of the world. She'd crumble to the floor and the crocodile tears would roll down her face.

"But that wasn't all. There'd be scraped knees from a fall walking to the mailbox, whiplash from an errant car that almost sideswiped her. It was as if a dark cloud hovered over her. Something bad always happened to her. Or at least, that's what she claimed. It was always 'poor Lynne.'

"Before we were married, I rushed to her after every emergency phone call, sometimes calling in a substitute because I was on duty. That was never fair to the men on my team but they might tell you I was blind at the time. I would've done anything for her."

He paused for a drink, wiped the moisture from his glass with the napkin and balled up the damp paper in his hand. "I'm not sure I can explain to you how hard I fell for her." He tapped the table with his index finger. "I developed tunnel vision and she was the only thing I could see."

He drank again and shrugged. "I'd only known her three months when I asked her to move in with me. The minute the door closed behind her, it all changed."

"What do you mean?"

"Every day, there was something wrong with her. A headache. Severe stomach issues. It was always something. I half expected to come home and hear her complain that her hair hurt. I was sympathetic at first but it turned old real fast. She was young and healthy but I swear she searched the Internet for information to manufacture disorders. She insisted she had symptoms of Parkinson's Disease. And various cancers, sometimes high," Blake touched his left breast, "and sometimes low," he grabbed his abdomen. "You name it, she suffered from it. She constantly complained. Until the dogs."

"You had dogs?"

Blake nodded. "Two. Lynne convinced me that she was afraid to stay alone at night when I was on duty so we rescued two dogs, because she couldn't have just one. Don't ask me why. She said the dogs provided for a safer, cozier home. They were beautiful Labradors, one yellow and one chocolate."

"What were their names?"

"Marlin and Dakota. They were a rambunctious pair and it

fell to me to exercise them and care for them. I didn't mind, though, but with my schedule, sometimes it was difficult. Lynne barely paid attention to them. She hated that they shed on the furniture and left hair on her outfits and she was outraged when Dakota chewed one of her shoes and Marlin shredded one of her precious handbags."

The memory caused him to smile and Noreen glimpsed his face free of worry. In that moment, he looked years younger and her breath caught.

"It didn't register with me at the time but, once Marlin and Dakota were in the house, Lynne's own emergencies occurred less often. But every day, it seemed, the dogs got into trouble."

"Didn't she have a job, Blake?"

"When we met, she had a part-time job with a rental agency. It was mostly men in the office and Lynne complained that they made passes at her. I convinced her to quit and find something else." He shrugged. "Another job never materialized."

Their food arrived and he repositioned his plate to show her a mound of homemade chips. He eyed her strawberry and spinach salad. "Try one of these chips. They're incredible."

The potato aroma tempted her taste buds.

"C'mon, Noreen. Step over the line one time and do something crazy. Your plate looks much too healthy. Dip one in this cup of sauce. You'll be hooked."

The warm, salty chip filled her mouth with flavor, enhanced by the restaurant's signature sauce. She grinned at him as she chewed.

"Good, huh? Stick with me kid. I know all the holes-in-the-wall that have the best food."

Stick with him. With Blake Matthews. The suggestion appealed to her.

Several minutes elapsed while they attacked their plates. Blake ordered a third round of drinks and they exchanged small talk about their dinners and the overall menu. But she wanted to know more about the Matthews' household.

"So, Lynne is home all day with dogs she ignores. But you must have been happy because ...." She didn't complete the sentence. She wanted to scream at him 'because you married her. Because you had a child with her.' But she tightened her lips together and curbed her outrage.

He shrugged. "I'm a proud man, too proud for my own good. I wasn't going to admit to my friends, my co-workers, or my mother that I'd rushed into something that wasn't working. Especially because my friends tried to tell me there was something off about Lynne. They all saw it. Besides, I thought it was working. At least between the sheets it was. We had some incredible, earth-shattering sex and, as thin as that sounds, I was willing to overlook everything else because of that. I'm not a man who is driven by sex but where Lynne was concerned, is still concerned to some degree, all rational thoughts disappeared when it came down to taking our clothes off."

There was no viable explanation for the crushed feeling that consumed her. He still loved his wife.

"So, you marry her and have a child. You haven't told me anything unusual about your life, nothing that explains accusations of domestic violence or child abuse."

The mention of his daughter caused him to smile. "The child came before the marriage."

He let that statement hang, waiting for her reaction. Men were so stupid about that kind of stuff.

"Make no mistake, Noreen, Gia is my universe. I don't regret for one minute that she exists and I wanted children. That's the bottom line." He tapped the table again with his finger. "I wanted to be married and have kids. I didn't give it a second thought to marry Lynne when she told me she was pregnant.

"But before that, practically as soon as Lynne moved in, I

knew it wasn't right with us even though I wouldn't admit it to anyone else. I wanted out. But I didn't get out fast enough."

"Are you saying she trapped you into marriage? C'mon Blake, you're a grown man. You know how babies are made. Weren't you using birth control?"

He nodded. "She was on the pill. I watched her take it every night. I discovered much later, after Gia was born, that Lynne stopped taking the pill because she said it caused her to gain weight and feel bloated. In front of me, like the dutiful wife, she swallowed a low dose baby aspirin."

The woman's deception shocked her. "Didn't that anger you when you found out?"

He'd destroyed his first napkin and moved onto a second, speaking to an unknown spot on the table. "Not really. Gia was born by the time she confessed that to me and I was so in love with that baby, I didn't care how she came to be. We went to Mexico for a winter getaway. One extended weekend that changed my life. My plan was to see how the four days went and if we couldn't make it work in sunshine and white sand, then I was ready to concede there was nothing between us." The memory caused him to smile and she felt like an intruder.

Blake spoke to the reminiscence. "Lynne was a different woman on that trip. The weekend was extraordinary. Gia is the result."

He fell silent, both of them concentrating on the napkin he'd mutilated. After a heavy sigh, he continued. "I told myself that marrying Lynne and having a baby was what I wanted. Things had gotten better. The clumsiness disappeared. She didn't have so many accidents. I thought we could make it work." He rested a fist over his chest. "My mind kept telling that to my heart.

"After we married, I pampered her more than ever. I hired a housekeeper who served her meals when I worked and I cooked on my days off. I picked up the mail and the groceries, did the laundry, paid the bills. To this day, as I look back on it, I've no idea what she did all day. After Gia was born, Lynne insisted she needed a nanny to help with the baby so I hired one."

Blake noticed her eyebrows shoot up and nodded.

"I can't explain it other than to say I was convinced my job was to take care of my wife and that's what I did."

More disappointment tugged at Noreen's heart. The commitment of this man was unfathomable and for an unexplained reason, jealousy overcame her. Did Lynne Matthews know what she'd ruined?

"You loved her. I understand." *Why couldn't a man love her like that?*

Blake raised his gaze to hers. "I did. I'm not ashamed to admit that. But things grew worse instead of better."

He spoke the next words as if lost in thought. "I should have seen it with the dogs."

"Seen what?"

He fortified his next statement with a deep breath. "The Munchausen's."

Noreen gasped. "The what?"

She knew the term, was familiar with the affliction from her studies but had never encountered a patient suffering from Munchausen syndrome. The mental illness causes the person who suffers from it to inflict bodily harm on themselves or manifest psychological symptoms. The disorder can be debilitating.

Blake whispered his words. "Are you familiar with Munchausen syndrome by proxy?"

His words set the room spinning. She'd studied the syndrome in nursing school, fascinated by the horror of the disease like people who can't tear their eyes from a roaring fire or tragic crime scene. Some considered Munchausen syndrome by proxy a form of child abuse. The caretaker, most often the mother, either fabricates fake symptoms or causes real symptoms to develop to make it look like the child is sick, in turn drawing attention to herself for the burden she bears in caring for the child. She'd read case studies in college about mothers who ultimately killed their children. She shuddered.

Her thoughts tumbled over each other as she searched her brain for specific details pertaining to Munchausen syndrome by proxy. She'd never seen a case of it, never treated a patient suffering from it or rescued a victim who was the object of it. Was that why their paths crossed, hers and the Matthews? Was she Argia's savior?

Sweat pooled beneath her armpits as Blake's hushed words launched her on a mental roller coaster ride.

"I can see by the look on your face that you know the syndrome."

She stared at him, too shocked to speak.

"It was there with the dogs. There was always something wrong with them, according to Lynne. She was constantly taking them to the vet's office for hundreds of dollars of appointments and medicines and ailments. I never saw it. Our job is twenty-four hours on duty, forty-eight hours off. I think you know that, I'm only making sure."

As if in a trance, she nodded and Blake continued. "I'd be on duty and she'd call saying Marlin was throwing up non-stop and she was on her way to the vet's. Or Dakota had an eye infection. Or one of them had injured their paw or their recently cut nails were infected.

"The men at the station used to tease me that I'd rescued two of the lamest dogs in the city. But they weren't lame, Noreen, they were beautiful creatures and I beat myself up now for not seeing how she abused them," his voice cracked, "and wondering what awful things she did that I don't even know."

She was afraid to ask. "What happened to them?"

"It became apparent that they weren't as friendly toward Lynne as they were to me and Lynne convinced me that the baby would be in danger with them around. Isn't that ironic? Labs by nature protect children but our dogs were monsters, according to her. I grew tired of hearing her whine about it so we gave them away before Gia was born. They went to a farm where they could run and where there were kids to love and play with them. I checked on them for a while after we let them go. Lynne never knew that. I enjoyed those goofballs."

The waitress cleared their plates and Blake asked if she wanted dessert or coffee. They each ordered coffee. Activity in the bar had picked up and the noise level required them to lean toward each other to be heard. A hint of cologne lingered on Blake and teased her. The physical attraction juxtaposed against her racing thoughts.

"So, after you found out she was pregnant you were married?"

He nodded and removed the stir stick from his drink. "I'll be honest with you. I was one happy son of a bitch. Even though there was an underlying feeling of dread, tying myself to this woman for all eternity, I wanted her and I wanted our baby.

"Lynne's pregnancy was not without complications. I'm not sure if they were real or manifested. It was her body and the doctors all supported her ailments. She was confined to bed for the last three months and required a round-the-clock nurse, even when I was home. Lynne insisted on the nurse." He held his hands out wide and shrugged. "What did I know? I'd never been around a pregnant woman before. My mother and my sister, when they chimed in, disputed every complaint and issue Lynne demonstrated. But I shut them down. I wouldn't listen to them."

"Wasn't that expensive? How did you afford full-time care?"

A crooked smile etched his face and he shrugged. "Not many people know this. I'm not certain why I'm telling you but, I have quite a healthy bank account thanks to a spinster aunt who adored me and my sister but doted on me. The woman scared me with her long, flowing white hair and her dark, shuttered house that smelled, ah, odd to a kid. But my folks made us visit her all the time. She was quite wealthy and she willed it all to the man-child, as she referred to me. I've invested well and already have a trust fund established for Gia that will pay for her college and more. It was easy to syphon money from the interest on my investments and never touch the principle and cater to Lynne's whims. Frankly, I was willing to do it."

The impact of his words threatened her dinner. He'd loved the woman with his entire being. She waited for more.

"Gia was tiny when she was born. She weighed less than five pounds. My mother swears to this day it was because Lynne didn't want to gain weight and refused to eat a healthy diet. Lynne refused to breast feed the baby and we had issues finding a suitable formula. She claimed that every brand we tried made the baby sick. Gia took a bottle fine from me but when I wasn't there, there'd be frantic phone calls about the baby vomiting. Or refusing to eat. Eventually, the doctors classified her as a failure-to-thrive baby."

Noreen was in the process of swallowing the last of her coffee and it flowed the wrong way when she gasped. She gagged and spewed liquid across the table in an effort to catch her breath. Her eyes watered and she coughed uncontrollably. Blake's eyes widened and he slid from his side of the booth onto her side. He thumped her on the back.

"Are you all right? Breathe deeply."

She wheezed. Her chest compressed and she struggled to fill it with air.

Blake grabbed her arms and lifted them to the ceiling. "Raise your arms in the air."

Her face was on fire. Her eyes bulged. But as her chest muscles stretched, the vise grip eased. Blake locked her wrists in one hand keeping them held high and applied pressure to her back, tapping it lightly. The coughing began to subside. Her nose was running and tears streamed down her face. Of all things to think about, she remembered that her mascara wasn't waterproof.

People around their table glanced nervously at her and

looked away. She'd be embarrassed if she ever stopped choking and regained her normal breathing.

All the while, Blake spoke softly. "Breathe. Relax. You're going to be okay. Panic only makes it worse. I won't let anything happen to you."

In all of his spoken reassurances, those last words shot to her brain. And into her heart like a targeted arrow. She leaned into him and filled her lungs with air, slowly releasing the oxygen. Heat emanated from his side and chest, his muscles taunt as he stretched his arms to keep hers extended.

Her throat felt raw when she spoke and her voice was hoarse. "Okay. I'm okay."

He remained in control. "Take a few deeper breaths. Slow. Inhale." She filled her lungs. "Exhale." She did.

He lowered his arms but the back massage continued. "Again."

Inhaling was easier this time. The crisis was passing. "I'm okay." At the sound of her voice, she attempted to clear her throat.

"You'll sound like that for a couple of hours. Likely you've irritated your throat and vocal chords. You're a nurse so that probably sounds stupid coming from me, doesn't it? Sorry. You fall into a habit of helping people."

Still wrapped in his embrace, she breathed normally, the warmth from his body igniting hers. She straightened, effectively moving away from the hand caressing her back. "Thank you. I can't tell you how embarrassed I am." She turned to look at him, not realizing their proximity. His face was inches from hers, his gray eyes dark with concern. His lips full, his mouth barely open, a hint of white peeking through. She couldn't tear her eyes away from that mouth.

The restaurant's special sauce remained on his breath and she smelled it when he spoke. Sweet and tangy. The urge to order more chips overcame her.

"There's nothing to be embarrassed about. I'm glad you worked through it."

Reluctantly, she lifted her gaze to his and edged away from his side, immediately sensing the loss of comfort.

Swallowing remained difficult. She coughed again. "Is that a modern CPR technique, lifting the arms? I didn't learn that one."

He dropped his arm from her back to rest on the seat, falling just below her waist, touching high on her butt cheek. An intimate position she didn't readjust.

Blake laughed, suddenly erasing the calamity, and lightening her heart. "Actually, that's a Carole Matthews' remedy. When we were small and regularly shoved too much food in our mouths and began to choke, my mom would immediately say "arms up in the air." I'm not sure if it actually opened the air passages or if it merely was a diversion—something to take our attention away from the feeling that we were choking to death. But it always worked. I use it for Gia if she swallows wrong."

She threw her head back and laughed. "I shall remember that for my patients." His eyes clouded at the raspy sound of her voice and she cleared her throat again. She averted her gaze to the bar crowd, who continued to cast curious glances her way.

"I provided a bit of entertainment for them, like rubberneckers at a car crash." Remembering the tears, she swiped at her cheeks. "And I must look like a freak from a B-rated horror film."

Blake grinned. "Please stop talking. You sound sexy as hell with that voice. Here. Let me."

He cupped her chin with his left hand and raised her face toward the ceiling, dipped the corner of a napkin in her water glass and gently dabbed at her cheeks. She studied him, confused by the sensations shooting from the hand on her chin straight to her female parts. Her nipples peaked and she tightened her thighs. Did he sense this innocent gesture was catapulting her into confusion? Christ, if he propositioned her, she'd accept in a heartbeat. She'd jump into bed with Blake Matthews at an Olympic gold medal winning pace.

Heat from his touch torched her face. And every other part.

"That's better." His words yanked her back to reality. "Not perfect but you look fine. Do you want to get out of here? The place has gotten pretty loud and it's getting late."

He stood without waiting for her to agree but he was right. The raucous crowd made it hard to carry on a normal conversation.

He extended his hand and helped her out of the booth. He signaled their waitress, pointed to the front of the room and the cash register and maintained his grasp on her hand, walking in front of her, leading the way to the counter. "We'll settle our tab up front. Dinner is my treat."

Once outside, Blake placed his hand on her lower back, riding just above her hips. "I enjoyed this evening, Noreen. You've restored my faith in the female species. My perception has been a bit skewed for the last few years."

Years? Was he serious?

They walked toward the parking lot adjacent to the ice cream shop. "What does that mean, exactly?" It was none of her business but she wanted to know and hoped the inquiry sounded playful instead of serious.

The look on his face indicated he didn't understand the question. "You said your perception has been skewed for a couple of years. Yet you've mentioned your mother and sister and I bet there's a female interest or two in there somewhere." What woman wouldn't want to spend time with this man? "Your reference strictly pertains to the unpleasantness with your wife, right?"

They'd reached her car. How had he known what she drove and where she parked?

Even in the darkness, his bright smile shone. "Ex-wife. Lynne refuses to use the term but the divorce was final more than a year ago. And sisters and mothers don't count as part of the female species. Sorry."

He winked at her and her stomach somersaulted. "I've had no girlfriends since my divorce if that's what you're wondering about. Lynne likely told you differently. I'm not about to parade a line of women in front of Gia. She's confused enough."

As if he were ending a business meeting, he shook her hand. Then he shoved his hands in his pockets and rocked back on his heels. "This evening didn't go at all the way I planned but I enjoyed myself. Thank you. I'll see you around."

He turned on his heel and strode into the night. The impulse to yell to him to stop died in her throat. She didn't want him to leave. There was so much more information she needed, so many questions he hadn't answered. Instead of resolving her fears for Argia, he'd ignited more. Like a campfire brought to life with added kindling, desire burned within her. For more answers. And for more Blake.

# 10

Noreen drove home on automatic pilot, dizzy from the scenarios galloping across the fields in her mind. Munchausen's. Her heart missed a beat each time the word repeated in her head. Munchausen's by proxy manifested a gulp of air and a hard swallow. If what Blake said was remotely true, Argia might be in imminent danger. Why didn't he see that? Why hadn't he contacted the authorities? Had Lynne arrested or at least investigated? How could he casually watch his child walk out of the ice cream store, her hand locked in that's monster's grip?

And the biggest question of all—how could he leave Argia in that house and move out? Deliberately abandon her? He professed his love for his daughter but what type of man walks away and leaves a child standing in harm's way?

The minute she arrived home, she kicked off her shoes, tossed her things on the couch and trudged to the basement where all of her textbooks and medical journals from college were stored. Granted, the information might be outdated, but it was a place to start.

She hauled the cardboard box off the shelf and searched

through the volumes, selecting the books that might contain helpful information. There were only three that seemed applicable so, leaving the opened box and pile of papers, notebooks and textbooks scattered on the floor, she carried the relevant ones to her kitchen table. Deliberately trying to calm her nerves, she brewed a cup of coffee, and then began to scan the pages.

Ongoing research changes the medical field almost daily and her books were all at least five years old. Still, the basic information frightened her. She'd recalled the specifics well.

A caretaker, most often the mother, deliberately causes a child to appear ill, sometimes by adding blood to the child's urine or stool. Had she read that in one of Argia's medical files? The caretaker might withhold food so the child didn't gain weight. Blake said Lynne refused to eat correctly during her pregnancy and claimed Argia wouldn't take a bottle. Tears blurred her vision when she read further.

The caretaker might claim the child suffered a high fever and as proof to medical personnel, warm the thermometer in hot water or apply heat to the child's face to redden its appearance.

A caretaker might deliberately make the child sick to cause diarrhea or vomiting. Argia had been rushed to the hospital for uncontrolled nausea. Reported by her mother.

A caretaker might infect an intravenous line to make the child sick. Noreen didn't suspect that but what had set off the emergency alert on Argia's monitors that night?

She pressed her fingers to her temple. The nurse in her couldn't conceive of this type of conduct and least of all, from a mother. She reached for her laptop and searched a private medical reference forum for physicians, finding an article that detailed signs and symptoms of Munchausen's. The adult caretaker, usually the mother, was often in the medical profession or was highly educated regarding health care and frequently detailed the medical issues of the child using professional references and terminology. The caretaker was actively involved in the child's care and regularly attempted to insert herself into the health care team.

Noreen sat back in her chair after reading the final sentence of the article, her pulse racing. "Given the devotion shown by the mother and attention to the child's well-being, a diagnosis of Munchausen syndrome by proxy is difficult and sometimes impossible to diagnose."

She took her search out onto the Web, knowing that an Internet search would not necessarily provide facts. But there might be news reports of arrests made or Munchausen's investigations that made headlines in other states. Plenty of articles about the syndrome itself popped onto the screen but she found minimal information about actual cases where authorities had suspected or proved the disorder. One headline declared a dozen shocking Munchausen's cases but as she read each one, the facts proved neglect and abuse. It appeared medical and law enforcement personnel hesitated to attach the actual syndrome to the crimes. The more she studied the information, the tighter her stomach knotted. Dear Lord. What if Blake was right in his assessment? How would he ever prove it? How could she help?

Their conversation tonight remained unfinished. Maybe he had contacted the authorities. She'd been unable to ask. If so, whom had he contacted? The police? Did they have jurisdiction? Had he spoken his concerns to Argia's doctors? Did they believe him? Would she have believed him that first night she met him in the hospital?

No, she wouldn't have. Lynne lobbied quickly to paint the absent father as a villain, a man who abandoned his sickly child and desperate wife. She flung medical jargon around like one recites the ingredients of a cherished recipe. Noreen asked her that night if she was a nurse and Lynne had lowered her eyes demurely and said no, but her investment in Argia's health necessitated an education. She'd been flattered that Noreen had mistaken her for a trained professional.

In retrospect, she'd viewed a concerned mother well-versed on her daughter's health issues. It had been refreshing. Now a cloud of doubt loomed over her impressions along with more questions than she could articulate. She needed professional advice.

While she attended nursing school, she'd worked as a part-time bank teller and became friends with Mackenna McElroy, a woman who'd been treated badly by her ex-boyfriend and then became the focus of an FBI investigation into a bank robbery ring. Most of their co-workers believed the worst, but Noreen had seen Mackenna's vulnerability and believed her. It had been a harrowing experience for Mackenna but one with a happy ending, considering she'd fallen in love and now lived with the FBI agent who saved her life. And she and Noreen remained friends.

Noreen felt comfortable calling Jake Manettia about Argia, even though she doubted the FBI had jurisdiction over this type of problem. Jake was trained to recognize criminal conduct and knew the law. She wanted reassurance that she wasn't fast becoming an eyewitness to crimes being committed against Argia. But after hanging up the phone, she still didn't have her answers.

"There's nothing illegal about an overzealous parent," Jake told her, "and you haven't told me anything to prove otherwise. You have no medical proof that she taints the child's food or that she abuses her. Until the broken arm, there was no physical injury that you know of. Kids fall down steps all the time. You're describing a mother who overreacts if her child gets a splinter and a divorce that, based on what little you know, is far from amicable. If anything, the father sounds more suspicious to me. If he thought the mother was harming the little girl, why'd he leave in the first place? Why not stay and build a case against her?"

It was a question she wanted answered as well. She'd ask Blake.

## 11

The overwhelming urge to kiss Noreen surprised Blake. He wasn't considering a simple peck on the cheek to say goodnight. No, he wanted an open-mouthed, tongue exploring, breathtaking lip-lock designed to leave no doubt in her mind about his desires. Because without a doubt he wanted to make love to Noreen Jensen. And not in a soft, slow, romantic encounter in front of a fireplace after an expensive dinner and bottle of fine wine. No, this urge was primal. His impulse leaned toward hot, heavy, sweaty sex right there in the parking lot if they'd stood there much longer.

Christ, his mind filmed an X-rated movie while they stood beside her car saying goodbye. Her hair falling into his face. Her breasts cupped in his hands and those long legs wrapped around his hips, high heels still on her feet. He'd turned and walked away quickly out of necessity.

His suspicions about Lynne floored her. He hadn't intended to confide in her like that but there was something about her that made him lower his defenses. She was so easy to talk to. Part of the problem was those blue eyes, the way they looked at him, drawing him out, putting him at ease, coaxing him to discuss the private portions of his life. He'd bet she was a detective in another life because she could easily lead him to confess to murder.

She hadn't felt the magnetism like he had because the look on her face was one of distraction while she mentally diffused the bombshell he dropped about the Munchausen's. He couldn't blame her there. Hearing that about a mother would throw anyone for a loop.

He'd been unfamiliar with the term Munchausen's until a couple of years ago. As if the Gods of Fate aimed to fortify his knowledge, one day after Gia had suffered another mysterious illness, a news story about a New Jersey mother killing her children made headlines. Authorities suspected Munchausen's by proxy. He'd lain awake beside his wife that entire night, staring at her, thinking about the dogs, wondering if he dared associate the words Munchausen's and Lynne. Then he began his research in earnest. And he'd enacted his plan. Divorce her and assume full custody of Gia, certain that Lynne would not prove a competent parent and provider.

Now that he was out of the house, he documented every sniffle and belly ache and the lack of any illness when his daughter was in his care. And for fifty-percent of the time, Gia was safely out of her clutches. If he doubted his suspicions, the sit-down with the men in his unit validated his fears. He'd always viewed Lynne through rose-colored glasses, but his men saw clearly. There was no 'maybe' anymore regarding Gia's issues. That talk cemented his beliefs and prompted him to share his concerns with Noreen.

He'd had time—more than a year—to assimilate the theory, complete with all its consequences. Tossing that term out tonight and linking it to Lynne was bound to shock Noreen. The fact that she practically choked on her drink proved that. At that moment, she'd been so vulnerable he'd jumped to her side like he'd respond to Gia in distress. Only the feeling summoned up by Noreen's red nose and smeared mascara was far from parental protection. Hot desire surged directly to his dick.

When her hand slid into his for their parting handshake, it was all he could do to keep from yanking her to his chest and covering that gorgeous mouth with his. Unlike the immediate physical attraction he experienced the minute he laid eyes on Lynne, the urge to know Noreen on a deeper level was more consuming, as if he needed to possess her because she could so easily own him. The connection was intense. Not an infatuation and not love at first sight. He didn't believe in that phenomenon and he'd learned his lesson the hard way with Lynne about relying solely on physicality.

No, the longing for Noreen may have been physical, but it was also spiritual. Despite their contentious first meeting in the hospital, when he viewed her as the enemy, he'd been aware of a profound level of familiarity. As if they knew each other in another life and their paths were destined to cross again in this one. He didn't discount the idea of reincarnation or the existence of the next world, simply because no one could prove the theory one way or the other. He controlled his destiny with the life choices he made, good and bad, but Noreen knocked him off balance. And from their first meeting, she stuck in his head like a melody. He'd planned for tonight's meeting to stop the music.

Instead the volume turned up to a higher level, even in the face of Lynne's intrusion and a police presence. Now what? This wasn't the time to foster a new relationship. Winning custody of Gia was his goal. Becoming involved with a woman when Children's Services or a judge might soon be assessing his capability as a parent would have a negative impact. But damn if he didn't want to risk it. He drove home pondering his next move.

~

Lynne begrudgingly provided the time and location of the autistic specialist whom she dragged Gia to see the next day. Blake arrived ten minutes early and dropped to his knees when Gia saw him and ran into his embrace. The feel of her arms locked around his neck and her silky curls smothering his face energized him. His daughter remained speechless but she beamed her happiness that he was there.

He and Lynne weren't permitted in the room while Gia performed several coloring and sensitivity tests, which locked them in a waiting room together. Alone. The Captain was on the warpath.

"You should have been arrested. I'm going to contact the mayor or the police chief when I get home and report those officers for dereliction of duty."

He knew better than to poke the bear. He reached for the morning newspaper.

"And what were you doing with Noreen anyway? She's Argia's nurse, which makes her *my* nurse. If she needs medical information, I'm more qualified than you to provide it."

The Captain apparently disregarded Blake's EMT and paramedic training and several state certifications.

Lynne droned on. "I'm going to have a talk with Noreen. That's a violation of hospital protocol, I'm certain."

As if she knew the protocol.

"The woman must be deaf to begin with to not have heard you threaten me. I don't want her to contact you again."

Well, that was unacceptable. Blake laid aside the newspaper. Lynne made concentration difficult anyway. "There's no need to involve the nurse in our differences, Lynne. She's already seen enough of our dirty laundry. Leave her alone." And Lynne didn't know the half of it.

The Captain's left eyebrow shot up in a perfect arch. "Leave her alone? That's an odd thing for you to say, Blake. Why so protective?"

He snapped to full attention. The tone of Lynne's voice set off a warning bell in his head. Best to throw her a bone. "I'm not being protective, Captain. It's called keeping our personal business private. It's unlikely either of us will ever see that nurse again."

But that was all he could think about. Seeing Noreen again. The doctor rated Gia's appointment inconclusive and conferred with them about further evaluative steps. Blake didn't want to take it any further but Lynne insisted and the doctor implied the consequences of not conducting more tests could be devastating. At a loss about what to do and deferring to the professional, which the doctor made sure to emphasize, Blake conceded.

Gia had come running out of the office and jumped into his arms and he carried her outside to his truck. The clicks of Lynne's high heels like fingers tapping a keyboard sounded on the pavement behind him.

"Wait. Where're you going? She needs rest. I have to take her home."

He buckled Gia into her car seat and tightened the harness. He closed the back door and spun around to face her mother.

"I'm not on duty until tomorrow morning. By the terms of our divorce agreement, I don't have to return her to you until six o'clock tonight. We'll see you then."

Without another word, he walked around the rear of his truck, climbed into the driver's seat, and drove away. Lynne disappeared in his rearview mirror, unheard threats spilling from her lips.

For him, it was a perfect afternoon. Gia was particularly clingy, which suited him fine, and they snuggled on the couch with Mr. Fox and Mr. Dog wrapped in her blankey, watched movies and ate cereal with chocolate milk. This was how it would be every day once he gained custody of his daughter. She'd know nothing but love. He already knew the people he could set in place while he was at the firehouse who could care for her.

He whispered his plans to her, caressing her silken hair and repeatedly kissing the top of her head. She turned her face up to him, those dark eyes round and wide, and smiled.

"Okay, Daddy," she whispered.

# 12

Blake was in the middle of an administrators' meeting downtown when his cell phone vibrated. The ambulance was on its way to his Riviera Road home. The call for a child in seizure all but paralyzed him.

He excused himself from the meeting, noting the frown that crossed the Fire Commissioner's face. Automatically, he dialed Lynne but it was useless. His call dropped into voice mail and he doubted his message would garner a response: "What the hell is happening? Call me."

Rob and Joe were already en route to his home but he didn't want to bother them with a phone call. Gia would be in good hands once they were on scene. That was a given. Seizures. The diagnosis carried potentially grave consequences.

Dammit. He was at least an hour away from home and rush hour traffic would slow him down. If he wore one of those gold badges sitting around the table in the other room waiting for him to return, he'd have an emergency light to pop on the roof. But without one, he'd be simply another driver on the road making his way to an unknown destination. He returned to the meeting, interrupted the presentation, and explained the emergency. Heads around the table nodded when he excused himself.

Five cars in front of him exiting the parking garage. Jesus, did no one use cash anymore?

Was his little girl frothing at the mouth? Trying to bite her tongue? Scared beyond belief? He banished those horrific thoughts from his mind. *Drive, Blake, just drive.* How he'd love to have that 10,000-pound fire engine underneath his butt right now forcing everyone to give him the road.

It was useless but he dialed Lynne's number again. She didn't pick up and he didn't leave a second message. They'd transport Gia to Children's. Maybe he had an ally there.

He'd wanted to contact Noreen after their dinner but with Gia under foot and work, he hadn't had the opportunity. More like he talked himself out of it once Gia was back at Lynne's and he had privacy in his home. What would he say anyway? That entire evening had been a challenge and he wasn't confident Noreen ended it on his side. So rather than hem and haw over the phone, he found reasons not to call. But there was no debate now.

By the third ring, he wondered if she saw it was him and didn't plan to answer. On the sixth ring, he mentally thumbed through his contact list for someone else at the hospital he might reach out to. He knew most of the emergency room staff but did he have any of their phone numbers? He'd never had a reason to contact them.

Ring number seven resulted in her breathless answer. "Sorry, sorry, I was just loading the groceries in the trunk and couldn't grab my phone. Hello? Are you there?"

"Noreen, it's Blake Matthews."

"I saw that. Hello. How are you? It's nice to hear from you."

Dammit, he should've phoned her before now. She interpreted this as a social call and he desperately wanted a favor. One that could jeopardize her career. "I wanted to call you after our dinner, Noreen, but for reasons I can't explain, I didn't."

"Why not?"

Always brutally honest. Despite the circumstances, he chuckled. "Call me a chicken. We can talk about that later but listen, I'm afraid I'm calling now to ask your help. I'll understand if you don't want to insert yourself in my problems. Lord knows I have no right to involve you in them any further."

She didn't hesitate. "What's wrong?"

"I'm downtown for an administrators' meeting and the squad received an emergency call from my house. Gia is having seizures. The paramedics are on their way and so am I but I'm at least an hour out with this goddamn traffic."

Mid-speech, Noreen gasped.

"They'll transport her to your hospital, I'm certain. The Captain, er, I mean Lynne, isn't returning my phone calls. I was hoping you'd be working but it doesn't sound like you are."

"I'm not scheduled until seven this evening."

"Is there any way you can find out what's going on in your ER? It's an imposition to ask you to try to assess what's happening. Hell, it's probably unethical and I don't doubt you live and die by some ethical code. I do too, for the most part. But where Gia is concerned, ethics go out the window. I need your help."

"Tell me everything you know." He recognized her all-business tone.

"Bare bones information, I'm afraid. Just what I told you."

"How long ago did the call come in?"

Blake checked his watch. Eighteen minutes.

"Okay, let me see what I can find out. The ambulance might not be there yet. I'll call you as soon as I know something."

"Call me if you know nothing. I'm losing it in this driver's seat stopping for every freakin' red light in this city."

She disconnected the call before he could add anything more. He scratched an imaginary spot on his right bicep, a nervous habit that manifested itself when he couldn't control a situation.

He checked his watch one more time. The fucking hands hadn't moved one minute.

The next thing he knew, his text tone sounded. Despite his cardinal rule to ignore the phone while driving, he read Noreen's message. "On my way to the hospital."

Why? Had she found something out? Could she find nothing? Why hadn't she shared more information? Jesus, everyone but him would be there for Gia.

He cursed at the car in front of him and slammed the steering wheel with his open palm.

Yet another glance at his watch. Noreen wasn't on duty for another few hours but she was making her way to the hospital. In uniform? Reporting to work early? Or, just as she'd jumped into action when she encountered a car accident, was she going the extra mile? For his daughter? For him? God, he hoped it was for both of them.

Noreen sped to the hospital. Two bags of perishables in the trunk might be lost but that was the least of her worries. Her mind flooded with the details of her Munchausen research. This symptom had been listed.

She rushed through the emergency doors intent on showing her badge to the admitting desk to determine Argia's location but there was no need. From down the hall, Lynne shrieked her name and ran toward her, flinging herself into Noreen's arms. Were it not for her grip on the counter, they both would have tumbled to the floor.

"Oh my God, I'm so glad you're here," Lynne screeched. "It's an answer to my prayers. Someone who knows my baby and will give me an actual prognosis. These nitwits here refuse to tell me what's going on and I'm beside myself. I almost fainted, I'm so distraught."

Noreen stepped back an arm's distance and out of Lynne's clutches. "Relax, Mrs. Matthews. The staff here is the best you can find but your daughter is their first concern, not you. You need to take hold of yourself. Tell me what happened."

"Oh Noreen, please, call me Lynne. We know each other well enough to be teammates."

She was taken aback by Lynne's assumed familiarity. And her demeanor. Now that she was being consulted about her daughter's condition, she was calm, taking the time to straighten her clothes and smooth back her hair before responding.

"She hasn't stopped regurgitating since her father dropped her off at my home last night. I think he might have poisoned her. She said she didn't feel well but I'd already sensed that. I have that perceptive ability where my daughter is concerned. And then, I'm certain I saw froth and she began to seize."

The reference to Blake caused Noreen's heart to skip. At the same time, the accusation against him shocked her. "Accusing someone of poison is a dangerous thing to say without substantial evidence, Lynne. Have you shared that theory with anyone else?" The real question she wanted to pose was if the police were on their way to arrest Blake. And had Argia, who wasn't speaking to anyone, actually told her mother she felt sick? Literally said those words?

Lynne waved off her concerns. "No. No one will listen to me. But it's so obvious. Argia wasn't home more than an hour when she fell ill. What else can I think?" Lynne flattened her hands against her abdomen. "The pitiful thing kept clutching her epigastrium."

The use of the medical term to refer to the upper abdomen sent up a red flag in Noreen's mind. What ordinary mother would describe their child's symptoms like this? Especially one who claimed to be distraught over the whole ordeal. Noreen wasn't a violent woman but this was the second time she fought the urge to slap Lynne Matthews' face. Instead, she grasped her shoulders and turned her toward the waiting area, gently shoving her toward the plastic chairs lined along the walls. It was no wonder several of the occupants already seated in the room stared at Lynne.

"Why don't you have a seat and let me see what I can find out." Without waiting for her approval, Noreen pushed through the hospital personnel doors. The individual cubicles buzzed with activity but three rooms down she spotted Paramedics Lystle and Yarnell. She smiled when they watched her approach without recognition.

"Hi boys. Are you here with Argia Matthews?"

Rob dragged his gaping mouth closed. "Oh. Noreen. I didn't recognize you in street clothes. Yeah, we brought her in. The doctors are debating whether to pump her stomach but the anti-nausea medication we administered seems to be kicking in. I hope they don't subject her to that procedure. She's so small."

"Pump her stomach?" Noreen gasped. "For a seizure?"

Rob's head jerked. "Seizure? What're you talking about? We didn't see any symptoms of a seizure. Just vomit over the poor thing's shirt and pants and all over the bed."

His response stumped her. "But wasn't that the initial call?"

Joe shook his head. "Well, yeah, technically, that's what the mother claimed but all we diagnosed was nausea. We've learned with this woman not to take her word for any medical situation." Rob jabbed Joe in the ribs and he turned away.

Nausea. That was slightly less severe but still cause for concern in a five-year-old. "Do you suspect poison? Or something toxic?"

The men studied her with narrowed eyes. She felt their unspoken accusation and sensed their loyalty to their lieutenant. She couldn't blame them. Based on her prior inquiries about Blake with these two, they likely suspected that she viewed him in a disparaging light. If they only knew.

"I'm not accusing anyone but you know yourself that the

dangers in a home are so many for a young child. Often parents are unaware of toxic chemicals contained in everyday items like cleaning products. I'm simply saying perhaps Argia was fascinated by something under the sink or found some prescription drugs. Maybe she ingested tobacco. Do either Lynne or Blake smoke?"

There was no mistaking the paramedics' unfriendly glares. When neither commented on her theory and didn't seem inclined to continue the conversation, she stepped around the curtain to assess the patient for herself.

Argia looked elfin in the hospital bed, her hair matted and face streaked with dried tears. They'd removed her clothes and wrapped her in a green hospital gown two sizes too large. Argia's soulful eyes leveled on her and as if drawn by them, Noreen rushed to her bedside, identifying herself when one of the staff asked. Argia reached for her hand and clung to it, drawing her closer, tugging until Noreen leaned toward her face.

"Daddy." It was barely a whisper and Noreen wasn't certain she'd heard correctly.

She inched back and looked at Argia. "What honey? What did you say?"

A wild scream and doors pushed open so forcefully, they slammed against the walls, startled everyone. Bursting through the curtains, Lynne shrieked, "I will not be kept from my daughter one second longer. Argia! Argia! Where's my baby?"

Argia squeezed Noreen's hand hard enough to hurt. She bent to the child again. "Honey, what'd you say to me?"

Lynne hurled herself into the cubicle, screeching at Noreen. "What's the matter with you? She can't speak. She's autistic. You have to confer with me." She clutched the foot rail of Argia's bed, literally shaking it. "Oh my baby. You poor, sweet thing." Then she glared at the surrounding hospital personnel. "What're you all standing around for? Do something, or I'll sue every one of you and this hospital too."

Everyone's attention focused on Lynne Matthews. Noreen looked down when Argia released her hand and saw the little girl swipe a tear from her cheek. Noreen's heart cracked.

The attending physicians began to shove everyone out of the compartment. Argia's eyes glazed over, as if to drown out the activity around her. One of the nurses spoke to her but she remained unresponsive. Lynne, on the other hand, wouldn't shut up. As much as it pained her to appease the woman, Noreen rushed to her side.

"Shh, Lynne, you're not helping and the doctors don't have time to treat you too." She ran her hands up and down Lynne's arms. "You're so distressed, please control your emotions. You're worrying me."

It was the formula for success. As if she flipped a switch, Lynne's behavior changed immediately. She gazed into Noreen's eyes and clung to her shoulders. "Thank you for understanding how devastating this is for me. I'm so frightened. I'm certain my blood pressure is elevated and my body temperature is spiraling. I should probably have a sedative but I want to be clear-minded for my daughter's consultation. What kind of tests do you think they'll run? I think a brain scan is dictated, don't you agree?"

Lying in the bed, Argia cried softly while the doctors inserted a fluid line into her arm and ran a second one in her thigh, since the cast prevented easy access to her other arm.

"Let's allow the doctors to make that determination. Why don't you and I take a walk. Some herbal tea will help calm you." As she spoke, she guided Lynne beyond the curtains into the corridor. Rob and Joe leaned against the wall, the looks on their faces failing to conceal their contempt. For Lynne or for her? She didn't want to alienate these two men, for whom she had the highest regard. Didn't they realize the way to extract Lynne from the equation was to play to her neediness? Or, heaven forbid, her mental illness.

Well, let them misread this situation and believe she sided

with Lynne Matthews. Blake most certainly would understand. What mattered now was removing Lynne from Argia's bedside so the little girl could be stabilized.

And she needed time to think. Argia had whispered the word daddy despite Lynne's insistence that the child didn't speak. Blake had affirmed that, for whatever reason, Argia had stopped talking and the child had remained silent at the ice cream shop. But there was no mistaking her whispered word. What did she mean? Did she want Noreen to fetch her daddy? Or was it her daddy who caused her illness? Did Blake Matthews poison his daughter?

# 13

Noreen lost track of time. Lynne was in no hurry to return to her daughter's bedside or to consult with her doctors regarding a medical diagnosis. The more attention Noreen lavished on her, the happier the woman acted. When she finally suggested they check on Argia, it was as if Lynne had forgotten her daughter was in the ER.

The serenity was short-lived. She drew aside the curtain to Argia's cubicle and Lynne's scream scared everyone. "Get away from her. You tried to kill her. Someone please, call the police."

Blake sat in bed in his uniform with Argia cradled in his lap, smiling while Argia tapped his cellphone screen. Of course, the phone dropped to the bed with Lynne's outburst. And people came running.

Despite Lynne's outrage, Blake ignored her and stared at Noreen, cold gray eyes rending her heart in two. At first glance, it certainly appeared that she supported Lynne but wasn't he smart enough to know she'd diffused the situation the only way she knew how? She scanned the room for the paramedics but they were gone. Likely they'd summed up for Blake what they witnessed, which truly was her comforting Lynne. But her motive was to remove Lynne from Argia's bedside. The poor thing had been petrified by her mother's rants. The only way to stop Lynne was to pretend to befriend her and walk away. Didn't Blake understand that?

The ER attending physician stepped in and grabbed Lynne's upper arm, squeezing hard enough to redden the skin. "Mrs. Matthews, please. We have the papers here to discharge Argia. You can take her home. There is no evidence that your daughter ingested anything toxic."

"Discharge her?" It wasn't a question but a yowl. "You can't discharge her. She's needs tests. This isn't the first time she's experienced uncontrolled nausea. She could have a bowel obstruction or gastro duodenal Crohn's disease. She never wants to eat. The girl isn't healthy enough to leave this hospital."

While Lynne ranted, a nurse removed the intravenous lines from Argia's leg and arm. She immediately swiveled in her father's lap and wrapped her arms around his neck, dropping her head to his shoulder. His bicep strained the sleeve of his uniform shirt when he embraced her with his left arm and retrieved his phone with his right hand. He swung his long legs over the side of the bed and stood, causing Lynne to go wild.

"Where are you going? You can't take her with you. He's harming her, don't you see? Somebody stop him."

With that, Lynne flung herself into Noreen's arms. "Oh, Noreen. I feel faint. I can't handle this."

Surprised by her actions and unprepared for Lynne's weight, she stumbled backward into an orderly who, equally surprised by the sudden physical assault, failed to keep his balance. All three of them crashed to the floor, toppling the hospital table in the process and sending its contents flying. Nurses and orderlies rushed to help them. From the middle of the pile, she peered over Lynne's shoulder.

Blake remained stoic, his jaw locked, a tiny muscle in his cheek pulsating double time. He strode past the commotion without a word. She wanted to chase after him but the medical emergency Lynne manifested prevented that. The woman clutched her heart and declared she suffered tachycardia, a condition where the heart beats above one hundred beats per minute. She plastered her free hand to her forehead and fell backward again into the orderly's arms, sending them tumbling to the linoleum a second time. Argia was forgotten.

An hour later, after the ER doctor pronounced Lynne healthy and she'd extracted a promise from Noreen to contact her the next day, Noreen circled to the rear of the hospital and dumped her milk, eggs, and other ruined refrigerator items in the dumpster. She'd already called in a sub to work her shift. Today's events needed sorted out.

Sitting alone in the dark at the rear of the building, she dialed Blake's number. It was too much to hope that he'd answer but her heart jumped when his deep voice filled her ear. "I don't believe we have anything to discuss, Miss Jensen. Please don't call me again."

"Blake, wait!" She held her breath until she was certain he hadn't disconnected the call.

"Please, Blake. I believe everything that you told me. Give me a chance to explain what happened today. What you saw, it's not what you think." He'd practically said the same thing to her in the ice cream shop. Didn't he remember?

"I think you are conspiring with my ex-wife to take my daughter away from me and what I witnessed tonight affirms that. I deal with facts, Miss Jensen. This conversation is over."

She screamed into the phone. "Argia spoke to me!"

Silence.

Her breath came so hard, she could barely say more. "She spoke to me, Blake, in the hospital."

Curiosity laced his voice. "That's unlikely. You know she hasn't been talking, even to me."

"I swear to you, Blake." Noreen squished her eyes together. His daughter was her one chance to reach this man. On any level. "She whispered to me. She knows she can trust me. You told me your daughter is your world. If she trusts me enough to speak to me when she won't talk to anyone else, not even you, then, for God's sake, you should trust me too."

His labored breaths carried through the phone. "What'd she say?"

A crack in his armor. A tiny opportunity to capitalize on. "She whispered, 'Daddy'. Please, Blake, give me ten minutes to talk to you. It's all I ask."

Hesitation, while he considered it. "Go ahead, I'm listening."

A quick hysterical laugh escaped her. "Not like this. I'm parked beside a garbage dumpster. My head is pounding and I'm starving. I haven't eaten all day. Can I meet you someplace?"

Now it was his turn to chuckle. "No, that's out of the question. For one thing, Gia is exhausted and I've just gotten her settled. My mother often babysits for me but she is away for a few days and even if she were available, I'm not leaving my daughter. Not after the day she's endured. And, sorry to say Miss Jensen, I don't trust you."

The use of her formal name cut to the quick and she flinched in her front seat. She couldn't blame him.

"Then give me your address. I'll come to you. I'll stay ten feet away. I'll stand on the sidewalk. I'll sit in my car and yell from the driver's window. I'm desperate to talk to you about this and embarrassed to admit it. But this is important enough for me to humiliate myself, which is exactly what I'm doing at the moment. Please give me an opportunity to explain."

The pause seemed endless. Thirty seconds at least that felt like an hour. Finally, he recited his address, giving her brief directions. Without another word, he hung up.

She programmed the address into the vehicle's navigation system and in about a half-hour, she eased her car into the driveway behind Blake's black truck. This was an upscale neighborhood in Plum Borough, a suburb of Pittsburgh that community officials touted as one of the top one hundred safest communities in the country. The porch light of the two-story house shined brightly.

She switched off the ignition and stepped out of the car, her eyes riveted to the front door. Would he make her stand outside to talk?

The front door swung open and Blake stepped out onto the porch, wiping his hands on a kitchen towel. "Have any trouble finding it?"

"No, none at all." She nodded toward the surrounding homes. "It's a nice neighborhood."

He shrugged. "My mom likes it. She lives on the other side of the community. My sister and I grew up in that house and she stayed there after she and my dad divorced. This was a little like coming home for me. I was comfortable moving here after Lynne and I split but it's temporary. I'm only renting."

"It must be nice, having Argia's grandmother so close." Small talk. They were making small talk but it was better than nothing.

"Gia is happy. That's all that matters."

She nodded. "Where's your dad live now?"

"Florida."

She stood in the driveway, not daring to move toward the first of two-sets of terraced cement steps that led to the porch, waiting for some indication she should. Blake appeared to be debating an invitation inside. She watched his chest rise and fall beneath a Pittsburgh Steelers T-shirt.

"You said on the phone you were hungry. I haven't eaten today either. I whipped us up a snack."

The light from the motion detector above the garage likely

illuminated the surprised look on her face. He smiled and a liquid warmth flowed through her body.

"Does that mean I can come in?"

He chuckled. "You better. We don't want the neighbors to gossip." As she climbed toward the front porch, he added, "But be warned Noreen. If you cross me, or betray me, you will live to regret it. Where my daughter is concerned, I'm a man you should fear."

## 14

Noreen stood in front of Blake, fully grasping the meaning of his words. At least they were back on a first-name basis. A five o'clock shadow highlighted his face, rendering his features more chiseled than she recalled. Tight blue jeans and bare feet added to his appeal.

There was more than one reason to fear this man. He had the ability to consume her.

He opened the screen door and motioned for her to step inside. The house smelled like fresh baked bread and her stomach growled loud enough for him to hear and laugh.

"Just in time, I'd say. The kitchen's this way." He placed his hand between her shoulder blades and nudged her beyond a staircase leading to the second floor. Soft jazz played through an intercom. "Gia's asleep."

Noreen gasped when she saw two place settings on the bar that was an extension of the black quartz kitchen counter. A bowl of fresh shrimp and a cup of cocktail sauce sat nestled in a second bowl of ice and positioned beside that was a small plate of cheese and crackers. Blake motioned to the high-top chair and moved to the oven, using the towel in his hand to remove a tray of toasted garlic bread. He quartered the bread slices, popped the lid on a jar of roasted red pepper pieces and skillfully spread the bruschetta topping on each piece of toast. Reaching into the kitchen cabinet, he retrieved several jars and bottles and seasoned each piece with a medley of spices. He topped each one with grated cheese and slid the pan back into the oven.

He was so at home in the kitchen, she couldn't contain her astonishment. "I'm impressed beyond belief. A kitchen is the last place I'd picture you."

A slow smile crossed his face, his white teeth a stark contrast to the dark stubble. "I love to cook. We take turns at the fire station, you know. But some of us step up more often. I'm pretty good at it, if I'm allowed to pat myself on the back."

She waved her hands to indicate the spread. "But this was so much work. How'd you do it in thirty minutes?"

He'd removed a tumbler glass from the cupboard and waited for the ice dispenser to stop. He filled it with water and set it beside a bottle of aspirin, pointing to the meds. "For your headache."

After filling a second tumbler with ice, he mixed a vodka soda and dropped a fresh lime into the glass, also setting it in front of her. "This was no trouble. The shrimp and garlic bread were in the freezer, toppings in the pantry. Cheese and crackers are a staple in this house. It's one of the few things I can coax Gia to eat." He removed the bruschetta from the oven, skillfully lifting each toast point onto a serving platter.

"It's not much. I can cook up something more substantial if you like but it's late and I doubt you want something heavy on your stomach. But if you do, just ask."

Considering the swarm of butterflies dancing in her belly and her racing heart, she doubted she could keep these snacks down.

She watched him pour a generous amount of scotch over ice, take a sip and lock his eyes on hers. This was the moment for the showdown.

"Does this mean you're no longer angry at me?"

Blake snickered. "No. It doesn't mean that at all. Let's say I am less angry but still suspicious of your motives."

She too sipped from her glass, wary of taking too big a gulp. This wasn't the time to drink herself into a tipsy state. Blake Matthews would keep her on her toes. "Then why the royal treatment?"

The right side of his mouth lifted in an appealing sneer. "Ever watch any of The Godfather movies? Michael Corleone says his father taught him to keep his friends close but his enemies closer. He's actually quoting a Chinese general but no one remembers that."

She felt her eyebrows spike. "I'm not your enemy, Blake."

A slow, excruciating sip of his scotch while his eyes pierced her heart. "Then what are you?"

She wanted to be so many things to this man. The realization excited her. Never had a man affected her like this, not one who displayed such obvious disdain for her. Tom had pursued her like a wild man, the same way he lived his life. This man standing before her wanted nothing to do with her and that attracted her to him like a moth to the light. She couldn't admit that though, not here, not now. He'd laugh her out the front door.

"That remains to be seen, I guess."

His head tilted ever so slightly before he smiled. "The toast is getting cold. Help yourself. Let's do battle on full stomachs, shall we?"

With that, he came around the island and sat on the high barstool next to her. Their knees touched and flames shot to her core.

He was in host mode again. "Do you eat seafood?"

She nodded and he heaped her plate with shrimp and five toasted pieces of bread. The sixth one he held between his fingers and edged toward her mouth. "Try this."

Like a bird being fed by its momma, she opened her mouth

and allowed Blake to feed her. The intimacy of the moment didn't escape either one of them, especially when his fingers grazed her lips. The combination of garlic, sweetness, and whatever seasonings he'd enhanced the toast point with were equally as intoxicating. She closed her eyes and reveled in the flavors, softly groaning her appreciation.

When her eyelids lifted, he stared at her with clouded eyes. Did the familiarity of his actions affect him too? Not wanting to pursue that line of thought, she attacked the remainder of items on her plate, relishing each bite. The man knew how to entertain.

They ate in silence, neither acknowledging the sizzling current that sparked between their rubbing knees, despite the denim of their jeans. Finally, when her dish was clean and she couldn't eat another bite, she edged the plate away.

"I don't know how to thank you for this. It was a delightful surprise. And much needed nourishment"

He leaned forward, and for one brief second, she thought he might kiss her. Instead, he clutched both sides of her chair and dragged it closer, essentially imprisoning her between his legs. "You can thank me with honesty. What went on at the hospital today?"

Concentration seemed lost with his legs braced against hers and his hands resting on either side of her thighs, clutching the chair. But this was her chance to establish a relationship with Blake Matthews. Something she desperately wanted.

"Let me start by saying I did a bunch of research after you and I had dinner the other night. I admit, I was leery of all that you told me but willing to give you the benefit of the doubt." One of his dark eyebrows arched skeptically.

The corners of her mouth tipped up but she contained her smile. "You said it yourself, Blake, you want the facts. The idea of a mother deliberately endangering her child is unthinkable. Even you didn't completely embrace it at first and you lived with it."

When he didn't respond, she continued.

"I didn't take what you said to heart because of you, mind you. I wanted to research it for Argia. You're right. That little urchin has a way of crawling under your skin. More like sneaking into your heart." That made him smile.

"I was shocked by what I read. The more information I gathered, the harder it was to comprehend that you believed this applied to Lynne. Maybe I didn't want to draw a comparison between the caretakers described in all of the Munchausen's research and your wife because that would make her a monster."

"Ex-wife."

This time she smiled. "Ex-wife. It frightened me when you phoned and told me Argia was at the hospital. When I called, there was too much activity in the ER for anyone to provide any details about her status. I'm not certain she had arrived there yet. Apparently, there was a highway emergency and there was so much commotion in the background I could barely hear whoever answered the phone. That's when I decided to go to the hospital and I texted you. You need to remember Blake, that you were the one who reached out to me and asked for help."

He nodded but remained quiet. His thumbs move idly in small circles against her thighs. Was it a conscious movement or was he unaware he was driving her crazy?

"When I arrived, I saw Rob and Joe and their faces were ashen, they were so concerned. And Lynne was a raving maniac. She flew down the hall like a bat out of hell and threw herself into my arms as if I was her long-lost soul mate. I was shocked and I immediately saw the looks on their faces. They told you about that, didn't they?"

Another silent nod.

"Based on the glare you gave me, I figured as much." She paused to catch her breath and straighten her posture and he slid his hands over her thighs and rested one on each knee. His thumbs continued their gentle caress.

She shrugged. “I didn’t know what to do. Lynne was out of control. There was no talking to her, no reasoning.”

“There never is.” She detected sadness in his voice. “She latches on to an idea and will argue her point until you’re in your grave. I gave up trying to reason with her one month into the marriage.”

A twinge of sympathy tugged on her heart. This man deserved so much more.

“Well, I gave up more quickly, stalled her by saying I’d check on Argia and rushed to her bedside. I’m not even going to tell you how frightened that baby looked. The minute I reached her, she snatched my hand as if she clung to a life preserver. That’s when she tugged and I bent over. That’s when she whispered the word daddy.”

His thumbs stopped moving and he tightened his grip on her knees. The muscle in his jaw resumed its pulsing. Impulsively, she laid her hands over his.

“I was so surprised I doubted what I heard. I asked Argia to repeat what she said. I’ll be honest, Blake, I wasn’t sure if she wanted her daddy or if she was telling me her daddy was the one who hurt her.” It pained her to admit that but there it was. He expected honesty. She’d present him with nothing less.

His intake of breath was loud and he held the air in his lungs a long time before releasing it slowly. She stood on the edge of a dangerous abyss being as forthright as this, especially with a man who had her yearning for more of his touch. Urges she’s hadn’t enjoyed in years pooled deep inside her. Even though her words could spell her doom, she continued.

“And then Lynne burst into the cubicle like a ranting wild woman and Argia seemed to zone out. Or recede inward. Take your pick. Medically, I’d list it as conscious but unresponsive.”

His fingers moved and interlaced with hers. His eyes were so telling, like his daughter’s. This was agony for him to hear. She willed her strength to flow between them and tightened her grip to his.

"I remembered what I'd read about the Munchausen's caretaker and that their actions were designed to deflect attention to themselves and I immediately knew the only way to protect Argia was to remove her mother from the scene. What the paramedics told you they saw was the truth. I comforted Lynne, I placated her fears and I led her away from your little girl's bed. And silently I prayed that you'd arrive sooner than later because I knew you were rushing to your daughter."

His eyes weren't tear-rimmed, but they were misted. That was her undoing. Without even trying, this man had won her heart. Too bad he'd never know it.

She shrugged again. "You know the rest. You saw the two of us together but what you didn't see was women who are allies. Or even friends. I believe everything you suspect about Lynne's mental illness." She flexed her hands, squeezing his. "I want to help."

"Why?"

"Because you can't do it alone. And because if Lynne convinces the right cop that you're the problem, you'll be in jail and that will leave Argia completely unprotected. And I don't want anything to happen to her."

"What's in it for you?"

*How about you?* She didn't have the nerve to say it. Instead, she attempted a light laugh, released one of his hands, and waved toward the remnants of their evening snack. "I'll take another helping of your hospitality."

Blake rose, released her other hand, and braced both of his behind her bottom. He slid her to the edge of the seat, causing her legs to spread and him to position himself between them. In that situation, so close, borderline intimate, she was forced to look up to see his face, his mouth inches from hers. He regarded her with hooded eyes, and she lowered her gaze to his lips.

If this was a dare, she's wasn't backing down. She already knew what she wanted. What did he want?

When his mouth touched hers, his lips were cool and wet and tasted like scotch. Tentative at first, barely making contact. And then, full on pressure when he slanted her head backward to improve his angle. The movement caused her mouth to open and his tongue plunged inside, a tangy combination of spices, alcohol, and lust sending her emotions spiraling. Her body thermostat hiked to boiling. He cupped her face with his hands while his tongue danced with hers and she grasped his biceps. Could she hold onto this man?

Suddenly, Blake stepped backward, his head canted and his eyes directed toward the ceiling. The house was quiet but he listened, returned his gaze to her face and brushed his thumb across her lips. "Excuse me," he whispered. He didn't attempt to conceal the bulge in his pants when he moved one more step backward, arching his back to see down the hall, and then proceeded in that direction. She grinned, pleased that she wasn't the only one physically turned on by this evening's events.

Blake's voice echoed from the front of the house. "Hey peanut. What are you doing up? Come here." In minutes, he returned carrying Argia, two well-loved stuffed animals and a frayed, burgundy cotton blanket. Sleepy-eyed, Argia smiled when she saw Noreen.

Blake planted a sweet kiss against Argia's cheek. "Look who's here for a visit. Nurse Noreen came to check on you." He settled Argia on his lap, tucking the stuffed toys between his abs and her body. "Are you hungry, honey? How about some cheese?"

The plate was closer to Noreen and when Argia extended her hand, one small finger pointing in her direction, Noreen twisted to reach the tray. To her surprise, Argia grabbed her shirt and began to crawl from Blake's lap into hers. Immediately, she braced her feet on the lower chair rung to level her legs and helped Argia onto her lap. She positioned her to face the plate and Argia reached on her own for a quarter-slice of cheese, her casted arm thumping loudly on the counter.

Blake's jaw dropped and her heart soared. When he spoke, his voice held a raw intonation. "I guess more than one Matthews wants to be in your arms tonight."

Forget the flutters. An outright explosion occurred inside her body, to include her female parts. The grin that split her face actually hurt. "I like the idea, too." She smoothed Argia's hair over her shoulder. "But Miss Argia has first dibs. How about a cracker with that cheese?"

Argia shook her head but reached for a second slice. Blake rose and walked to the refrigerator. He faced Argia with a carton of chocolate milk and an empty glass. "Gia? Chocolate milk?" He raised the carton an inch, and then the glass. "Or water?"

She pointed to the glass and he filled it with ice and water from the door dispenser. The two of them watched as she finished her cheese, held the glass with both hands to gulp a drink, and opt for a third piece of cheese.

"Can I make you something else, Gia? I'm trying to impress Nurse Noreen with how good a cook I am. You know we're a team and you're the leader. How about some pas-ghetti with butter and cheese? Does that sound good?"

Without looking at her father, she shook her head. "C'mon honey, you have to help me out. We want Nurse Noreen to visit again, maybe for a real dinner next time but if she thinks I can't cook, she might not. What about a juicy scrambled egg? Please peanut? We want Nurse Noreen to come back, don't we?"

Her head lifted and Argia gifted her with a wide smile. Then she looked at her father and agreed.

In seconds, Blake had an egg sizzling in a frying pan. When Argia returned her attention to the cheese in her fingers, he mouthed a silent 'thank you' to Noreen.

This felt so natural, it scared her. Cradling a five-year-old in her lap, watching her father putz in the kitchen, being a part of a family. Sure, she'd held her niece and nephew from the time they were born, fed and diapered them, even babysat them overnight. She'd fixed breakfast for them a hundred times. But this was different. These moments etched themselves inside her heart, burning as hot as a soldering iron scorches a piece of wood so that it will never be the same.

Argia had no attachment to her. Barely knew her. Yet she willingly crawled onto her lap and was content to stay there. This night would be hard to reconcile with her mantra of independence and detachment. Blake set a plate in front of his daughter with a child's fork beside it on a paper napkin. He waited, but Argia ignored the bright, yellow fluffy egg.

Noreen rubbed small circles on the child's back. "Wow. That looks delicious. May I have a bite?" When Argia agreed, she lifted a small piece of egg from the edge with her fingers and popped it in her mouth.

"Oh my goodness, Argia. You have to try that egg." She leaned close to the girl's ear and whispered loud enough for Blake to hear. "Wait until your dad isn't looking and pick up a piece with your fingers. Don't use the fork. It's much tastier that way. Watch for him to look away."

Blake cleared his throat and announced he needed a drink of water.

Now part of a conspiracy, Argia watched her dad turn his back on them, giggled, and snatched a piece of egg. "Quick, Gia, let's grab another piece before he turns around." She pretended to help herself to more while Argia grabbed a handful of egg and jammed it into her mouth.

Blake turned, eyed the diminishing pile, and smiled.

She leaned into Argia once more. "Watch this." She raised the level of her voice. "Um, excuse me, Blake. I'm rather thirsty also. Would you mind pouring me a glass of water too?"

"Certainly, Nurse Noreen." He turned his back on the pair

again and took an extra-long time retrieving a glass and filling it. By the time the glass was full, Argia had cleaned her plate.

He mocked surprise. "What the heck? What happened to that egg? Gia, did you eat that?"

The child erupted in laughter, throwing her arms up and falling against Noreen's chest.

Blake continued his amazement. "When did you eat that?" He propped a hand on his hip. "Did Nurse Noreen eat all that?"

Her curls flew when she shook her head.

"You ate it all? I can't believe it. I'm shocked."

He came around to them and planted a wet sloppy kiss on the top of Argia's head and dropped a light kiss on Noreen's mouth, electrifying her. Argia raised her arms and he lifted her into his embrace. "Would you like something else, honey?"

She shook her head and dropped it on his shoulder, eyeing Noreen from the safety of her father's arms. "Are you ready to go back to bed?"

Another negative head shake.

Noreen eased off the high-top chair. "Well, I am. It's past my bedtime. I should go." She raised her eyes to Blake, wondering if they revealed her feelings. How she wished she could be a part of this man's life. And his daughter's.

"Thank you for a nice evening."

"We have to finish it. Sooner than later I hope."

Her heart launched like Kennywood's Sky Rocket—ninety-five feet in the air in three seconds. She felt lightheaded.

He walked her to the front door. "Do you have to work tomorrow?"

"I'm on at seven tomorrow night. You?"

"Off the next two days. Then on duty at eight. Do you know your way home from here?"

"I think so." She caressed Argia's back. "I'm glad you're feeling better, Argia. May I come and visit you again?"

Argia straightened and reached for her as if to hug her. She stepped closer and Argia kissed her cheek. Blake's eyebrows shot up and her heart puddled.

"I'll take that as a yes. You take good care of your daddy, okay?"

She'd resumed laying her head on her father's shoulder but it moved up and down. Noreen looked at Blake, wondering why his eyes had darkened but his face was laced with a smile.

"Goodnight, Blake."

"Yes, it was."

## 15

Blake couldn't define his feelings regarding Noreen beyond the fact that he wanted to make love to her. And that impulse mystified him. He didn't completely trust her, although watching Gia crawl into her lap sent a wave of paternal love coursing through him. His daughter's faith in Noreen went a long way toward reassuring him his feelings were justified, whatever they were. Gia was rather intuitive when it came to people, even as young as she was. She possessed a knack for seeing a person beneath their surface, as if looking into their soul, and intuitively distinguished evil from good.

As a baby, only he and Lynne could hold her. It took more than a year before Carole Matthews earned her trust and to this day, Gia doled out hugs for her grandmother in measured rations. Forget distant relatives or a stranger's attempts to cuddle her or even gain her attention. Gia remained aloof from most adults. For her to eagerly go to Noreen last night surprised him. It also excited him. He'd never share his life with another woman if Gia wasn't comfortable with her.

He choked on the coffee he sipped. What the hell? Now he

was thinking about sharing his life with Noreen? He barely knew the woman.

He ignored a phone call from Lynne, opting instead to listen to her voice message reminding him that Argia should be returned to her by six o'clock that night. Like some unwanted purchase he'd take back to the store. Lynne's formality irked him. Why hadn't he seen how cold she was beneath her creamy breasts and long legs when he met her? And what made him equate ice with Noreen? He used to be an excellent judge of character. Maybe he was getting old.

Tiny footsteps caught his attention and erased further conjecture about both women. The only lady in his life demanded some attention. He used Noreen as an excuse to feed Gia another egg, saying practice makes perfect, and they took a long walk hand-in-hand around the neighborhood. Cuddle time on the couch watching a princess movie and naps for both of them filled the remainder of the day. The closer the time approached to take her back to her mother, the more withdrawn Gia became.

"I'll see you in two nite-nites, peanut, I promise." He lifted his daughter from the truck and walked her up the walkway to the front door. It was too much to expect that Lynne would greet them at the door and welcome her daughter home. He knelt in front of Gia.

Stray strands from two pigtails blew across her face and he whisked them away with his finger. "Maybe you won't understand this, Gia, but it won't be like this much longer. I promise I'll take you out of here. It will be you and me all the time." Those wide brown eyes searched his face. Did she comprehend the meaning of his words?

"I won't take you away from your mother. I would never keep you from seeing her. But you'll be with me. It won't hurt anymore." He kissed her right cheek, then her left. Placed a kiss on her forehead and then kissed her mouth. The front door swung open.

"What on earth are you doing? She's going to catch pneumonia out here."

Blake gazed directly into Gia's eyes, their special stare. "I love you, Gia."

"Love you, Daddy."

He barely heard it. Lynne couldn't have because she was shrieking about Argia needing dinner and a bath and ordering him to release her daughter and leave.

He didn't press Gia to repeat her declaration. It was enough to know she spoke to him again. And she'd chosen to whisper to Noreen as well. There was a message there, somewhere, if only his thick skull could figure it out. His daughter opted to not speak except for a word now and then parceled out to only two people. Her silence made her rescue that much more imperative.

Noreen likely would be tired after working a twelve-hour shift but Blake didn't care. He barely slept and somewhere between dawn and his fourth cup of coffee, he decided he needed to see her. He calculated the time it should take for her to drive home, taking a chance she went there directly from the hospital, and drove to her apartment. If no one answered his knock, he'd wait.

The door swung open and he looked over Noreen from head to toe. Her blonde hair tied neatly back in a bun instead of falling over her shoulders in curly waves as it had the other night. No makeup that he could identify. No gold earrings. Barefoot instead of in the peep-toe pumps that teased him. Green animal print scrubs. The surprised look on her face stirred him, not that he needed more temptation.

"Blake! Is something wrong?"

"Yeah. We have some unfinished business to take care of and I can't wait much longer. May I come in?"

She stepped aside, confusion etching her features. When the

door closed, he turned and reached for her. "I hope you didn't work a killer shift last night." His lips swooped down over hers, the urgency of his desire stunning both of them.

In seconds, she responded, opening her mouth to allow his tongue to explore inside and wrapping her arms around his neck. He eased his hands down her sides and cupped her bottom, his hips edging toward hers to dance a slow grind. She pressed into him and he felt the tips of her breasts through their clothes, peaks that fueled him to a hotter flame.

He kissed her hungrily, moving off her lips for mere seconds to run his tongue along her jawline or nibble at her earlobe, but always returning to her mouth for more. He'd suffered smoke inhalation in the past and, much like he gulped the pure oxygen to clear his lungs, restore his breathing and alleviate the discomfort in his chest, he sucked on Noreen's mouth as if she breathed fresh life into him and eased his pain. He moaned when she rolled up on her tiptoes to lessen the height difference and kissed him harder.

His hands roamed beneath her shirt to caress her silky skin and he unhooked her bra. Now it was her turn to moan when she allowed him to caress her breasts and he tweaked and teased her nipples into hardened nubs. Finally, she nudged him backward, gasping for breath, her face flushed.

"Bed? Or sofa? Not the floor."

The room spun around him. "Bed."

She nodded in agreement and whispered, "Follow me." Pivoting, she walked through the living area, snatching the hem of her shirt and dragging it up and over her head. Her light laughter floated as easily as the garment did to the floor. The bra followed and in seconds, Noreen sat on her queen-sized bed topless, looking up at him expectantly.

Visions of his childhood days diving into the community swimming pool drifted through his mind as he extended his arms to the mattress for balance and buried his face between her breasts. She laughed at his eagerness and ran her fingers through his hair. As if sensing a primal need, she didn't speak, nor did she interfere with his ministrations. She turned her body over to him completely, allowing him to set the pace of undress. In turn, his desire demanded speed.

Only when he moved to enter her did she place her hand in the middle of his chest to stop him and whisper, "Protection?"

Thank goodness he'd stopped on the way over, feeling as awkward as a teenager buying a box of condoms. The variety of products had surprised him. It'd been quite some time since he shopped for them.

With the condom in place, he slid into heaven. Christ, he was that fumbling teenager again, nervous as hell and hard as a mountain. His palms sweaty. Only now, he was a man who knew how to please a woman. This woman.

Fleetingly, he considered taking his time, refining his techniques more along the lines of a deliberate seduction. But his raw desire dictated his actions and Noreen's equally passionate responses fueled the flame. When she clawed his back and screamed his name, he exploded in ecstasy inside her.

They panted in unison, both slowing their heart rates to normal, sharing a mutual sheen of sweat. He lifted his face from the crook of her neck and playfully kissed her lips. "I'm sorry. Apparently, you drive me crazy."

They were still connected, her hands clinging to his biceps. Her quick laugh jostled his stomach. "I'm sorry are the wrong words to use after taking me where you just did. I hope you're not sorry about this. I'm not."

He kissed her again, more slowly this time. "No, I'm not sorry about that. We have such an odd relationship, if we have a relationship at all. One minute I think you're my enemy and the next, I'm watching you embrace my daughter. And then all I can think to do is knock on your door and ravage you when you open it."

He lifted his weight off of her and rolled to his side. Spotting the bathroom to the right, he swung his legs over the edge of the bed and walked to it to dispose of the condom. Peering around the opened door he watched Noreen sit up and reach for her panties.

"Want a warm washcloth?"

"Yes, please."

He sat beside her and reached for his jeans. "There are things I want to say, Noreen, and none of the seem appropriate. You confuse me."

Her head shot up and she stared at him. Then she rubbed her palm the length of his bare back. "Good. Now the playing field is perfectly level."

# 16

A pang of disappointment shot through her as she watched Blake draw his shirt over his torso. He likely spent hours in the gym and it showed. Of course, in his line of work, he'd be expected to stay in shape. He rippled with muscles from broad shoulders to a slim waist and tight abs. Close up and personal was much better than the shirtless newspaper picture of him on the rooftop.

That photo hadn't revealed the tribal tattoo inked over his left shoulder. All black and fierce, it covered his shoulder blade in back, spilled down toward his nipple, and ended just above two small X's and several other letters positioned over his heart. The design covered his upper arm, ending where the sleeve of a pullover shirt would touch. She'd never seen it because his shirt-sleeve concealed the geometric design on his arm. The tattoo had been a surprise turn-on.

"You have a nice physique, Blake. What are the letters on your chest?"

His gray eyes shone. "Thank you. Those are Roman numerals. That's Gia's birthdate. One of the best days of my life."

She loved that he unabashedly adored his daughter. He leaned in to kiss her. "Today might be right up there, too. May I take you out for breakfast? Or make something for you here?"

She stood, bare from the waist up, and watched his eyes roam over her, the effect of the view visible in his crotch. A craving to have him inside her again surged through her.

"I better get dressed or you're going to find out the color of my bed sheets and we'll both go hungry."

A red flush spread across his cheeks and he dipped his head. "Sorry. I'm a bit out of control this morning." He stood and straightened the bedspread that had just held their combined weight, retrieving the throw pillows from the floor and propping them up against the headboard.

She shrugged into a T-shirt, choosing to remain braless. Might as well keep the ardor stoked. "That's the second time you've used the word sorry for your actions. I don't accept either apology. C'mon, let's see what's in my pantry and we can talk."

Blake scoured her refrigerator for omelet ingredients and gathered onions, cheese, and a plastic container of leftover cooked spinach. He pronounced his cache perfect. While he whipped the eggs, and lit a fire beneath two individual frying pans, she retrieved two plates and the necessary silverware and started a pot of coffee.

"You know, Noreen, it occurs to me that I know very little about you. I've spilled some of my darkest secrets to you and you're somewhat of a stranger to me." The eggs dropping into the pans sizzled and popped.

"We've been naked together. I'm not such a stranger."

He chuckled. "Well, that's true. But I want to know something about the person, not the sex goddess."

It was her turn to laugh. No one had ever implied she was sexy. "What is it you want to know?" Sharing personal information was uncomfortable. Her nurse's training enabled her to ask the correct questions for a diagnosis. She lacked the skills to properly answer personal inquiries. Nerves fluttered in her stomach.

Blake focused on his cooking. "I don't know. Where did you grow up? Do you have brothers or sisters? What made you go into nursing? That kind of stuff."

Those were answerable. "I grew up here. I have an older sister, married with two kids whom I adore. My mother used to say that nursing was in my chromosomes. At an early age, I had a doctor's kit and regularly took my baby dolls' temperatures and bandaged my stuffed animals."

Blake laughed. "If that's what a career is based on, then Gia is going to be a hair stylist. She combs and re-combs her dolls' hair. She trimmed the tails on two of her stuffed animals and," he paused and laughed harder, "one night when Lynne was snoring away on the couch, Gia cut her bangs. Oh my gosh, it was a mess. She had about an inch of growth left at her hairline. Lynne was furious."

Noreen whirled around to face him. "What happened? Did she punish Argia? Did she physically hurt her?"

Blake eased two perfectly cooked omelets onto their plates, sprinkled a parsley garnish on top of each and positioned the dishes on the placemats she'd laid out. "Breakfast is served."

He poured them both another cup of coffee and piled the dirty pans and cooking utensils in the sink before joining her at the table. "Blake? What happened?"

"Lynne would never strike her, if that's what you mean. I've never condoned physical punishment and I was there so it's not as if Lynne could spank her or anything. Gia isn't a child who needs spanking anyway. When she does something wrong, I speak to her like an adult. I always have. Even before she could talk, I'd explain what she did wrong and ask her never to do it again and she'd always say 'yes, Daddy.' Or give me a hug to let me know she understood.

"If it was a serious infraction, like the time she took the butcher knife outside to play with, I'd take a privilege away, like her favorite bedtime cartoon. I'd ask if she understood why she was being punished and her bottom lip would pop out and huge tears would fill her eyes and she'd nod slowly. And the behavior would never repeat itself. Gia is an easy child."

Noreen sampled the sweetest omelet ever. "What's in this that it tastes so good?"

He winked and her stomach somersaulted. "It's a secret ingredient. I can't tell you."

They ate silently until she asked a nagging question. "How did Argia get hold of a butcher knife?"

He stopped chewing, dropped the hand that held his fork to the table and stared at her. He swallowed. "I asked Lynne that too. For Gia to reach inside that drawer would have required her to drag over a chair and climb up on it. It's unlikely a four-year-old would take the time to return the chair, especially if she knew she was doing something prohibited. Besides, I installed strap locks on all of the drawers. I don't think Gia's little fingers could have released the mechanism."

Noreen processed his words. "This happened last year?"

"Un huh. The day after I told Lynne I wanted a divorce."

"Blake! Aren't you afraid to leave Argia with her? How could you abandon that poor baby and leave her with that monster?"

He crushed his napkin between his hands and dropped it on his cleaned plate. Leaning back in his chair, he cocked his head. "Now you sound like my ex-wife, Noreen. I didn't abandon my daughter. Leaving her is the only way to save her. As long as I lived in that house, Gia was with her mother full-time. When I was off duty, I couldn't keep Gia by my side all the time. I already told you I grocery shopped and mowed the grass and did laundry and pretty much everything you do on your days off. And I'm no saint. Every once in a while, I like to go out and have a beer with my friends. Now that I'm single, maybe even see someone."

He flashed her a quick smile and heat crept across her cheeks.

"Once I walked out that door, it placed me in a position to have Gia fifty percent of the time. Sure, I still have routine chores and tasks that need completed, like cutting the grass, for example, but while I'm in the front yard, Gia is visiting my mother or my mother is at my house, inside with her. My mother, not Lynne. And now I can legally fight for full custody and, when I'm working, I have people who will care for her. I'll control her time with Lynne. That's the only way I can protect her."

"Wouldn't it be safer to keep her completely away from her mother?"

Blake shook his head. "I would never forbid my daughter from seeing her mother." Suddenly, he looked weary. "Lynne loves Gia. I don't doubt that for a second. If you did any research, you know that once the child is old enough to talk and let people know what is happening to them, the person suffering from Munchausen's moves on to a new host. Gia is almost at the age where she'll be able to tell me if Lynne deliberately hurts her. But I believe in my heart Lynne wouldn't do that."

His comfort level surprised her. "But Blake, you know it's a tough fight taking a child from the mother. How can you be so sure you'll gain custody?"

He rose and began clearing the table. "The clock is ticking for Lynne. She has to be out of that house in thirty days. She has no job. Hell, I'm not sure she has any friends. Per our divorce decree, I pay child support and alimony but that doesn't add up to enough to allow her to live the lifestyle she desires. Designer clothes and cleaning people, expensive shoes, and more jewelry than you can imagine. What's the saying? Champagne tastes on a beer budget? It's never enough for her. She doesn't have a college education and she's going to have to find a full-time job, maybe more than one to afford her preferences. That strengthens my case to be named the custodial parent because of my work schedule."

"Aren't you afraid of what might happen until you are awarded full-time care of Argia?"

"That's a chance I have to take, Noreen."

# 17

"Enough about me. I want to know more about you." Blake nudged her while he ran hot water over their plates. They stood side by side rinsing and loading the dishwasher.

She bristled. "I don't like talking about myself. I'm not that interesting and I don't allow people to get personal with me."

He grinned and dropped a kiss on the back of her neck. "Making love isn't personal for you?"

"That's not what I meant." Thankfully, her cell phone rang, giving her a reprieve from Blake's questions. The spot on her neck where he kissed her sizzled. Through their entire conversation over breakfast, she'd studied him, watching his eyes light up when he talked about his daughter and his features turn serious as he revealed more about his ex-wife and their failed marriage. He spoke without anger or the need for revenge. What pushed his buttons? What would it take to make him mad?

Clearly, his daughter was his top priority. That devotion excited her. She wanted nothing more than to drag him back into her bedroom for more of his lovemaking. Frowning at the unfamiliar number displayed on the screen, she answered the call.

The level of Lynne's voice was so loud, Blake heard. "Noreen? Thank God I found you. I need to discuss Argia's medical records with you. I'm going to have her father arrested and I want you to support me."

He stood at the sink, the soapy cheese slicer clutched mid-air in his hand. He eyed Noreen. The euphoria of the last few hours evaporated.

"What? Lynne, what're you talking about? That's a serious accusation to make against your husband. I can't support something like that. I won't."

"Once you see the facts I've gathered you will. Meet me and I'll show you. Are you home? I'll come to your apartment."

Blake's eyebrows shot up.

"You know where I live?"

Lynne laughed, sounding a little possessed. "Of course. There's so much information out there on the Web, you were easy to find. I'm not far. I could be there in about twenty minutes."

The breath caught in her throat. Lynne couldn't find Blake here, in a T-shirt and barefoot, at home in her kitchen. And she didn't want him to leave, especially not under these circumstances. She fell into nurse mode, straightened her spine, and leveled her voice.

"That's unacceptable, Lynne. I worked a twelve-hour shift and I was just ready to attempt some sleep. One more minute and my phone would have been silenced. I need my rest to adequately care for my patients and yours is not an emergency. We can arrange to meet when it is mutually accommodating for both of us."

Did Blake just release a breath he'd held? She wasn't sure.

On the other end of the line, Lynne stuttered. "I-I'm sorry, Noreen. It's just that I'm so concerned for my daughter. Her father brought her home last night and she wouldn't eat and was listless. I thought she might throw up and—"

The cheese slicer clattered to the bottom of the sink and a

thin line of bright red blood oozed from Blake's palm. She grabbed a cloth towel from the counter, rushed to him and pressed it into his palm. She couldn't interpret the expression on his face. Aside from that telltale tick in his jaw, he was unreadable. He turned and leaned against the sink and she nestled into his side, adjusting the phone at her ear so he could hear better.

"Did she vomit?"

"No, no she didn't. But her pallor was ashen and she was so withdrawn. She—"

Noreen interrupted again. "Where is she now?" If Lynne planned to discuss her evidence against Blake right now, she wouldn't do it in front of Argia, would she? The girl couldn't be beside her. And she certainly wasn't with her father.

Lynne paused before responding. "She's with her little friends down the street. She loves playing with them and those parents will watch her while you and I confer. She has no one to play with when she's with him." She spat the last word, as if it was a disease.

This conversation needed to end. Now. "Then she's fine for the time being. I don't have a day off until Friday. I'm willing to meet you then, in the afternoon, say one o'clock at the diner on LaMarido. Do you know it?"

Lynne whined into the phone. "Yes I know it but Noreen, this is important. Friday is four days away. I fear my daughter's life is in danger."

She raised her eyes to watch Blake while she asked her next question. "And will Argia be in her father's care between now and then?"

Blake shook his head while in her ear, Lynne responded. "No. He'll pick her up after school and have her for the weekend. But—"

"Then we have time. I'll meet you on Friday."

"Noreen, you aren't considering my well-being and what I'm dealing with."

She cut her off. "That's exactly what I'm focused on, Lynne. I know this is important to you and I'm anxious to hear what you have to say. But I want to give you my best and that will happen on my day off. I'm really too tired to concentrate right now." She gazed at Blake.

"I've had some distractions this morning that have thrown me off balance and I'll need a clear head if we're going to resolve this issue together. You deserve my undivided attention. I'm certain you understand." She didn't wait for Lynne's acknowledgement. "I'll see you Friday. I'm going to bed now."

She punched the end button and Lynne's phone number faded from the screen. She stood silently beside Blake, waiting for his reaction.

His voice, when he spoke, was a low growl. "How'd she get your phone number?"

Maybe this was what pushed his buttons. The lust in his eyes a minute ago was gone.

"I gave it to her at the hospital."

"Why?"

The unspoken accusation irritated her. She swung around and pointed an accusatory finger at him. "You said it yourself. Keep your enemies close. Whether you know it or not, Blake Matthews, I'm on your side. Rather, I'm on Argia's side. But I will not stand here and be silently accused of siding with that, that monster."

He opened his mouth to speak and she raised her fist at him. "You be quiet and listen to me. We just came from my bedroom. If you think I carry on like that with anyone who knocks on my door first thing in the morning, then you need to leave. Make up your mind which side of the road you walk on but get off the yellow line, dammit. Decide once and for all where you stand regarding me. But know one thing. I've listened to everything you told me and I believe you. I will not stand by and let Argia be hurt anymore. Whether that means taking her mother down, taking you down or fighting the system, I'll do whatever I have to. So now, you can either stand beside me or get the hell out of my way."

Her chest heaved. Her face heated. She stared at him, surprised by the realization that she meant every word.

Blake's Adam's apple bobbed when he swallowed and the corners of his mouth edged up. "If I say I'm sorry one more time, I think you'll throw me out."

Her shoulders relaxed and the tension that had tightened her body like a taut piano string snapped. "You're right. I will. Think of something else to say."

He shrugged and grinned. "What has you so distracted this morning, Nurse Jensen?"

Her feet propelled her toward him and she reached for his towel-wrapped hand. "You're terrible at communicating, you know that? Let me take a look at this."

While she looked down, Blake placed a kiss on top of her head. "It's fine. The wire cut through my palm, that's all."

Noreen worried her lip. "It might need a stitch, Blake. The cut looks deep."

He nudged her hands away and rewrapped the wound. When he drew her into his embrace, she enfolded her arms around his waist and peered up at him.

His smile was devilish. "You told Lynne you were on your way to bed." The heat of his kiss burned to her core. "Let's not make a liar out of you."

# 18

Fresh out of the shower, Blake stopped abruptly in the middle of toweling himself dry and stared at his reflection in the vanity mirror. He'd been whistling. The last time he'd done that was, well, he couldn't remember. Maybe the day Gia was born. But sure enough, today he felt as if he could click his heels together and perform a Fred Astaire-worthy dance routine around the house.

In about two hours he'd pick up Noreen for a dinner date. Christ, as nervous as he was you'd think it was the first time he ever took a woman out. They'd talked every day since that morning at her apartment about their jobs, the emergencies and monotony of their hours. And always, they talked about Gia.

He'd made one ambulance run to Children's Hospital and sneaked up to Noreen's floor but she was on duty and all business. Even that had been a turn on. Especially when she discreetly squeezed his fingers before he stepped onto the elevator. Her touch sent an electric current up his arm that diverted straight to his zipper.

Little by little, Noreen dropped her guard, sharing tidbits about her childhood and her life experiences. She avoided details about a prior relationship with a man she thought she'd marry. He pieced together that the man was a bit of a free spirit, which surprised him considering Noreen was so conservative and straight-laced, and that she'd witnessed the accident that took his life. She hadn't been able to save him, which turned her career path toward nursing.

He asked why not become a doctor and she laughed and said nurses did all the real work. He didn't argue differently.

Tonight was the first night their schedules allowed them to meet and he wanted something simple but intimate. He chose a neighborhood Italian restaurant that offered lighted candles in wicker-wrapped wine bottles and checkered tablecloths. Dinner was all that he planned, despite his yearning to hold Noreen again and make love to her for hours.

Her meeting with The Captain was tomorrow afternoon and she'd stressed that she wanted to be clearheaded. He'd smiled through the phone when she used that word. Able to think clearly was exactly what he couldn't do when he thought about her. Jesus, he was falling hard for her. And fast. Where she fell on the emotional Richter scale was still an unknown. Maybe tonight, he'd clarify that.

Dressed in the skinny jeans he remembered from the burning car incident, with her hair combed up in a ponytail and falling in ringlets down her back, she looked like a teenager when he picked her up. He was certain the face-splitting grin he wore appeared childlike. He couldn't have been happier. Leave it to The Captain to burst his bubble.

Halfway through dinner, she called Noreen's cell phone to make certain their meeting was still on.

"I almost went to the police today. I've received three anonymous letters threatening me. So be very careful tomorrow. I'm certain he's watching me."

He listened to the conversation and rolled his eyes. Noreen's eyebrows furrowed. "Who?"

"Blake, of course."

"Are you certain Mr. Matthews is behind the letters? What if someone else means you harm?"

Lynne laughed. "I have no enemies, Noreen. Only an abusive husband."

Noreen smiled when he mouthed the word ex and blew her a kiss.

"We'll discuss this tomorrow, Lynne. I'm in the middle of something right now. Goodbye."

She folded her napkin and laid it beside her plate. "She's on a vendetta, Blake. You can't simply sit back and wait for her to make the first move. You have to be more proactive."

"Don't think I haven't tried."

He recounted the time he decided enough was enough and called the county sheriff, only to encounter the same roadblock as anyone else purporting wrongdoing. Without actual proof, he only had vague accusations about his Munchausen's suspicions. The deputy was sympathetic but it was a bizarre he-said-she-said situation until Lynne literally hurt Gia. Much the same as a protection order can't be issued until actual abuse occurs. Noreen declared that unfair.

He understood her frustration about the police and tried to explain why it was so difficult to take legal action. The advice her FBI friend gave her was spot on.

Months ago, one of the hospital doctors hinted that he suspected Lynne deliberately made Gia sick. He mentioned that incident after they left the restaurant and walked hand-in-hand to his truck. The Captain had ruined both their appetites.

"I thought the doctor might finally open the door for someone to take notice, but he wouldn't risk it."

"Tell me," Noreen urged.

It had been another rush to the hospital for non-stop vomiting that resulted in the doctors admitting Gia for a thorough evaluation. But not Children's. Lynne had driven her to a different facility. After listening to Lynne recount Gia's medical history, everyone agreed the nausea occurred too often in a child so young, especially one who rarely ate. He'd wondered out loud what there was in her stomach to expel. Of course, he was never around when the sickness reared its ugly head and the doctors took Lynne's word as gospel.

"She stayed in the hospital for five straight days, missing more school. She's behind in her studies. It was hard to keep her spirits up. She was restless and sad and perfectly healthy. I begged the doctors to let us take her home, as we were still married, and when they seemed inclined to do that, Lynne ran out of Gia's room that afternoon declaring she'd had another vomiting episode."

"Did she?" Noreen whispered.

"There was no evidence. Lynne claimed she took Gia to the sink to wash her face and Gia upchucked in the sink. Lynne acted flabbergasted and insisted that, with the water running, it immediately diluted the vomit and sent it down the drain. That's when the doctor threw up his hands, pointed directly at Lynne and said he was suspicious of her. I thought for sure he'd file a report and at least the hospital might initiate a follow-up. Maybe launch an official investigation. I waited a couple of weeks and when nothing materialized, I checked. He told me a false report would jeopardize his career."

She reached across the console and squeezed his shoulder. "In a way, I can understand his hesitation. It's hard to prove. And an unfounded accusation against a parent like that, well, that would stay with the doctor for the rest of his career. I see now, it's similar to the position the police find themselves in."

And just like that, Noreen announced she had an idea.

# 19

They had a plan. Noreen was right. They needed real evidence against Lynne if they wanted to involve the authorities. His goal wasn't so much to have Lynne arrested and charged with a crime. It was to build a case for custody. He didn't give a damn what happened to Lynne.

They drove back to Noreen's apartment hashing out the details. He hadn't planned on staying, didn't want every meeting with Noreen to end up in bed. But she invited him in for a nightcap and once she wrapped her arms around him, there was no tamping his desire. Or hers.

They made love slowly, neither of them closing their eyes as if they needed reassurance that they were in this together.

The mom-and-pop diner where Noreen was to meet Lynne was located on her side of town, taking Lynne as far from Riviera Road as possible. That was necessary to allow him time to search the house while Lynne was gone.

"Look for anything," Noreen instructed, "not just medicines or toxic products. Search the refrigerator for moldy food. Smell Argia's toothbrush. And her pillow. Is there an office? Look for papers, research on how to make a child ill. Lynne isn't smart enough to read it and retain it. She'd want it written down. Look everywhere, Blake. In Argia's room, in Lynne's room, in her drawers. You lived with this woman, you should be familiar with her habits. Check her purses, her shoeboxes. You're bound to find something."

He'd laughed at her. "Once I wondered if you were a detective in another life. Now I think you might have been a hardened criminal instead." He kissed her lightly. "Don't worry Ma Barker. I'll be thorough."

He'd waited for Noreen to text him that she was leaving before he set out for the house he still paid the mortgage on. That had been part of the divorce decree, that he provide a place for Lynne and Gia to live. This house was too big for the two of them and too expensive for him to maintain and also afford his own home. He'd given Lynne until June to find another, more affordable place to live. If she'd started looking, she hadn't shared that information with him.

She still hid a spare key under the solar-powered welcome rock in the front yard. Exactly where a burglar would find it.

Blake closed the door behind him and waited. Lynne had never mastered the security alarm system and he didn't hear it beeping. Another bill he needlessly paid every month. He withdrew a pair of disposable gloves and a flashlight from his back pocket and headed to the kitchen. He opened cabinets and searched behind the plates and glasses, riffled through the silverware drawer, and dropped to his knees to inspect the pots and pans. He peered behind cans and boxes in the pantry, not sure what he looked for but hopeful that he'd know it when he saw it.

The freezer had very little food in it and the refrigerator contained more takeout cartons than leftover plastic containers. What was she feeding Gia? From the kitchen, he moved to the bathroom and searched the medicine cabinet, surprised at the number of prescription bottles bearing Lynne's name. He found capsules to help her sleep and tablets to energize her, a prescription for a weight loss supplement and, surprisingly, one for birth control. Whom did she need that for? She'd quit the pill when she was with him.

He hadn't considered that Lynne might have attracted another man. Didn't think there was another one on earth stupid enough to fall in love with her, like him. If she'd enticed someone into her bed, that could improve her financial situation as well as her custody eligibility. He was banking on Lynne's lack of income to affect her ability to care for Gia.

The spasm that grabbed his stomach made him uneasy and he considered swiping an acid-reflux pill from Lynne's stash. When had she developed acid reflux? Maybe the boyfriend needed it.

Finding nothing, he walked to the master bedroom. Standing in the doorway he examined the room for signs of a male presence, but it seemed exactly as it had the day he left. He opened bureau drawers and inspected her closet, now looking for evidence of a man's intrusion as well as a clue to Argia's unstable health. Lynne still required three drawers chock full of cosmetics and beauty products that had irritated him when he lived there and seemed fuller now. He'd bet Noreen didn't use these various creams and lotions and makeups. All high-end brands too. And likely all purchased on his dime.

Christ, she could conceal a gold bullion brick in here, it was so cluttered. He moved items and shifted the contents without concern that she'd detect his hand had been in the drawer. She'd never be able to tell. Just as he was about to slam the bottom drawer closed, his fingers shifted the objects in the back and a small box of charcoal granules slipped into view. Activated charcoal? What did she use this for?

He examined the plastic bag that sealed the box inside, noting a black powder residue. The back panel of the box instructed users to crush the granules into a liquid in the event of poisoning and drink to induce vomiting. An extensive cautions paragraph followed, warning the user of potential interactions and dangers.

Curious, he walked back to the bathroom adjacent to Gia's room, the one always referred to as hers. It held her bath products and hair accessories and the tub was rimmed with her floating bath toys. He looked inside the medicine cabinet. Sure enough the bottle of syrup they always stocked in case she ingested something poisonous stood on the shelf. The seal had never been broken. He scanned the glass shelves and grabbed hold of the edge of the sink to keep from falling backward when his eyes fell on two prescription bottles. He recognized the drug names. One was an anti-seizure medicine and the other, tranquilizers. Both labels listed Gia's name as the patient. Both written by different doctors.

Gia didn't have seizures. And she didn't require tranquilizers. He snatched the medicines and shoved them in his jacket pocket. Let Lynne wonder where they went. For that matter, let her suspect he'd taken them. She wouldn't give Gia another one of these pills.

His hand shook as he returned the charcoal box to the cosmetics drawer. The ugly possibility that he'd discovered the cause of his daughter's sicknesses and the non-stop nausea hit him like a sledge hammer to the gut. He didn't need the product to clean out his system. He rushed to the toilet and expelled his breakfast.

It still wasn't proof but it sharpened his suspicions. Returning to the closet he yanked each one of her designer purses from the shelf and inspected the insides. This striped one was the last he'd noticed her carrying. But aside from some used tissues and stray coins at the bottom, the bag was empty.

What had he expected? The proverbial smoking gun? A blatant list of steps detailing how-to-poison-a-five-year old? Lynne was more devious than that.

He conducted a cursory search of the remaining rooms, laughing at the dust on top of the desk in his former office and curious about the stack of mail with his name on it. He didn't dare look through it. Too easy to see the pile was disturbed. But he made a mental note to ask his ex-wife if he had any mail at the house. He didn't waste time in the basement. Lynne hated the unused space below the ground, even the portion he waterproofed and renovated for his man cave. She said it felt like she was in a grave and she refused to go down there. He eyed the four-digit combination padlock that swung from a newly installed latch. Who mounted that for her? The new boyfriend? He doubted Lynne did it. She wouldn't know a wood screw from one used for sheet metal.

He yanked on it but it held fast. It was probably a good idea to keep Gia upstairs. The basement spanned the entire length of the house and the unfinished portion was unlighted, damp, and leaked water when a hard rain fell.

After he returned the key to its hiding spot, he drove home hoping Noreen was having better luck.

Noreen forced a smile when Lynne strolled into the restaurant, spotted her and approached the table, catching the attention of several male diners as she walked by. The nearer Lynne stepped, the tighter the vise-like grip on her stomach grabbed.

"I'm so sorry to be late," Lynne purred. "Thank you for waiting."

She crinkled her nose when she sat across from Noreen and unceremoniously freed her silverware from the cloth napkin that encased it. The utensils clattered to the table, catching the attention of diners nearby.

"How have you been? Are you adequately rested?" While she spoke, she dipped the corner of the napkin in the glass the waitress filled ten minutes earlier after Noreen arrived. Lynne sponged her fingers clean with the wet corner.

Noreen nodded. Once Blake extracted himself from her bed with a promise to return soon she'd slept like a baby. And awakened energized. And maybe, a little bit in love. The possibility equally frightened and excited her.

She eyed the woman across the table, conceding that Blake was right when he said Lynne was stunningly beautiful. Highlights in her hair caught and reflected the light, creating the illusion of an aura that complemented her face. The long, false eyelashes drew attention to her smoky shadowed eyes, which screamed seduction. Noreen recognized the designer suit from a magazine ad she'd drooled over as well as the trendy purse that Lynne dropped on the floor as if it were a throwaway plastic grocery bag. Everything about this woman shouted high-class but, based on Blake's accounts, it was all superficial. She understood how a man would be drawn to a woman like Lynne, someone beautiful who seemed perfect.

What would attract that same man to her, a bargain shopper, dollar store regular, buy-one-get-one fanatic? In Lynne's presence, Noreen deemed herself dowdy.

Frowning, Lynne relocated her water glass to the edge of the table and ordered fresh cucumber water. She raised her perfectly tweezed eyebrows when Noreen requested black coffee. "I limit my coffee and tea intake. I have my teeth whitened regularly and products like that might discolor them. That's why I avoid any type of berry, too. A woman can't be too careful about letting herself go, you know." Her dark eyelashes drooped lazily over her brown eyes and lifted slowly. They were Argia's eyes without the intense depth the child possessed. Without emotion at all.

Since Noreen regarded this as a business meeting, she'd tied her hair back and opted to dress down. Now she regretted her lack of jewelry and minimal makeup. Sitting across from this woman, she felt inferior.

Lynne studied the lunch menu, ticking off the items she refused to eat because they were high-fat, high-carbs, too greasy or just plain unhealthy. It was no wonder Argia was such a picky eater.

She attempted a friendly smile. "It's good that you are nutrition conscious. What do you usually feed Argia since a growing child needs a balance of fats and carbs as part of a healthy diet? And how do you avoid picking off her plate? I confess I give into the urge when my niece or nephew enjoy fast-food chicken nuggets."

Lynne's dark red outlined lips curled into a sneer. "I forbid Argia from eating any type of fast food."

Healthy or not, wasn't that an occasional delight of childhood?

"Argia is food sensitive. Her diet requires precise planning on my part. It's an arduous task that I sacrifice hours of my day to accomplish."

She'd asked Blake how Lynne spent her time. Perhaps that was the answer. But she recalled Argia's eagerness to snack on cheese and devour her father's scrambled egg and wondered if the sweet child went hungry when in her mother's care.

"That's admirable of you, Lynne. I hope you supplement her diet with vitamins if her meals are so restricted. What does Argia normally eat?"

"Absolutely not," Lynne declared loud enough to again attract the attention of the group at the next table. "I will not have my child ingest synthetic products even if they are manufactured as beneficial vitamins." Her head bobbed in slow motion. "The more acquainted you become with me, the more you'll realize the daily challenges I overcome for my daughter. I guard her health with my life, unlike her father. Every minute she spends with him strives to undo all that I achieve. I must make you understand that. Have you seen him?"

Noreen's heart clutched in her chest and heat immediately

radiated across her face. Involuntarily, she tightened her thighs, taming the fireworks she'd felt where Blake had kissed and touched and loved her hours earlier. She was a terrible liar. Would Lynne notice?

"Who? Mr. Matthews?" Her voice sounded higher than normal in her ears and she cleared her throat. "No. Not since the incident at the ice cream shop. Why do you ask?"

Lynne stiffened. "That was the perfect opportunity to have Blake arrested and you botched it, Noreen. Why did you lie for him?"

The tone of her voice was surprising. She switched from sweet to accusatory in the blink of an eye.

"I didn't lie for him, Lynne. I was speaking to Argia, trying to distract her from what was going on between her parents. I didn't hear Mr. Matthews threaten you in all the commotion and that's what I told the police."

Lynne's head canted to one side. "Really?"

The waitress delivered their lunch plates, thankfully ending Lynne's inquisition. She'd ordered a spinach salad, without the egg, water chestnuts or bacon dressing, requesting lemon juice on the side. Noreen resisted puckering or comparing this sour woman to her entrée.

Instead, she dove into her own strawberry spinach salad, savoring the first bite of the garlic breadstick on the side and adding the extra hot bacon dressing to the bowl. Lynne appeared to cringe.

Without looking up, Lynne announced, "I want to discuss Blake with you."

She gulped her mouthful of food. Blake and Lynne Matthews were divorced. The guilt for having slept with her ex-husband and enjoying every blissful moment of it was unfounded. Still, it felt as if she'd committed adultery and Lynne knew.

"You mentioned that you suspected Mr. Matthews of poisoning Argia. That's quite an accusation, Lynne. You said you had proof but it doesn't appear you have any files or medical records with you. I thought that's why we were meeting this afternoon."

Her chin lifted to the ceiling and her eyes rolled into the back of her head. She emitted a spine-tingling laugh. "Are you really going to continue calling him Mr. Matthews? You of all people?"

She must know something. But how could she? "I don't understand."

Lynne's fork poised in mid-air and she emphasized each word with a stabbing motion. "I saw the two of you at the ice cream shop. It presented a cozy little scene. After a meeting like that, I'm sure you're on a first name basis with my husband. Maybe even closer."

She sensed her eyebrows coming together and half-expected Lynne to chastise her for wrinkling her forehead. And then Blake's voice echoed in her ears. *"Ex-wife. Our divorce was final some time ago. Gia's mother refuses to accept it. But she's my ex."*

Her shoulders relaxed. "He did suggest I call him Blake but I'm not comfortable doing that. If he's as diabolical as you claim, I prefer a more formal reference."

"Oh, it's no claim, Noreen. I can prove my position." She stabbed the bare spinach leaves with her fork as if trying to kill them. They floated in mid-air when she waved them to emphasize her words. "I have to make you understand first what kind of man he is."

She was beginning to draw a pretty good picture on her own and she liked what she saw. Kind. Caring. Dedicated to his daughter. Handsome. In incredibly great shape. Loving. And one hell of a lover.

"He uses people. He'll use you if you let him."

Lynne's words cut into her musings and, suddenly, her appetite disappeared. The tone of this conversation left her uneasy. Raised a Catholic, the guilt of her time spent in Blake's arms hovered in her conscience and likely led her to read more into Lynne's statement than was actually there. Her heart refused to entertain thoughts of regret and instead, embraced the possibility of a new beginning. She took a deep breath and checked her watch while Lynne's hollow eyes bore into her. Had she allowed Blake enough time to search the house? She no longer wanted to be the diversion for their plan.

"Perhaps we should meet again when you have tangible evidence with you, Lynne. Until then, I can't consider wild accusations and I won't risk my career by becoming mixed up in the aftermath of an unsavory divorce. If Argia is truly in danger, I'll do anything to protect her. But I need facts."

She reached for her purse resting at her ankles and slid her chair back. Lynne watched her rise.

"I'll do anything to protect Argia too, Noreen. Remember that."

Squaring her shoulders, she turned and walked away from the table, feeling Lynne's gaze penetrate her back like a dagger. She took a deep breath once she was outside, grateful for the cleansing cool air diffusing through her body. She resisted turning around to see if Lynne also departed the restaurant and then realized she hadn't paid for her lunch. But she wasn't going back inside. She'd apologize and offer to reimburse Lynne at another time.

Years earlier, after her friend's handbag was snatched while she walked through a parking lot, Noreen adopted the habit of keeping her keys separate from her purse, usually dropping them in her coat pocket or simply keeping them on the table beside her. She clutched them now so tightly, the metal edges cut into her skin. Her trembling hand missed the ignition slot twice and she released her breath when it finally slid into place and she turned the key. Until now, she hadn't acknowledged how unsettling this whole meeting had been. The faster she could drive away from here, the better.

The engine began to grind. Surprised that the car didn't start immediately, Noreen released the key and studied the illuminated panels on her dashboard. A second attempt and the engine revved slowly and then stalled. The gas needle showed a full tank. The other gauges for water, oil, engine performance and the like all displayed normal levels. A third attempt resulted in more cranking. There was no use. Her car wouldn't start.

She twisted the key halfway and rolled down the windows since her nerves had gotten the best of her and she'd begun to sweat. Nothing to do but dial the auto club and wait for help. She scanned the parking lot. If Lynne exited the restaurant after her, she hadn't noticed. No matter. She wouldn't reach out to that woman for help anyway. This meeting had spooked her.

She located the membership card and dialed the emergency roadside assistance number. And then she locked her car doors and waited.

# 20

Blake expected her to text him when she left the restaurant but they underestimated the time she might spend with Lynne and then, in all the confusion with her car, she forgot. After all, she wasn't used to reporting her whereabouts to anyone. Wasn't used to having someone who cared where she was or what time she locked her apartment door behind her at the end of the day.

When he finally called, he sounded concerned, starting off the conversation by asking if it was safe to talk. After learning that she sat in her disabled car waiting for roadside assistance, he overreacted, in her opinion. His first instinct was to drive to her location and rescue her, which made her smile. A part of her heart leapt at the notion that he wanted to be her knight in shining armor. It was such a macho response, as if she wasn't capable of dealing with the emergency herself. She handled emergencies every day at the hospital.

Sitting alone in the middle of the parking lot with nothing but time, she'd dissected this inconvenience from every angle. There was no plausible explanation for her car's failure. It had run fine on the way to the restaurant and she diligently kept it on a regular maintenance schedule. She explained all that to Blake.

She didn't tell him that something didn't feel right. The hairs on the back of her neck stood on edge but she couldn't explain why. It added to the uneasiness of the entire day, starting with the minute Lynne sat down across from her. She convinced Blake they couldn't take the chance that Lynne remained in the vicinity, although why she'd hang around in a parking lot was unclear. Unless she waited to see the outcome of Noreen's emergency. She didn't share that last conjecture with him either. It was as unfounded as Lynne's accusations that he poisoned Argia.

In response to his query, she didn't know if Lynne lurked somewhere in the shadows. She'd been preoccupied with trying to start her car.

Sensing her unease, he admitted his concern. "I don't want you there alone."

"I'm fine, Blake, really. I'm locked inside the car and I've got a can of pepper spray on the seat beside me." She decided against telling him the container had rolled around in her glove box for more than a year. Her sister gifted her with it one Christmas after she switched to the seven-to-seven shift.

"Besides, it's still daylight and there's plenty of activity around me." By now, people were heading home from work and running errands along the way. A steady stream of cars filed past her. Probably why the auto club's arrival was taking so long.

"This restaurant sits in front of a shopping plaza and there is a good amount of car traffic passing all the time. Please stay where you are. I'll wait for the tow truck and call you when I'm home again."

Blake disagreed. "You're right, it's risky if I show up but I'm calling someone to come for you. I'll call you right back." He hung up before she could argue the point.

That only intensified her angst. No one knew they were seeing each other, if that's what they were doing. Did one Italian dinner and several hours spent making love translate to dating? Or was this just a fling for Blake, a way to entice the enemy onto his side. After all, he'd admitted he regarded her as Lynne's ally. The look in his eyes, the memory of his kisses and the yearning for his touch negated that suspicion. They'd shared too much for it to be a ruse.

But Blake couldn't possibly call someone without offering an explanation about why he was searching for help for a nurse he barely knew. And what sort of reason would he offer that sounded acceptable? Whom did he trust that much? She jumped when her cell phone rang less than five minutes later.

"You know Joe Lystle, don't you? The paramedic from our station? He's on his way to meet you. He lives about ten minutes from that shopping plaza. He'll wait with you until the tow truck arrives and he'll drive you home. If you're okay with me going to your apartment, I'll wait for you there. I don't pick up Gia until later. I want to see you."

Noreen's breath caught in her throat. It was one thing to share her concerns with Blake about his ex-wife and daughter but to allow a third party into the loop seemed reckless.

"He's hardly a third party, Noreen. He's like my brother. Every man in that fire station is someone I trust with my life. By default, I trust them with Gia's life and yours. It'll be fine."

"But isn't he going to wonder why you know that I'm stranded and why you're helping me? I don't think he holds me in the highest regard right now, not after the last time he saw me with Lynne at the hospital. What's he going to think?"

"He actually asked those same questions, honey. I told him I needed him to do this for me, no questions asked. That was good enough. If the table was turned, Joe could ask the same of me. It's how it works at Station Twelve. He's on his way."

"I think he's driving up now. Yes. It's him."

"Good. Let me speak to him."

She stepped out of her car grateful that the activity could

account for the blush she felt on her face. She forced a smile. What must Joe think? A woman stayed in the passenger seat, smiling at Noreen when their eyes met.

"I'm so sorry about this, Joe. I don't know how to thank you." She held up her phone. "Lieutenant Matthews is on the phone. He'd like to speak to you."

The briefest smile crossed Joe's face. She sounded ridiculous referring to Blake as Lieutenant Matthews. Joe likely saw right through that subterfuge. He stepped around her while he greeted Blake, reached inside to pop the hood, and walked toward the front of the vehicle to bend over the engine.

"I'm looking now. All cables seem intact. I'm not a mechanic but nothing jumps out at me."

She looked away when Joe's passenger stepped out of the car. "Hi, I'm Brittni. Joe thought you'd feel more comfortable if I came along, rather than him showing up alone." Brittni smiled and offered her hand to Noreen. Her firm, warm handshake was reassuring. She liked the woman immediately.

"I'm sorry I ruined your evening. I'm sure I would've been fine waiting for the tow truck by myself. I didn't ask Lieutenant, um, or rather Blake, to call anyone." She shivered and clasped her arms across her chest. "I admit, though, I'm glad you're both here."

Brittni smiled and rubbed her arm. "You didn't ruin anything. We were just thinking about what to do for dinner. I'm on a vegetable kick and wanted a salad and Joey is hungry for a burger. He welcomed the interruption. This isn't an imposition at all. Joey would do anything for Lieutenant Matthews. So would we all. Everyone has the utmost respect for him."

Joe slammed the hood, advised Blake he'd let him know when help arrived and ended the call. The three of them stood awkwardly in a tight circle beside the driver's door until flashing yellow lights caught their attention and the salvage truck advanced on them.

After exchanging the necessary auto membership information, Noreen and Brittni waited in Joe's truck while he stood with his hands in his pockets until Noreen's car was loaded onto the flatbed and secured. Before Joe's arrival, Noreen called her sister to share her dilemma. And to hear a friendly voice. Her brother-in-law recommended an auto service shop and Joe nodded his approval when she provided the address.

She declined Brittni's invitation to join them for dinner, and they drove to her apartment in silence. He slowed the car in front of the entrance and Blake jumped up from the terraced steps leading to the front door.

"Brittni, it was nice meeting you. I don't know how to thank you, Joe."

Joe waved off her gratitude. "Glad I could help. Have a good night, Noreen. I'll see you around." He waved at Blake and drove off. Neither spoke as they climbed the stairs, entered the building, and made their way to her apartment.

The second the door closed behind them, Blake reached for her. In his arms was exactly where she wanted to be and she didn't resist. They didn't move. Simply stood still, their bodies pressed against each other. He kissed the top of her head and tightened his embrace.

This wasn't foreplay, designed to entice her to bed. This was comfort, safety and reassurance enveloping her in two strong arms and seeping from his body to hers.

Despite the security of Blake's hug, her mind whirled. Was he wrestling with the same questions she'd been rehashing all night? Was it a coincidence? Or did Lynne have something to do with her disabled car?

# 21

Blake cuddled Gia in his lap while they waited in yet another doctor's office. This appointment was to remove her cast and he tried to share the excitement about that with her. But she seemed more withdrawn than ever. Even the games on his phone didn't interest her. And so he held her, massaged her back, and whispered his love. She'd arrived with her hair in a frizzy mass and he'd used his fingers to comb and braid it down her back. Lynne scowled, sitting one seat away, the chair between them holding her oversized designer tote. For once he was thankful for her endless handbag obsession.

"Don't coddle her," she snapped, causing him and Gia to jolt. "She shouldn't have fought me when I tried to comb her hair this morning."

He kissed the top of his daughter's head and immediately smiled, recalling the kiss he placed on top of Noreen's head several nights earlier and the passion it led to. He'd enjoyed an incredible sex life with Lynne and, drunk enough, might share a bed with her again. But there likely wasn't enough alcohol in the world. She was wild and uninhibited and he didn't regret their time naked together.

Making love with Noreen transported him to a whole different plane. He'd sink inside her and stay perfectly still, the two of them saying more with their eyes than words could express. Slowly, he'd lower his lips to her mouth and the kiss would be deep, as deep as he probed her body. It strengthened that link between them that hooked him the first time she blocked him in the hospital hallway.

Noreen had refused to explore possible reasons why her car malfunctioned that night, instead asking him to simply hold her. His consolation led to one hell of a bedroom romp.

"What're you looking so dreamy-eyed about?"

Lynne's sarcasm smacked him back to reality and he sighed, speaking more to his daughter than responding to his ex-wife. "We're going to celebrate tonight, aren't we Gia?"

After working a double, he finally had two days off to keep Gia with him. He wanted to fit Noreen into that downtime too.

"Honestly, Blake, sometimes you're so naïve. Argia's arm will be weak. She probably won't be able to use it and require therapy to rebuild it. A celebration is out of the question. You see how she is. Autistic children have special needs. I wish I could get that through your thick skull. Argia isn't like other children. Look at her. She's more frightened than a rabbit of everything around her. You want to celebrate and that will only upset her more and send her further into her own soundless world. Pretty soon she'll withdraw so far, we won't be able to reach her."

Gia tightened the fingers grasping his shirt.

"She's not autistic, Lynne. And she's exactly like other children. Anyway, it's none of your concern how I spend my time with my daughter." He winked at Gia. "We're celebrating."

Lynne bolted to a standing position and towered over them. Gia immediately shrunk into his chest as if she wanted to crawl beneath his shirt and hide. "Of course it's my concern. I'm her mother. And don't think I don't know what you're up to, Blake Matthews. But your scheme to undermine me won't work."

"As usual, Lynne, I've no idea what you're ranting about."

Her closed fist braced on her hip. "Oh really? Don't think you can get her on your side. Or do you prefer her underneath you? I wouldn't have pegged her for a whore but I guess looks can be deceiving."

His throat closed. What did she mean? *Who* did she mean? He deliberately responded in a monotone.

"You're not making any sense, Captain, and it doesn't sound like something I want you to explain or debate with you." He returned his attention to Gia, hoping to end the dialogue.

"It's a beautiful bridge, isn't it? The Sewickley Bridge?"

His heart caught in his throat. Noreen lived in Sewickley and access to the town from the highway was via the bridge. He raised his gaze to stare at his ex-wife. Her chin lifted ever so slightly but she refused to be the first to blink.

The nurse called for Gia, ending the silent standoff, and he dropped her feet to the floor and held her hand while they walked to the exam room. But his heart raced. His only trips to Sewickley were the night her car broke down, their one dinner date, and that initial morning when he arrived unceremoniously on her doorstep. The morning they first made love.

How could Lynne know that?

The cast came off without a hitch. The doctor remarked that Gia's flexibility was good and instructed he and Lynne on some exercises designed to strengthen her arm. He masked his surprise when Lynne inquired about rehabilitation and explained that Argia's arm would strengthen naturally the more she used it. He expected it to recover in a week or so. Lynne tried to object but he assured her children are resilient. He suggested her parents give her time.

Lynne's flippant bridge reference concerned Blake but this

was neither the time nor the place to confront her. Instead, he retrieved Gia's blue backpack from the SUV, buckled his daughter into her car seat and drove off without further conversation.

Pleased that Gia agreed to lunch he waited in the drive-thru when his text tone sounded. Noreen had her car back from the repair shop and she wanted him to call as soon as possible. He'd prefer Gia not be privy to the conversation over the hands-free speaker so he texted back that he was driving home and he'd call within thirty minutes.

Once Gia was settled at the kitchen table and he challenged her to take turns picking up a nugget with the "new" hand and the "old" hand, he wandered to the other side of counter, which opened to the living area. His daughter began to devour the food.

Noreen answered on the second ring and dispensed with a greeting. "My car was vandalized. Someone filled the gasoline tank with water, Blake. That's why it wouldn't start."

He took a minute to process her words. "I'll make some calls and find out if there were similar reports that day in that parking lot. It could merely be a juvenile prank. Maybe a herd of delinquents getting their jollies."

"Or it could've been Lynne."

His body reacted with a jerk and he immediately keyed in on Gia. She couldn't hear the conversation. The same theory had flashed through his mind but he dismissed it immediately. Lynne knew zero about cars.

"What makes you think that?"

Her voice paused as if she fought for control. "Because she was late for our lunch meeting. And when she finally arrived, the first thing she did was cleanse her hands. She wet her linen napkin and wiped her fingers. I thought maybe she was a germaphobe. But now I'm questioning that."

In all the meals they shared, he'd never seen Lynne do that. He didn't want to alarm Noreen by sharing Lynne's reference to his visits to her hometown but now, this made two question marks he linked to her mysterious behavior. Why had Lynne casually made the Sewickley comment?

"Did you file a police report?"

"Yes. The chief mechanic at the auto repair shop is my brother-in-law's friend. He insisted and he documented everything for me."

That was a relief. He hesitated to use her name, remembering his mother's adage "little ears hear big things."

"Have you discussed us with anyone, honey?" Gia raised her gaze to meet his and he smiled.

Noreen released a nervous laugh. "I'm not sure what I'd tell someone. I've no idea what you and I are about."

He'd wondered the same thing. "Yeah, I hear you on that."

Her plate was clean and Gia happily raised her greasy hands in the air. He snagged a kitchen towel from the sink and rushed to her. "I can't answer that either. Listen, after tonight you're off work, right?"

"Only for one day."

"Gia, I'm talking to Nurse Noreen. She's happy to hear that your cast is off." In his ear, Noreen said 'that's great.' "She'd like to see you tomorrow, if that's okay with you. Do you like that idea?"

Gia grinned and bobbed her head.

"Why don't you call us when you wake up tomorrow, Noreen, and let's see if we can't get together." His daughter stared up at him while he spoke. "Wait until you see how well Gia's arm has healed." That made his little sweetheart smile and she skipped off to her room.

"Be extra careful tonight, please. Be cautious of your surroundings when you leave the hospital and when you get home."

"What are you thinking, Blake? What are you afraid of?"

It was just a hunch and a crazy one at that. "I don't know. Just take extra care. I'll be glad to see your face tomorrow. Don't forget to call."

The conversation ended and as a chill crawled up his spine, he involuntarily glanced over his shoulder out the window. Calling for Gia to follow him outside, he grabbed a flashlight and walked to his truck. He lifted the hood and shined the beam underneath it, unable to pinpoint what nagged him. Why would Lynne reference a bridge she'd probably never driven across? They lived on the opposite side of the city.

Finding nothing unusual, he searched the interior, running his hands beneath the seats, under the dashboard and peering into the glove box. Then he examined the truck bed. Finally, he dropped to the ground on his back and peered underneath the chassis.

The flashlight beam reflected off the bright red swirl logo. The compact tracking device was barely two inches long, locked in a waterproof case and held to the underside of the truck by a powerful magnet. He'd seen advertisements for this kind of equipment, touting its ability to allow parents to discreetly track their teens' whereabouts from anywhere by syncing with their phone or computer. Was Lynne smart enough to use this? He couldn't imagine her prone on the ground snapping it to the underbelly of his truck. She hated to get dirty.

Did the new boyfriend install it? That seemed more plausible. How long ago? And where? He didn't recall a time when Lynne might have free access to his truck. But this tracking device was definitely how she knew he'd driven to Noreen's apartment.

Fury surged through him as he yanked the tracker from the metal frame. He emerged from beneath his truck and focused on Gia, sitting on the bottom step with Mr. Fox and Mr. Dog wrapped tight in her arms. Did she know about the boyfriend? Had she met him? Did he dare ask?

She eyed him as if she knew what he'd discovered and waited

for his next move. Fortunately, his actions weren't dictated by his anger.

He didn't want to tip off The Captain that he'd found the device. No, better to confuse her.

Blake scooped up his daughter. "Whaddaya say we go visit your Uncle Rob, peanut. We're going to accessorize his vehicle."

They waited for Noreen the next afternoon at the park on the Boulevard. Gia was halfway down the slide when she spotted Noreen walking toward them. She jumped off the edge and ran to greet her. He felt a wave of warmth surge through him watching Noreen drop to her knees and embrace his daughter. Followed by an upsurge of physical desire. Gia never greeted her mother like that.

He couldn't hear their animated conversation but imagined the praise Noreen lavished on Gia's cast-free arm while she jumped up and down, held both arms out, raised them over her head and dropped them to her side. Hand and hand, they walked toward him, all three of them grinning like dopey kids. Before he could stop himself, he reached for Noreen's waist and kissed her lightly on the mouth. Gia erupted in a fit of giggles and Noreen's cheeks turned fire engine red.

"I'm glad to see you. Any trouble last night?"

Gia tugged and Noreen moved toward the slide. "None. Even the hospital floor was eerily quiet. What have you two been up to?"

He escorted Gia to the four-step ladder at the rear of the slide and Noreen positioned herself at the foot. Hands in the air, Gia zoomed earthward toward her.

"We've been enjoying this beautiful sunshine. Gia ate an entire scrambled egg without you and she's promised to eat some dinner if you spend the rest of the day with us."

Noreen pretended to think about it, laying her index finger against her chin. “I don’t know. I’m awfully busy today but I guess I could change my schedule. Would you like that Gia?”

She shocked them both. “Yes, honey.” The words were as clear as could be. Then she grabbed Noreen’s hand and dragged her toward the swings.

Hours later, after a spaghetti dinner, a coloring competition and one book that Noreen read out loud while Gia nestled in her father’s arms, they tucked Gia in and poured themselves a drink.

Noreen slipped her feet beneath her on the sofa and wiggled into the crook of his arm, a position he’d never shared with The Captain. This was a good fit.

“We have a lot to talk about, starting with the fact that you’ve enchanted both me and my daughter. It makes me happy. Thank you.”

Noreen laughed softly. “Me too.”

“I spoke to my contact at the police department today. It seems yours was the only car vandalized.”

She stiffened beside him and he rubbed her arm. The ice in her glass clinked in her shaking hand.

“Do you think it’s possible, Blake? Could she really do something like that? Why?”

There was no need to identify the subject of the question. They were on the same wavelength.

He kissed the top of her head. “Why would she attach a tracker to my truck?”

Noreen gasped. “What? Are you sure?”

“I found it last night.”

“How’d you know to look for it?”

Now he straightened and twisted at the waist to face Noreen. “It was a hunch after Lynne made a reference about the Sewickley Bridge.”

Noreen’s eyes bugged wide and she held the breath she inhaled. He drew her forward and kissed her forehead, then ran his nose along hers. "I don't want you to worry. But I do want you to be careful. I don't know what bizarre scheme is going through her mind or what she's capable of."

"Are you going to ask about the tracking device? Is it still on your truck?"

He couldn't resist laughing. "No. Tomorrow it's traveling about a hundred miles to Lake Erie. Rob's going fishing."

# 22

Blake signed the last of the custody papers and pressed his finger between his throat and the knot of his tie. He hated wearing suits. But a meeting with his attorney dictated his attire.

"This is going to ignite a firestorm, you know that, don't you?"

The lawyer nodded. "It's best to start the wheels turning now. The juvenile court is overloaded and locking in a calendar date for a hearing could take at least a month. You said Lynne has to be out of the house by June so the timing will work to our advantage. Whether she's mooching off of someone or living in a substandard apartment, it gives us more ammunition."

Blake faced a possibility he'd been avoiding. "What if she moves in with another man?"

The lawyer's forehead wrinkled. "Is there one?"

He shrugged. "I'm not certain. Just an inkling I have."

"Based on?" He left the question hanging.

He certainly couldn't reveal he'd unlawfully searched Lynne's home for evidence that she abused Gia, although the argument could be made that he paid the mortgage and therefore had the right of access. But Lynne also had the right to privacy. He shrugged, deciding not to reveal his conduct. "Think about it. Her options are limited. She doesn't have a job yet, at least not one I'm aware of or one that changes her schedule with Argia. She's made no mention of apartment searching or complained that I'm forcing her out of the house so I suspect something is going on. It's possible she's used her feminine wiles to convince a man to take her in. Take it from me, she's a pro at that kind of stuff."

After about thirty seconds to weigh the alternatives, the lawyer shook his head. "That wouldn't play well with a judge. A man she just met, moving in with him, allowing him to support her and her child. We could have a field day with that."

He cringed. It wasn't his intent to destroy Lynne but this attorney was sharp and his reputation was to go for the jugular. He cautioned Blake at the onset of the custody proceedings that their battle cry had to be no survivors.

"Can you find out more information about that?"

Blake shrugged. "I'll do my best but it might not be fact." He nudged the legal documents toward his attorney and they both stood to shake hands.

"I'll have these filed by the end of the day." A ring bell sounded in his head. Round one in the fight for full custody of Gia was about to begin. Fighters. Take your corners.

Two days later, Blake stood at the commercial stove in the firehouse kitchen sautéing ground beef while Joe chopped onions and opened cans of kidney and pinto beans. A giant pot of chili with fresh biscuits and a salad was on the menu tonight for the team. The kitchen smelled wonderful.

He recognized Gia's school instructor's number when his cell phone rang. Laurie was more friend than teacher. They'd shared long conversations about Gia's abilities and the fact that her enrollment in this special school for children with learning disabilities seemed misdirected. That was an argument he'd vehemently waged with The Captain but once she hinted that Gia had developmental issues, the so-called experts erred on the side of caution. More like covered their own butts to sidestep liability.

Laurie thought the pace of the program essentially was a disservice to Gia, who seemed gifted and more advanced than her classmates. He hated that all Gia seemed to do was color all day, even though she excelled at it. Hers was artwork truly worthy of a prominent place on the refrigerator door.

But the academic curriculum didn't challenge Gia and Laurie had seen no concrete evidence that she wrestled with learning disabilities. Gia's lapse into silence was the first behavior that concerned her. She'd admitted some time ago that Gia was a different child when her mother dropped her off at school than when Blake brought her in after spending time with him. They secretly plotted to mainstream Gia next year.

"Hey Laurie, how are you?"

"I'm surprised you didn't let me know about Argia's vacation, Blake. You're the primary guardian on our records and you've been so good about sharing information. It was your responsibility to let us know she'd be gone so long. I would have assembled a study plan to send with her so she at least keeps up with the syllabus."

The wooden spoon stopped in the middle of the pan. "I don't know what you're talking about, Laurie. Who's taking a vacation?"

She hesitated a moment before responding. "Argia and her mother. Don't tell me you don't know about her plans? Blake, I'm sorry. I assumed you were aware of the trip."

The spoon hit the floor. Blake stepped away from the stove and motioned for Joe to take over.

"What trip? Start from the beginning, Laurie. What are you talking about?"

With each word she spoke, his heart pumped one beat faster. Heart attack fast. Gia wasn't in school today, Lynne's day to take her. Over lunch, Laurie called the house to check on her student but there was no answer. After school, she tried the number again and when there still was no answer, she dialed Lynne's cell phone. Lynne had never given the school her personal cell but he'd shared it with Laurie.

"She said Argia wasn't in school today because they're taking a trip. She didn't know how long they'd be gone and when I inquired about Argia's schoolwork, she said that didn't concern her. I offered to send some assignments to wherever they were going and Lynne said that wouldn't be necessary. I admit, the conversation stunned me. I wished her well, hung up and that's when I dialed you."

He was speechless. His worst fear might be coming true. The constable served Lynne with the custody papers yesterday.

"I'm as stumped as you are. I'll call you back." His finger trembled as he tapped the button to end the call.

In his heart, he knew Lynne loved Gia and would never physically harm her. The broken arm and how that all happened still mystified him. He hadn't asked Gia about it but he didn't believe The Captain's story. Gia wasn't a clumsy kid. However, he refused to entertain the theory that Lynne deliberately caused the accident.

What did haunt him was the fear that the mother would simply disappear with the child. Break her arm? No. Runaway with her? Absolutely. Gia turned every trip into an adventure, even a grocery store run or dry-cleaning pickup. She'd be thrilled if her mother told her they were going on a surprise getaway. So excited she'd never think to call Daddy and say goodbye.

"What is it, Lewey?" Joe wiped his hands on a dish towel. In the kitchen, Shaemus manned the stove.

"I'm not certain. Gia is unaccounted for." Joe's curse echoed in his ear as he touched the keypad number to speed dial Lynne. His call jumped to voicemail. Better to placate The Captain and not tip his hand. He left a message saying his schedule at the fire station might change and he needed to discuss rescheduling the days he was supposed to take care of their daughter.

"What do you want to do, Lewey?"

All he could do was shake his head. In the past, a phone message like that would generate an immediate and angry response and actual quotes from the divorce decree reminding him of the stipulated custody times. He stared at his phone, willing it to ring. Nothing.

Sweat pooled on his upper lip. Something was terribly wrong.

"Find someone to cover for me, Joe."

About an hour later, Blake let himself into the house, calling out Lynne and Gia's names as he opened the door. It looked exactly as it had the last time he sneaked in here and searched it. He checked Gia's room first, feeling some relief when he spotted her blue backpack hanging on its usual hook. The only things unaccounted for were Mr. Dog, Mr. Fox and her special blankey and those went everywhere with her.

Lynne had tried to wean her off the blanket and witnessed one of the rare moments when Gia lost her temper. In a sheer showdown of wills, Gia screamed non-stop until Lynne relented and threw the blanket back at her, calling it a filthy rag. Of course, he wasn't home for the confrontation and when he laughed about it, The Captain turned her frayed nerves on him. Gia came by the attachments necessity naturally. His mother said he clung to his baby blanket at night and some old moccasin until he was almost eight. That explanation hadn't pacified Lynne.

Next, he went to the master bedroom, again calling out their names and remaining curious if another man had privileges in this house. It was impossible to determine if one of her many totes was missing and it didn't appear the level of junk in her cosmetics drawers was lower. The charcoal granules remained in the rear of the bottom drawer. Another sigh of relief escaped him.

He dialed Lynne's cell phone a third time, deciding against

leaving a message. Now he regretted installing the tracking device on Rob's vehicle. He should've attached it to Lynne's SUV.

Locking up the house, he walked three doors down to the neighbors whose daughters Gia played with. They hadn't seen Lynne or Gia all day and the mother acted surprised when he inquired about a trip. He returned to his truck to wait. He knew one or two of Lynne's friends, couples who used to be both their friends but fell by the wayside as casualties of the divorce. Lynne had been a loner with no girlfriends to speak of. Rob's wife stood as her maid of honor at their wedding.

Their phone numbers remained in his contact list and he called them one by one. Each one said they hadn't spoken to Lynne in months and wouldn't know about her travel plans.

His stomach turned despite not having a meal since breakfast. He'd been out on a call at lunchtime and hadn't bothered to eat upon his return to the fire station. Eating now was not a consideration. Nothing would stay down.

He closed his eyes and tried to tap into the special bond he shared with Gia. *Where are you peanut? And why is Daddy so frightened?*

# 23

Noreen's shift was five minutes from ending when her cell phone rang. Seeing it was Lynne Matthews, she frowned. All she wanted to do was go home, sleep a few hours, and hopefully see Blake later today. He worked last night too and would be off in another hour. She ignored the call, swiped her badge as she left her floor and headed toward her car.

The phone rang again. And again. Cursing the woman for her persistence, Noreen settled into her driver's seat, opened her car windows, and stabbed the 'accept' button. She willed her voice to sound friendly.

"Good morning, Lynne. I'm just clocking out of the hospital and heading home to sleep for a few hours. May I call you back later?"

"Argia is ill." She relayed the information as calmly as if she were telling someone the time of day. Usually, she'd be frantic.

Noreen's pulse bumped. "What do you mean she's ill? What's the matter?"

"I don't know what the problem is. I'm not a doctor. Or a nurse. Will you come to check her?"

She felt her eyebrows come together in confusion. Lynne typically offered a medical diagnosis for her daughter's condition and demanded tests. This conversation was odd.

"What are her symptoms? Have you called her doctor? Where are you? At the hospital?" She resisted referring to it as her home away from home. If Argia suffered a hangnail, Lynne interpreted it as a medical emergency that required transport. Noreen had already figured that out.

"No, we're at home. She's too sick for me to move her."

Noreen caught her breath. "What do you mean too sick to move. What are her symptoms?"

"I'm asking you to come and help my daughter. You're a nurse so it shouldn't be that difficult. I'll text you the address. Please hurry."

She hung up, leaving Noreen with a slack jaw and her phone pressed against her ear. She didn't need Lynne's text message to start driving toward the Matthews' house. The address remained in her car's navigation system from the time she drove by trying to complete that welfare check that opened a door to a hell of a lot more than she ever imagined. It led her to Blake. Was he there? Why hadn't Lynne followed her usual pattern of calling an ambulance and shipping Argia off to the hospital?

A co-worker interrupted her speculation with a phone call and questions about one of the children on the floor. By the time she hung up, she'd parked in Lynne's driveway and turned off the motor. Did Lynne know that her car failed to start after their lunch meeting and would she inquire about it? That would be a dead giveaway.

The door swung open and Lynne emerged on the porch. "Don't just sit there. Argia needs you."

Leaving her purse on the passenger seat and her cell phone in the cup holder between the seats, Noreen locked the doors and walked into the house. This home was different than Blake's rental house, newer, more modern, and colder. The front door opened into a small entryway with a three-foot tall, blue porcelain vase that held artificial grasses stretching almost to the ceiling. It was frightening at first glance. To her right was a room with a baby grand piano and on the left, an oval oak dining room and eight chairs that she could count. A matching hutch, dry bar and auxiliary butler crowded the space. Down the hall in front of where she stood, Noreen saw the kitchen.

All the furnishings and accouterments looked expensive and professionally decorated. None of it reflected Blake's warm, down-to-earth character. Blake told her that once he moved out, Lynne hired an interior decorator to refurbish the entire house, forwarding all the bills to him after the fact.

She nodded toward the piano. "Who plays?"

"Argia will someday. Unless you let her die."

Icy fingers of foreboding crawled down her back. What an awful thing to say.

Now she raised her gaze to the stairs leading to the second floor. "Where is she, Lynne? Upstairs? If she's that ill, perhaps we should call an ambulance immediately." Anything to get someone else in this house. "Have you called her father?"

"I called you." Lynne opened a slim door in the rear left corner. "Down here. She knows she's not allowed to play in the basement but she never listens."

Shock forced her to focus on Lynne. "Argia is down in the basement? Is her father with her?"

Lynne smirked. "Of course not. Why would he be here?"

Her feet drove her toward the door. "You left Argia down in the basement by herself when she's not feeling well? What the hell is the matter with you?" She'd reached the top step when Lynne shoved her hard from behind and she plummeted head first to the concrete floor.

Excruciating pain paralyzed her leg and she screamed. Lynne hurried down the steps.

"Oh my goodness, Noreen. What happened? Did little nursey nurse have an accident?"

The room spun in the darkness. Mold and the universal musty smell of a cellar clogged her nose. Dampness seeped up from the cement beneath her. To her left, an unfinished floor-to-ceiling wall. On her right, exposed beams and chalk marks from the home improvement dealer were legible on the plywood panels. The framed wall turned at a ninety-degree angle, effectively containing the space beyond it. The opened door allowed her to see inside to a carpeted, finished room. It held no furniture. Nothing. A small window at the ceiling provided the only light and, off to the side, it appeared a panel had been torn from the wall. A faint sound from that direction attracted her attention. Whimpers.

Lynne propped her hands on her hips. "I thought I was going to have to restrain you but I don't think that will be necessary. There's blood on your pants and I'm rather certain that distended bulge in your pant leg is your tibia." She smirked and tossed her hair. "See? You're not the only medically educated person around here. My knowledge is superior."

Noreen fought the urge to vomit and blinked several times to keep her eyes focused.

"Now, Noreen. Here's your first challenge. You're Argia's nurse. She's on a mattress behind the boiler in that room back there. You came to check on her. I suggest you do it."

This was a nightmare. She didn't recognize the woman standing before her with bulging eyes and a twisted grin. "Lynne, what're you doing? What's going on with you? I don't understand." Each question came out in a huff as her body tried to compensate for the raging agony of her shin bone protruding from her leg. "Lynne, I think you're right. My leg is broken. I need an ambulance. Please help me."

She dropped her head back and laughed. "Oh, so now it's all about you? Don't you care about Argia any longer? I thought as much. Your overt attention to my child was a scheme to sleep with my husband, wasn't it?"

This was too much shock for her to handle. The ringing in her ears rivaled church bells. How did Lynne know she'd slept with Blake? And was this solely about revenge?

Somewhere in her foggy brain, Blake's voice replayed, *"Ex. She's my ex."* Noreen checked her own smirk and a subdued sniffle drew her back to the moment.

"Where's Argia?"

"I told you. In the room in the back. There's no light in there. She has sensory issues, you know."

She stretched her hand toward the woman she was certain had lost her mind. "Lynne, she's your child. She must be frightened to death. I need you, Lynne. Help me reach Argia. I can't walk. We're both dependent on you."

Her attempt to flatter the woman and psychologically appeal to her fell flat. Lynne released another eerie laugh and dropped her foot on the bottom step. "Crawl to her, bitch."

With that, she stomped up the stairs and slammed the door.

Noreen dropped her head on the floor and closed her eyes. In the silence, the muffled cries sounded louder. She rolled over, only then realizing that the fall down the steps had done more damage than merely breaking her leg. Her torso ached and she prayed she hadn't broken a rib. That's what it felt like.

"Argia? Honey? Are you back there? It's Noreen, honey. Can you hear me?"

Nothing but quiet sobs. She must reach her. Bracing her arms on the floor she used her good leg to force herself forward onto her elbows. The dragging motion on her broken leg burned as if a welder's torch seared it. She dropped to her stomach, squeezed her eyes against the pain and waited for the room to steady. At least she hadn't broken her arms.

She raised herself up on both of them and scooted forward another inch, crying out as her immobile leg resisted movement. Her vision blurred with tears and each breath came in a huff. Midnight blackness surrounded her and she wondered if she was about to pass out or if the basement was simply opaque.

"Argia? Sweetie, I'm trying to get to you honey but I'm hurt. And I can't see you. Honey, make some noise so I can find you."

The whimpering ceased and a stream of light spilled from under a closed door, casting a shadow along the floor like an airport runway. Lynne must have left a flashlight with Argia. A benevolent move on her part.

"Good girl, Gia. I'm coming in that direction so turn the beam off until I tell you to shine it again." Her guiding light disappeared. With every ounce of energy she had, she hauled her contorted limb along the carpet, sputtering when a cobweb crossed her face and coughing at the dust each forward motion disturbed.

"It's going to be all right, honey. Don't be afraid. Your daddy is going to find us and fix this. Honey, are you hurt?"

Speaking through her clogged throat was difficult but it refocused her fears and some of the pain from this insane skulk across the finished room that yielded only inches with each attempt. "Gia, I know you can talk. This is really hard for me, honey. I'm hurt. My leg is broken. Remember how bad it hurt when you broke your arm? That's how it is for me right now."

Another three inches of forward progress. Maybe. She couldn't see but sensed a barrier in close proximity to her face.

"Talk to me, sweetie. I need to know you're okay." The dead weight of her body shifting along the floor and the loud exhale each time she dropped her chest to the ground to regroup rolled around the room and echoed off the cinder block walls.

And then, a surge of relief. "Noween? Is Daddy here?"

Tears of gratitude glided down her cheeks. Despite the bleakness of the situation, she whispered 'thank you God.' And she propelled herself another few inches. "No, honey. But I know he'll come. He's probably looking for both of us right now." *Please, God, let it be so.* "Gia, turn the light on again for me."

The flood of light showed the door about six inches away. Which way did it open? “Argia. Are you hurt? Please tell me.”

“No. But Mother hurt Mr. Fox.” She started to cry.

“It’s all right, honey. We’ll fix Mr. Fox. Listen to me, Argia. Can you open the door for me? I can’t stand up.”

The silence deafened her. “Argia?” Muffled movements in the room but the barricade remained between them? “Talk to me, Gia.”

“I can’t weach it. Mother made it so I can’t.”

If she survived this ordeal, she’d claw her mother’s eyes out for this. “It’s okay. I’ll do it. Keep the light on.”

The average doorknob is three feet from the floor but in these shadows, this round black orb looked as high as the Empire State building. Undaunted, Noreen nudged closer. And closer. And then she stretched her arm, straining every muscle along her side and thigh to turn the knob, screaming when pain ripped through her leg as she fell face first into the room when the door swung inward. Bile clogged her throat and Argia’s scream matched her own. She lay on dirt, panting, willing herself to ignore the excruciating throbbing, ordering her body to overcome the distress. She spit wads of dust from her mouth.

Sneakered feet dropped into her line of sight and she raised her head to see a bungee cord tied around Argia’s right ankle and anchored to the leg of a rollaway bed. Argia extended the line as far as she could, squatted, and reached for her, her five-year-old fingers playing invisible piano keys in the air. Noreen overextended her left arm, groaned when the muscle tore, and grasped the child’s hand. “It’s okay, honey. I’m here now.”

Argia’s clothes were filthy, no doubt from this room and the grimy mattress on top of the cot. Her face was streaked with old and new tears and she crushed her blankey and cherished stuffed animals underneath her armpit. The fox’s head swung ludicrously from four strands of thick cord.

“Sit back down, Gia. Give me a minute and I think I can free your leg." What mother in her right mind would tie her daughter to a bed in the basement? Well, perhaps that question answered itself. Lynne was a lunatic.

She dragged herself farther into the room until her feet cleared the door and it slammed shut, scaring them both. She looked at the closed portal in horror. No door latch on this side. Now they were both locked inside.

There was no floor in this room, only compacted dirt settled in uneven waves. One wall was lined with shelves and hundreds of containers of nuts, bolts, and screws all covered in dust. These jars hadn't been opened in years. A rusty boiler occupied the opposite corner and behind it, an old push broom, its bristles worn down to two inches, a yardstick, and a leaf rake. Pipes rose out of the top of the tank but connected to nothing. It hadn't operated in years.

It was unimaginable that this room was part of the clean, modern Matthews house upstairs. Why would Blake keep such a chamber like this?

Finally, willing herself not to blackout, she flipped herself over and edged backward on her butt until her shoulders hit the cot. Argia fell beside her and threw her arms around her neck, sobbing. Noreen wrapped the child in an embrace.

"It's all right, honey. Don't cry. It's going to be fine." The child's chest heaved and her body wracked with her unchecked fear. Noreen allowed the storm to run its course, fully understanding Argia's terror. She was scared to death too.

## 24

Blake took two deep, calming breaths before answering Lynne's phone call. He'd only called her every hour on the hour from five o'clock last night until three in the morning when he tired of sitting in the driveway staring at the darkened house. He drove home hungry, thirsty, in desperate need of a shower, and fighting a pounding headache. Fear and fury wrestled for equal time in his head.

Noreen had been unreachable all day as well, which irritated him. She'd assured him she'd clock out, grab a couple hours of sleep, and then spend the day with him and Gia. He supposed an emergency at the hospital could've changed her plans but he expected her to be courteous enough to let him know that. Maybe this relationship meant more to him than her. It hadn't felt like that though when he was wrapped in her arms.

Once he drove home, he didn't sleep. Only dozed on the sofa until the phone jolted him to full consciousness. He stretched to release every ache and kink in his back.

Keeping his anger in check, he tapped the screen and stopped the funeral dirge that played as Lynne's distinctive ringtone. "Captain. I've been trying to reach you. Where've you been?"

"Cut the crap, Blake. How dare you take Argia out of school and not tell me. What're you trying to pull?"

His response caught in his throat and he choked on his words. "Wh-what did you just say?"

"You heard me. The school notified me this morning that you took her out of class yesterday and she's absent again today. You know she's behind as it is and every minute in that school is important. How dare you interfere with the individual education plan I approved? Where are you anyway? And where is Argia?"

Her voice was like a foghorn, droning and muddled and monotonous. Maybe it was the buzzing in his ears. The headache resurfaced.

"Slow down, Lynne. Gia isn't with me. The school called me yesterday and said you informed them that she would be absent. They said you planned a trip for the two of you. Why do you think I've been calling you every hour? What's going on?"

She screeched into the phone. "That's absurd. I did no such thing. Who told you that?"

Lynne despised Gia's teacher, manifesting an unfounded jealousy toward Laurie after their first meeting. This wouldn't help. "I spoke to Laurie and she—"

"She's a liar."

Her harsh response stopped him short. They'd argued about Laurie before. Lynne's insecurities were irrational.

"Where are you, Lynne? If Gia isn't with you, we have to find her. Nothing else matters right now."

"You can't fool me, Blake. I know exactly what this is about. You're jealous. And you're using Argia as your revenge. Stop playing games and take my daughter back to school. Or I'm reporting you to the authorities."

He shook his head to clear his thoughts and squeezed his eyes shut. None of this made sense. "Calm down, Lynne."

"I'm perfectly calm."

Amazingly, she was. The Captain's usual tirade over the smallest irritation was absent. As if this call was calculated.

"Laurie told me yesterday—"

"That whore. I wouldn't believe a word she said. You know she has eyes for you. If Argia is missing, she probably has her stashed away some place hoping her big, strong daddy will come find her. The woman can't attract a man otherwise."

Never mind that Laurie was married with two children of her own. Or that this was an old argument Blake didn't care to revisit. He reorganized his approach.

"Yesterday was your day to take Gia to school and—"

"And I did just that. And then I left you the message to make sure to collect her after school because I had evening plans. Be honest, Blake. That's what this ridiculous charade is all about, isn't it? You don't want me but you won't allow another man to have me. You're pathetic."

The junkyard in his brain overflowed with trash. What message? He'd received none. What man? Had his suspicions been right that Lynne had attracted a lover? What did that have to do with anything? He didn't care who Lynne slept with or spent time with unless the guy mistreated Gia. And where the fuck was Gia?

"What message, Lynne? I never received any communication from you about Gia. I was at the station all day. You know my schedule." Well, he was there until he flew out of the building and camped out in her driveway until six hours ago.

She exhaled loudly into the phone. "Well don't blame me if one of those incompetents you work with failed to relay my message. I left you one telling you I'd be out all night."

Without needing to check at the station, he knew that couldn't be true. No one in his unit would fail to give him a message, especially one pertaining to Gia. Lynne hadn't called.

Now, she purred into the phone. "Honestly, Blake. I know that's why you constantly rang my phone all night. You can't stand the idea of another man touching me." She giggled and his skin crawled. "You always were so possessive. Darling, if the thought of me spending the night with another man upsets you this much, we can fix that. Come back home and we'll be together again as if none of this divorce stuff ever happened. We can make love like we used to. Maybe even have a child. A son. Would that please you?"

He'd lost his mind. Either that, or he was living an episode of *The Twilight Zone*. They had a child. She was the reason his heart beat and at the moment, she was unaccounted for. But as usual, the Captain reconfigured the situation to be about her.

"We have a beautiful daughter, Lynne, remember? Where is she?"

# 25

They huddled in the dark together, Argia tucked beneath her right arm and her head against Noreen's breast. One look at the grimy sheet and paper-thin mattress stained and discolored and Noreen opted to drop to the floor and use the cot to brace her shoulders. After a few minutes, she hardly noticed the metal rail digging into her back.

She'd taken a quick survey of their surroundings, and then explained to Argia that keeping the flashlight off would save the battery. When switched on, the light shined brightly. Maybe Lynne ensured the battery was new for her daughter's trip into hell. Of course, in total darkness, the beam was a beacon.

She reassured the trembling little girl as best she could that together, they were strong and there was nothing for them to be afraid of. If only that was the truth.

In reality, she wasn't certain what was happening or what the next few hours would bring. Was Blake looking for Argia? Would anyone miss her?

The level of numbness in her leg rendered the pain minimal as long as she didn't dwell on it. She tried to recall her medical training about broken bones that pierced the skin and untended wounds. How soon did gangrene set in when tissue was damaged? Especially in a place this dirty. The knowledge didn't immediately come to the forefront of her brain and she was too distracted to concentrate. Several hours, at least.

Instead, she contemplated the monster who'd tied her five-year-old daughter to a piece of furniture and abandoned her in a pitch-black, filthy cellar with a flashlight, a bucket for waste, and three unopened bottles of water. It was beyond comprehension. What made Lynne Matthews desert her child like this? Furthermore, why had she subjected Noreen to this torture?

That answer was obvious, if somehow Lynne found out that she'd slept with Blake. Jealousy was one of the oldest motives for thousands of crimes. But why drag this frightened baby girl into the mix? Just take out her vengeance on Noreen. At least then, it would be an even match. Woman to woman.

She tried to imagine Blake loving Lynne Matthews. He'd confessed to her that he was myopic where his wife was concerned, he'd loved her so deeply. A pang of jealousy pierced her heart when she'd listened to him describe his devotion and suspected he still loved Lynne on some level. Now, after she'd enjoyed the pleasure the man's mouth, hands and body could evoke, the twinge of jealousy threatened to rend her soul. Passion seeped from the man's pores. And ice water poured out of his ex-wife's. How could he have loved her so? She hadn't seen an ounce of compassion in the woman.

Proof of that clung to her now in the dark, confused about why her universe had turned into a living nightmare. And likely unsure who, if anyone, loved her.

She squeezed Argia tighter and dropped a kiss on the top of her head. She loved this little girl. And she'd die protecting her.

"Hey?"

Argia's head moved against her side to look up.

"Does anything hurt?"

She shook her head.

"You didn't stumble down the steps or fall on this uneven floor?" She resisted asking if that witch of a mother shoved her from behind as she had Noreen.

A second negative headshake.

"Did your mom carry you down here or did you come down on your own?"

Argia shook her head again and Noreen placed another kiss in her hair.

"Talk to me, Argia. It's important to know so I can figure out how to get us out of here. Please honey."

The silence lasted so long she didn't think Argia would speak. When she finally did, she whispered in staccato sentences. "Mother said it was a game to play with Daddy. We're not allowed down here."

"We who, honey?"

"Me and Mr. Fox and Mr. Dog." She crushed the toys to her chest and whimpered. "Mother hurt Mr. Fox."

"It's okay, don't cry. We'll make Mr. Fox as good as new once we get out of here."

Argia sniffled. "Weally?"

"I promise. I'm a nurse, remember? I helped fix your arm when it was broken, didn't I? We'll make Mr. Fox all better, you'll see."

Slowly, Argia's sniffles stopped. Only their breathing sliced the silence.

"Why did your mom hurt Mr. Fox, honey?"

"I cwied and I'm not allowed to cwy. Mother told me to listen or she'd hurt me too. Like Mr. Fox." A shudder ran through her tiny body and shot into Noreen's frame. The fiend.

She kissed the child again. "It's okay now, Gia. Your mom isn't going to hurt you. Not if I can help it."

If Lynne Matthews returned, she'd go down protecting this little girl. Broken leg and all, she'd attack first. Years ago, a self-defense class bolstered her confidence when she exited the hospital at midnight and walked alone to her car every night. She already had the psychological mindset to fight. And survive. Thumbs in eye sockets. She didn't need two good legs for that and the attack would throw Lynne off balance. Take her by surprise. And then, Noreen would simply beat the woman senseless. Her fists clenched now as if ready to strike.

She'd need better balance though to overtake a woman standing in two sturdy designer shoes.

"Gia, we have to do something about my leg. You'll have to help me. Do you think you can do that?" Against the fleshy part of her breast she felt rather than saw Argia look up at her.

"Your daddy is going to be so proud when I tell him how brave you were and how you helped me."

Argia sat upright. "Is Daddy coming?"

Whenever Argia spoke, she whispered, as if weeks of silence hurt her throat to talk. Or perhaps she feared that speaking louder would disturb whatever unknowns surrounded them. In the dark, even she could imagine monsters.

She flicked on the flashlight, stroked Argia's hair, and kissed her forehead. Blake lived for his daughter. If she, practically a stranger, was ready to fight for this child Blake would be unstoppable in his quest to find her. There was no doubt about that.

"I'm certain of it, honey. It may take him a little time to find us because he knows you're not allowed in the basement and you're such a good little girl, he won't think to look down here because you don't go against his wishes."

"Mother made me."

She brushed the hair off Argia's face. "I know that, Argia. When your daddy finds you, he'll understand. Don't worry about that. In the meantime, do you think you can help me?"

Noreen shined the light toward the boiler. "See those sticks over there? Can you bring them to me?"

Argia's grip on her hospital shirt tightened.

"Don't worry, I'll keep the light on and watch you every step.

You'll be fine. Just be careful because they might be heavy. You might have to make more than one trip, honey, but you can do it. Start with the smallest stick."

The faded yellow yardstick beckoned. Argia didn't move.

If forced to, she could butt crawl over and back but the disturbance to her leg would be excruciating and sap her strength. She'd need every bit of it to face off against Lynne. "Please try, honey. I'll hold Mr. Fox and Mr. Dog and protect them. You can have them right back."

Wide eyes filled with terror stared back at her. Argia eased the partially decapitated fox into her hand but clung to the dog. She glanced at the corner where the tools stood like emaciated guards and back at Noreen. Noreen nodded. "You can do it, honey."

Argia rose cautiously and eyed the distance. It was no more than ten feet but to a frightened child it was a chasm of terror she was asking her to cross. With Mr. Dog smashed against her chest, Argia tiptoed to the boiler and reached for the yardstick, easing it from a nest of cobwebs.

"Good girl, Gia."

Triumphantly, Argia smiled and squatted beside Noreen, laying the retrieved treasure beside her thigh.

"I think you'll need two hands for the next one, honey. It will be heavier than this stick." She extended her hands outward. "Let me keep Mr. Dog safe so you don't drop him."

Argia considered this major leap of faith for a full thirty seconds before relinquishing the beloved toy.

"Just knock them both over, Argia. Then you can drag them closer."

The clatter from the broom and leaf rake falling to the dirt floor and the resulting dust cloud scared Argia and she rushed back to Noreen, hurling herself into her arms. Her weight sent a surge of agony down her broken leg but she crushed the child to her chest and squeezed her eyes shut against the throbbing.

With Mr. Dog and Mr. Fox safely ensconced in her arms once

again, Argia tugged and yanked until the push broom and rusty rake were within Noreen's grasp. She drew them closer. The broom would serve as her Excalibur, King Arthur's magical sword. Legend had it that, when first drawn in battle, the blade blinded Arthur's enemies. A blinding blow to the back of Lynne's head would suffice.

The yardstick snapped easily in half. Noreen placed each piece along the side of her injured leg. Not enough support. She eyed the brittle rake handle and prayed for the strength to crack it.

"Gia, can you stand up for a minute? I have to adjust my position."

Dutifully, the child stood, watching her intently. Using her hands to lift her bottom and her good leg as a propeller, she raised her body off the floor and readjusted her position to an angle with the cot. Her head dropped back against her shoulders with renewed agony and every nerve in her injured limb screamed in protest. This would have to do. She couldn't maneuver to a better position. Cringing, she tugged the two-inch thick mattress away from the bed frame and waited for the coughing spell caused by the cloud of dirt to subside. Taking the rake in both hands with the tines at her stomach, she cautioned Argia to stay behind her and cover her ears. Summoning every ounce of strength, she crashed the rake against the metal edge. The crack sounded like an explosion and the top of the handle flipped into the air, spun in an arc, and dropped on her good leg. What was one more bruise?

Without thinking, Noreen twisted her upper body and grabbed for Argia, wrapping her arm around the girl's waist and hauling the trembling child into her lap. She hugged and rocked her until the shaking subsided. "I'm sorry. I didn't mean to scare you." She kissed her forehead. "Are you okay?"

Argia nodded.

"Good. You can help me fashion this leg brace." The rake

handle was so dry, twisting the metal tines fastened to the end easily loosened the rivets attaching it to the stick and with a few yanks, Noreen freed it from the handle. She eyed the metal fingers spread wide in the shape of a fan. They might come in handy for something. She set it within reach on top of the cot.

With the round handle pieces on either side of her leg and the yardstick halves positioned on top and below her leg, she wrapped the bungee cord around the makeshift struts. But the bungee cord wasn't thick enough or long enough to securely hold the wood in place. This required ties.

Argia helped her tug the sheet off the bed and they tore it into long strips, each of them holding their breath as long as they could while they handled the grimy fabric. Argia's face, arms and hands were smudged with dirt and her hospital scrubs as dirty as the ball uniform she'd first seen Blake wearing. Thinking of him, she smiled.

Cautious of the jagged edges that protruded from the ends of the broken rake handle and with Argia's pointer finger assisting with the knots, Noreen tied the four pieces of wood into place. It didn't hold tight enough against her leg to brace it. The gaps needed filled.

She ran her palm around the sides of the mattress, praying bed bugs didn't feed on her fingers. It was unlikely any living thing could survive in this room but she held her breath and finger-walked the circumference of the pad. No zipper. She dropped her hands to her shirt, knowing even as she touched the fabric that it wasn't thick enough to provide a pad between her leg and the sticks.

Seeing that Argia watched, she explained. "I need to pad the space between the sticks and my leg otherwise, it won't hold. Something bulky."

As if understanding her plight, Argia dropped her coveted blanket into her lap. Noreen fingered the cotton. "Gia, will you let me use this?"

She hadn't seen that toothy grin in a while and when Argia flashed it, Noreen leaned over and kissed her forehead. "This will be perfect. You're an angel. Will you help me wrap my leg with it?"

Argia crawled to her ankle and worked to loosen the bedsheet ties already in place. Once they had all the strips untied, Noreen eased the blanket beneath her leg, biting her lip against the fire that took her breath away each time she moved the broken bone. Pulled tight, Argia's blanket wrapped around her leg twice.

"Let's tie it in place first." As thin as it was, the tight fabric encompassing her bones offered some comfort. Or maybe she willed herself to think that.

She tore more strips from the sheet and repositioned the wooden canes, laying the rake handle, which was thicker and heavier, on the front and back of her calf. The yardstick pieces butted against each side of her leg and Argia carefully held each one in place while she wrapped and tied the bedsheet strips. With the blanket beneath as padding, the sticks fit close to her leg.

As long as the wood held out, it was a suitable brace. But sitting on the floor with her legs outstretched still left her at a disadvantage. And the cot was positioned on the wall opposite the door, leaving too much distance between her and the entrance.

Time to test the brace. With both hands on the cot behind her, she lifted herself off the floor, thankful for the hateful triceps exercises she regularly performed at the gym. She might never complain about triceps dips again. Argia jumped up to perch beside her. Noreen rubbed small circles on the girl's back and asked for the push broom. Using it as a crutch, she hoisted herself into a standing position, her right leg bearing all of her weight. So far so good.

If she relocated the cot to the wall at a ninety-degree angle to the door, she'd have the advantage on someone entering who wouldn't expect the bed or an occupant to be so close.

"Gia. Can you show me how strong you are? Will you help me drag the bed over there, to that wall? We'll be closer to the door that way."

The lightweight folding bed shifted easily and in minutes, they aligned it against the cinder block. She jumped around on one leg and dropped to the cushion, hearing a wooden support slat crack beneath her weight. Argia scrambled up beside her and crawled into the crook of her arm.

The flashlight beam appeared duller and she switched it off, plunging them into midnight again. Argia inched closer and she tightened her arm around the child.

"Wait until I tell your daddy what a helper you've been."

Argia's voice quivered. "When's Daddy coming? I want to go to his home."

"I don't know when, honey, but I'm sure he's coming. I bet he's looking for you right now. You're going to have to be brave until he finds you. Do you understand?"

Her forefinger poked Noreen in the chest. "You, too. Daddy will find you, too."

Noreen's heart skipped. "He'll find us both, sweetheart. Don't worry."

Her head bobbed. "Daddy likes you, Noween."

Of all things, in this dark, gloomy, dank room, she laughed out loud and immediately felt lighthearted. Dear Lord how she wanted this child to be right.

"I like him, too."

Minutes crawled by that felt like hours. She wasn't sure if Argia was asleep until she moved against her.

"Noween, I'm hungwy." What Blake wouldn't give to hear his daughter ask for something to eat.

"I'm a little hungry too. I hope your daddy shows up with food. Let's try to guess what he might bring." If she could keep

Argia occupied with other scenarios, maybe her own growling stomach wouldn't be so intense. But Argia shook her head and fell silent again.

"Here, honey, drink a sip of water. That might help." She twisted the cap off the bottle, shaking her head over the tight seal. How had Lynne expected Argia to open this? She barely managed. She tilted the bottle as Argia lifted it to her mouth with two hands.

After Argia had a healthy drink, she took a teaspoon of water in her mouth and swished it around like mouthwash before swallowing. Argia should have every drop possible.

Nothing to do but wait. But for how long?

"Hey, Lewey, Lynne told the police that Argia was abducted from the school," Joe said, jumping right to the subject as soon as Blake answered his phone.

Blake shook his head. "Where the hell she'd get that notion?"

"I don't know but that was the call that went to the station. Two patrolmen met her at the school and questioned her and the staff. Your ex was dressed to the nines for that performance and really put on a show. I'm told it almost came to blows with one particular teacher who Lynne accused of conspiring with you to kidnap Gia."

He ran his hands through his hair. Poor Laurie. "Jesus Christ, maybe I'd better get over there."

"No, you're better off staying at the fire station, Lewey. Lynne agreed to take the cops to the house so they could see Gia's room. She's cooperating fully and your temper would give her an edge. I've got this."

Waiting around for something to happen was unacceptable. He

was a proactive man, not someone who reacted to a situation. Even when summoned on an emergency call, he raced to the scene formulating a plan of action. He refused to remain on the sidelines where his own daughter was concerned.

He stood at the white board in the firehouse training room, overwhelmed by the show of support by his coworkers. Men from every shift spilled into the firehouse the minute word spread that Gia was unaccounted for. Blake refused to use the word missing, especially since he suspected Lynne played a part in this mystery. Directly or indirectly.

A handful of firefighters from neighboring communities also arrived ready to assemble an unofficial search party. Officially, the police were in charge of the matter. An Amber alert had been issued so the authorities as well as the ordinary Joe citizen knew his precious girl was lost. The FBI had been contacted.

The police interviewed him and his mother. They asked to see Gia's room at his house, just as they'd done with Lynne. They assured him they were doing everything possible. He wasn't satisfied that was enough and so he enlisted the squad's help. Legal restrictions tied the police department's hands. Blake had no limits.

Every member of his unit lined the walls, their faces etched with concern. All except Joe who was staked out at Lynne's house. Watching. Waiting. Joe had the patience to sit and bide time until Lynne tipped her hand. Blake was convinced she would. Neither he nor Joe believed her claim that she had no idea what happened to their daughter.

His first and only conversation with her ended when he hung up on her after she whined about how distressed she was. She might never recover from this trauma.

The local news station interviewed her for the six o'clock news and Lynne played the role of distraught mother to the hilt. He couldn't help but notice her hair was styled perfectly, she'd applied makeup and wore her diamond jewelry. Hardly the picture of worry.

He, on the other hand, hadn't shaved, wore yesterday's clothes, and had breath that rivaled a cow pasture.

He'd contacted Gia's school and learned Laurie organized a group of teachers who were calling parents and questioning classmates. She waved off his attempted apology for Lynne's accusations.

He focused on his impromptu cavalry and handed out street lists so the men could canvass the area near the school as well as the houses in Lynne's neighborhood. Even though he'd already contacted all of them, iridescent yellow marker highlighted the names of neighbors and nearby friends where Gia might have walked.

But she wasn't a child who wandered away on her own. She'd promised Blake she'd never scare him again after that time she wanted to hide in the house to surprise Grammy. When his mother arrived and played along trying to find her granddaughter and Gia wasn't in the usual hiding spots waiting to jump out and holler surprise in a fit of giggles, a cold terror literally paralyzed him. She had to be in the house but she didn't come out from hiding when he called and the irrational dread that something evil happened—something he couldn't identify or explain—gripped him and twisted his gut.

Gia had recognized the fear in his voice when he demanded she come out of hiding immediately and came running down the hall from a back room. His relief was so great he dropped to his knees and crushed her to his chest. She studied his tear-rimmed eyes while he asked her to never, ever do that again. He'd laid his hand on his chest and explained she deeply frightened him and it hurt his heart. Her round chocolate eyes filled with tears that spilled over and her bottom lip protruded in sadness. She'd flung her arms around his neck and choked out her apology between sobs.

No. Gia would never simply wander off and hurt him like that again.

Yet, his daughter had disappeared without a trace.

His men grilled him about possibilities, manufacturing situations much like they did when they designed a new training program and exhausted every 'what if' question. He was out of ideas.

Shaemus wasn't. "What about the hospitals? We should check them. Between all of us, we all know someone who can give us information on the q.t. Maybe she was admitted as a Jane Doe, found wandering along the road somewhere. She hasn't been talking so they wouldn't know her name. Or maybe your ex manifested another emergency but signed her in under an assumed name. Those are both viable theories."

Rob chimed in. "Blake, what about Noreen Jensen? Have you spoken to her? She'd have access to admissions at Children's Hospital and the five-hospital network."

Blake collapsed into a chair and caught his head in his hands. He'd almost forgotten about Noreen. "No, I don't know where Noreen is. I called her several times but never reached her. We planned to hook up yesterday but I didn't hear from her and with everything else that unfolded, I gave up trying."

Rob's eyebrows rose. "Isn't it odd that she wouldn't return your calls? Try her again now. I'll check the hospital." Without waiting, Rob dialed his cellphone and moved to the doorway to inquire about Nurse Jensen. Blake dropped his head back to stretch his neck and closed his eyes listening to Noreen's voicemail message. "I'm trying to reach you. Call me. It's an emergency."

He disconnected as Rob returned, shaking his head. "The hospital hasn't heard from her. She didn't report to work last night and she's not answering her phone."

Shaemus stood. "Do you know her address? I'll go there, now."

Blake blinked twice at their reaction. "You don't think Noreen has something to do with this? I've watched her with Gia. She has nothing but affection for her."

Rob sat beside him. "You can't rule out the possibility that she's involved. She had an intense interest in Argia. Even you were suspicious. We told you about her alliance with your ex-wife at the hospital. Maybe Lynne isn't lying when she tells you she doesn't know where Argia is. But maybe Noreen Jensen does."

It was inconceivable. He'd made love to the woman, shared a connection beyond the physical act. Gazed into her eyes and felt a grip similar to the link that chained Gia to his soul. He knew this woman, despite barely knowing her. She wouldn't harm Gia or destroy him.

"Blake?"

Rob brought him back to reality. He was right. Every option had to be eliminated. Shaemus waited at the door. He recited Noreen's address. "It's an apartment building. Maybe the super will let you in if there's no answer."

"Don't worry," Shaemus shrugged, "I'll get in."

Minutes later, Blake's phone rang. Joe reported that Lynne was leaving her house. "Follow her. I'm coming over to have another look around."

With Rob silently riding shotgun, Blake sped to his former family home. Approaching it from the street he was struck by its ghastly appearance, as if suddenly it was haunted. He hadn't been on hand to perform routine maintenance and the yard was overgrown, the windows in need of a good cleaning, paint peeled from the porch columns, and a shutter on the upstairs window hung haphazardly from a bottom nail. This place no longer felt like home.

Retrieving Lynne's hidden key, he opened the front door.

"What are we looking for?"

"Anything that might hint that Lynne is part of some horrific scheme to kidnap Gia. I was here the other day, before Gia went missing, but I didn't see anything out of the ordinary."

He opened the refrigerator and studied the level of milk product. Was it half full the last time he eyeballed it? He frowned, recalling its nasty taste. Everything was untouched in Gia's room. Her backpack still in its place. He ran into the master bedroom and yanked open the lower cosmetics drawer. The box of charcoal granules slid to the front.

"Dammit." He slammed the drawer closed. This was a dead end.

Rob waited by the front door. "What about the basement?"

He ran his hand through his hair in frustration. "There's nothing left down there. We emptied it when I moved out, remember?" He strode to the slim door leading to the cellar and flipped the shiny silver lock. "I'm guessing The Captain installed this to make sure Gia didn't wander down there. Probably too lazy to keep an eye on her all the time. God forbid the kid would interrupt her mother's beauty sleep."

"Any windows down there?"

"Just one. There's a semi-circle window well that allows for an emergency exit. It's why we were able to include the basement as living space in the square footage, because it counts as an egress. It's about four feet long and extends about three feet from the house. It'll be cramped but you can drop down into the window well and see inside. The window is below the ground on the outside but about a foot below ceiling level inside. I never covered the window on the inside with a curtain or anything."

Rob ran out the door.

He wandered back into Gia's room and glided his hand along her yellow daisy bedspread. Drawing it away from her pillow, he flattened his hand where her head would settle and closed his eyes, willing himself to reach her on their special level. Slow, deep breaths as if easing into a meditative state.

"Gia, honey," his mind messaged, "where are you, peanut?"

# 26

Argia bolted upright, startling Noreen awake. "Daddy!"

Her back and neck ached. Her leg throbbed. Her sinuses were overloaded with dust and her head clogged. The flashlight lay beside her thigh and she switched it on, sending a weak beam of light along the floor and creating soft shadows in the room.

"What is it, honey?"

Argia eased off the rollaway bed and stared at the door. She repeated her exclamation. "Daddy."

How long had they slept? She shined the light on the face of her watch. They'd been here since yesterday, which meant she'd missed a shift at work. By now, someone was looking for her, too.

She opened the second bottle of water and took only a mouthful as she'd done every time she offered Argia a drink. Funny how the longer her body was deprived of food and water, the less she craved it. Last night she forced herself to empty her bladder in the bucket and Argia had used it five times. The room reeked of stale urine.

"Sip some water, Argia." She held out the bottle to the child's back but Argia remained fixated on the door. When she didn't move, Noreen angled her ear toward it. Did Argia hear something she didn't?

"Gia? What're you doing?"

She waited but Argia didn't move a muscle and remained silent, her eyes riveted on the wooden barricade. "We have to save the battery, honey." Noreen switched off the flashlight and stared at the child's form. That was another marvel of the human body. Her eyes had adjusted to the darkness, like a bat, although she read once that a bat's ability to fly in a cave was based on its hearing, not its eyesight. Maybe she imagined she focused on Argia's shoulders. She certainly didn't hear anything. But Argia must. She stood as still as a statue.

Finally, the threadbare mattress sagged and Argia crawled back on it and tucked in beside her. Noreen nudged the water bottle into her hands and lifted it while Argia drank. Then she capped it and propped it against the wall beside her where only one full bottle remained. Did Lynne plan to let them die of starvation or thirst down here?

Noreen whispered in the darkness. "Did you hear something, honey?"

Argia nodded. "I was talking to Daddy."

Was the child sick from all this sour air and hallucinating? She pressed her hand against Argia's forehead. No fever. "I wish I could talk to your daddy, too. You pretended that's what you were doing, right honey?"

Settled in beside Noreen again with Mr. Fox and Mr. Dog cradled in her arms, Argia shook her head. She patted Noreen's thigh. "Don't worry, Noween, Daddy's coming. I'm hungwy."

"I am, too. Do you want more water?"

Argia silently declined. Besides food, they needed to keep hope. If Argia believed she communicated with her father and had faith that he would rescue her, she wasn't going to dispel that. She had to believe too. Blake would crawl to the ends of the earth to locate his daughter. She closed her eyes to summon up the memory of the passion she and Blake shared. She released her breath slowly, knowing he wouldn't stop until he found her too.

Just as Blake returned the house key to Lynne's welcome rock hiding place, Joe called to say she was on her way back. Blake waited for a face-to-face confrontation. He and Rob leaned against the back of his truck, their arms crossed over their chests, each man lost in his own thoughts.

A smile exploded across Lynne's face when she turned the SUV into the driveway and parked beside his truck. While she checked her hair and makeup in the rearview mirror, Joe cruised by and turned at the end of the street.

He expected a tirade but The Captain addressed him with measured words when she exited the front seat. "I wasn't expecting company. What're you doing here?"

Company? Their five-year-old was missing and she regarded him as company? He gripped her by the shoulders. "Look me in the eye and tell me you don't know where Gia is."

Beside him, Rob stepped forward and seized his arm. "Easy, Lieutenant."

Lynne frowned and shrugged off Blake's hands. "You're hurting me, you brute." She turned to Rob. "You saw it. I'll probably have contusions on both my arms in a couple of hours. It's not the first time he's physically abused me, you know."

Rob rolled his eyes. His phone rang and he stepped away to take the call. Judging by the look on his face, he welcomed the distraction.

Blake blocked The Captain's attempt to step around him and walk toward the front door. "Lynne, I'm asking you again. Where's Gia?"

"If you don't know, I don't know. The police are handling it. They've assured me they have all of their officers on alert looking for her. It would seem to me that instead of waiting in my driveway to harass me, you'd be doing the same thing. After all, you're the one who wants full custody."

He lost control. "Is that what this is about? You little bitch, what have you done with her? I swear to God, Lynne, if one hair on her head is harmed I'll kill you." He moved so close to her, his breath bounced off her face back into his and he smelled the cinnamon mint in his mouth. He squeezed her shoulders and propelled her against the side of his truck. "As sure as I'm standing here, I'll wipe the street with your dead body."

Lynne screamed and Rob bolted over, jumped between them, and shoved against his chest, pushing him backward. "Blake, calm down. Threatening her will backfire on you, you know that."

Her second shriek sounded louder and brought a neighbor to his front door. He stuck out his head and stared at the three of them. Lynne screamed that she feared for her life and ran to her front door while Rob shoved him farther down the driveway. The old man disappeared inside his house.

"C'mon, man, walk it off. You getting arrested isn't going to help Argia. You know, she's probably inside calling the police. That neighbor might be calling as well. Get control of yourself."

Blake pressed the palms of his hands against his forehead, then raised them in the air, palms out. "I'm fine, Rob. I'm fine. Sorry. You're right. I'm good."

He paced the sidewalk, willing himself to cool off and waved Joe onward when his truck crawled past again and Joe motioned from inside to park or keep moving. Rob was right. Losing his temper with The Captain could have dire consequences. But Christ, she knew how to push his buttons.

"That was Shaemus on the phone. He spoke to the building superintendent and he let them into Noreen's apartment after admitting he's been wondering about her. He noticed her parking spot was vacant longer than is normal and a package below her mailbox went uncollected. Guess the guy keeps an eye on her. He said it's unusual for Noreen not to let him know if she's going out of town. It seems her neighbors haven't seen her either, although she must keep to herself. Shaemus said some of them didn't know who she was but as near as he can figure, it's been about forty-eight hours since anyone has seen her at the hospital or at home. No sign of her car at either location."

Blake's head snapped up. "Are you saying Noreen is missing too?"

Rob shrugged. "Is she missing or is she hiding Argia? I know you like the woman but it's a question that has to be asked. If this whole mess involves Noreen, what's her role? Do you trust her, Blake?"

He scratched his upper right arm, which had become a target for his anxiety and now appeared as an angry, red, oversized mosquito bite. Did he trust her? He had faith in so few people beyond the men in his squad. His mother. His sister. Without a doubt, he trusted them. Did he trust Noreen?

The sensation of her fingertips gliding over his bare chest resurrected itself in goose bumps along his arms. His pulse quickened with the memory of her taste, her scent, and the lazy, satisfied way her eyelids drooped after they made love. The way they entwined their legs and arms and lay together, only needing skin on skin and their mingled breathing to communicate. Speaking in whispers or not talking at all.

Yes. Noreen Jensen was a woman he could trust.

He walked back to Rob. "She's not in on it. If she's missing, it's connected to Gia but she's a victim too. Somehow, she's a part of it, I can feel it. But she's not aiding and abetting Lynne. We have to let the police know."

As if on cue, The Captain emerged from the house. She'd changed her clothes from the yoga pants she exercised in to tight blue jeans and a snug V-neck tee. She leaned over the porch railing presenting a generous view of her breasts.

"I just spoke to the police, Blake, and they advised me to ask you to cease being a nuisance and leave the premises. If you don't go quietly, I'm to call them back. And I promise you, I'll have you arrested. Your girlfriend isn't here to lie for you again and provide an alibi." He wanted to slap the smug look off her face and took two steps toward her but Rob blocked his path.

Rob waved at Lynne. "We're leaving now, Lynne."

She drew in her arms alongside her breasts, generating an uplift.

"By the way, I asked them if we should offer a reward for Argia. I think it's a good idea. People always respond to money and I'm sure I could persuade that news crew to come back. They understood my pain."

The curse he wanted to scream died on his lips and Rob urged him toward his truck. When he reached for the door handle, his hand froze in mid-air and his eyes jumped to the façade of the house. It looked as dilapidated as when he arrived but something caught his attention. Movement in a window? He focused on each opening. Nothing.

Lynne stared at him. "What are you waiting for? Get out."

His heart exerted pressure against his chest, it pounded so hard. He squeezed his eyes tight. Gia.

"I'm calling the police." Lynne raised her cell to her ear and Rob shoved him between the shoulder blades. "C'mon, Blake. Don't give her this advantage."

The sensation disappeared. As if on automatic pilot, he threw the truck into reverse and backed into the street, his eyes never leaving the structure in front of him. Gia was inside. He felt it.

# 27

When they drove by, they waved at Joe parked around the corner from Lynne's house. The men had already drafted a surveillance schedule so that Lynne was never left unmonitored. Blake smiled. His brothers.

Joe somehow learned that the police walked through Lynne's house assessing Gia's bedroom and the overall living quarters. It wasn't a search, more of an assessment. He'd agreed to a similar evaluation and his mother was posted at his front door waiting for them. That lock on Lynne's basement door still puzzled him but if the police looked downstairs, they didn't find anything that raised their suspicions. For now, he and Lynne weren't suspects, as is the first assumption when a child disappears. He didn't agree Lynne was innocent. Noreen's disappearance added to the confusion.

He called the investigator assigned to Gia's case while he and Rob drove back to the firehouse. The officer didn't recognize Noreen's name and his department had no report on her missing car or her. Blake didn't have sufficient information to file an official report, especially since he didn't know what he knew. He advised the cop he'd be back in touch.

The lack of a report of record didn't matter. His men at the station had enough backdoor connections to run their own inquiry. Joe was the best example of that.

As if in answer to his wish, Shaemus called.

He declined to elaborate on how he obtained the details he shared beyond saying he had a friend who hacked the phone company, but a ping on Noreen's cell phone pinpointed her location to a struggling shopping mall in a blighted neighborhood north of Sewickley. Crosstown traffic was with them and he and Rob arrived at the plaza in under an hour. They discovered Noreen's locked car parked behind a dumpster in the rear of the smattering of stores that remained open in this failing shopping center.

Blake picked his arm while they waited for the local police. "She'd never shop here to begin with. And no ordinary customer would park back here."

Rob agreed. "That doesn't rule out the possibility that she is part of the conspiracy." He raised both hands in surrender when Blake glared at him. "Listen, Blake, when it comes to Argia, you think with your heart first. As for Noreen, I think it's your dick doing the reacting so allow me to be the devil's advocate and think out loud. I know Noreen Jensen too and she's a top-notch professional dedicated to caring for kids, not hurting one. I agree with you that this doesn't feel like it's part of a master plan to abduct Argia but let's leave the door open to the possibility and wait for proof otherwise."

They discovered that proof after the police arrived, pried open Noreen's driver's door, and unlocked the trunk. Her cell phone and purse lay inside. Noreen Jensen became an official missing person and possible kidnap victim thirty-two hours after his daughter went missing.

The face of her phone offered no clues. They could scroll on the screen and see nine missed calls and messages from Blake and two calls that displayed the word Sis. The phone required a passcode to unlock, which the police said would take time to override. Shaemus' friend might have better luck but Blake kept that to himself.

He couldn't draw a clear correlation between Noreen's disappearance and his daughter's unknown whereabouts nor could he convince the police that The Captain was a common denominator in both equations. Meeting Noreen for lunch days earlier didn't implicate Lynne in Noreen's absence, the cop pointed out. Maybe it was the desperate look on Blake's face or his conviction that the two were related that convinced the small-town detective to reach out to city police and suggest they compare notes in the event they'd need to coordinate their investigations on down the road.

It was better than nothing. At least now all police agencies knew about Gia and Noreen and classified them both as missing. He still wasn't satisfied. He and Rob returned to the firehouse planning their next moves.

Blake jumped on social media, searched Noreen's name, and found a social page that included pictures of Noreen with two young children. She'd talked about her niece and nephew. It appeared to be the kids' mother's page whose middle name, presumably her maiden name, was Jensen. Blake studied the woman's face and the strong resemblance to Noreen. The pictures of Noreen in a bounce house made him laugh. She looked as happy as the two kids floating beside her.

And then his heart caught. Where was she? Was Argia with her? Were they both safe?

He typed an instant message to Noreen's sister asking her to contact him about Noreen, trying to express urgency without alarming her. In less than a half hour, his phone rang. Her sister was as cautious as Noreen about sharing information and he experienced a twinge of disappointment to learn that the sister was unaware that he and Noreen knew each other outside of their jobs. "You're the fireman who was at that accident scene," was the only offered recognition.

"That's correct. I hoped you might know a little bit more about me."

"Like what?"

Good question. Like they were involved? They were lovers? They were more than that? It was too soon to think of Noreen in more permanent terms, wasn't it?

"That's not important now. I'm concerned about your sister and I'd like your help. Have you heard from her?"

The woman on the other end paused. "Is there reason for your concern?"

"I think so. I'll explain but please, tell me, have you heard from Noreen?"

"No. She usually returns my calls but...tell me what's happened."

The phone call was grueling but by the time he hung up, he had several possible combinations that might unlock Noreen's phone. Understandably upset, her sister planned to call the police herself and then she and her husband were coming to the firehouse. He assured her he'd wait for them.

Meanwhile, the police had kept Noreen's phone as evidence so he called them. The detective gladly tried the diverse number combinations Noreen's sister suggested. The third set—the date Noreen graduated nursing school—was the winner.

The detective refused to share Noreen's call history, saying it was part of an ongoing investigation, but after a little persuading and a promised bottle of single malt scotch, he agreed to confirm information if Blake already knew it. Yes, there was a record of Noreen receiving recent phone calls from the cell number Blake provided, which was Lynne's. Three calls on one day and one solo call. The trio of calls were made two days earlier, shortly before seven in the morning. About the time Noreen was clocking out and the last time anyone reported seeing her.

For the police, it wasn't proof of anything. The detective suggested they could be girlfriends making plans or Lynne could simply be asking for free medical advice. Until they obtained a transcript of the actual conversations, the police had nothing to go on. The process of securing a warrant to serve the phone provider was in the works.

Blake resisted screaming that one of the women was his crazy ex-wife and one was his current lover and how likely was it that they'd be girlfriends planning an outing? About as likely as him quitting the fire service and opening a coffee shop, despite his love for coffee. But revealing his involvement with Noreen would only muddy the waters. Better to keep that fact to his immediate family—his squad mates.

In his mind, the calls connected The Captain to Noreen's disappearance and were enough to convict Lynne. He'd gladly sit on that jury.

But even with that additional clue, he was no closer to finding Noreen or Gia.

He sipped his black coffee and grimaced at its bitter bite. For the last few days he'd lived on the stuff, and his stomach protested yet another cup. "We missed something in that house, I know it."

Rob and the other men stood in his office, each one looking as disheveled as he felt. They had barely slept themselves. "The only place we didn't search was the basement and you said yourself, we emptied it when you moved. I looked in the window. It was dark but I didn't see anything. If they were down there, they would've seen me looking in or certainly they could hear us walking above them. They would've yelled or made some type of noise."

Blake cringed when his fingers dug into the bloody sore on his arm. If he didn't find Gia soon, he'd pick through to the bone. "Maybe they're tied up and gagged." He shook his head the minute the words were out of his mouth. But talking out and offering ideas and suggestions without judgment was how the men in this family worked out all of their problems.

Rob shrugged. "That's possible."

No. Not really. "Possible but not plausible. Noreen is in better physical shape than The Captain. She regularly exercises." He didn't add that her strong thighs wrapped around his hips in a cocoon of heat validated her physical prowess. He cleared his throat while the men waited for him to continue. "Noreen is stronger than Lynne. She'd never manage to get the best of Noreen. Unless she drugged her. Or somehow knocked her out."

Rob negated that concept. "There's still the problem of luring Noreen to the house and dragging her somewhere to hide her once she's unconscious. Dead weight is hard to maneuver, we all know that. I can't picture your ex-wife moving an unresponsive body."

The corners of Blake's mouth edged up. Noreen's body was anything but unresponsive. He looked away from the group when his cheeks heated.

That's when Shaemus burst in the room waving sheets of paper crumbled in his hand. "Don't ask me how, Lieutenant, but my friend tapped into Nurse Jensen's phone. Your ex-wife called her and said Argia was sick. She asked Nurse Jensen for help. Your daughter wasn't sick enough to go to the hospital, but your ex insisted that Nurse Jensen needed to check her out. I took notes while I listened to the dialogue. Noreen sounds surprised at the phone call and that your ex didn't call an ambulance or drive Argia to the hospital. You can listen to it if you want. It'll take my friend about twenty minutes to tap you into it again but based on what I heard, Nurse Jensen is not a conspirator. And I don't suggest you waste time listening to these words. We need to get moving."

Blake catapulted to his feet. "Where? Where did she tell Noreen to go?"

"The house on Riviera Road."

# 28

Argia and Noreen heard the rustling sounds at the same time and sat upright.

An object struck the door with a loud thud. There was another thump, not a direct hit this time but audible. Now two clunks in rapid succession. The racket was muffled but someone was definitely out there.

The flashlight lay between them and Noreen switched it on. The bright beam was now dull yellow, like a white T-shirt never laundered with bleach.

Noreen reached for the push broom and slid to the edge of the cot. Argia mimicked her movements, her beloved stuffed animals plastered to her chest. Using the broom as a crutch, Noreen cautiously lowered her left foot to the dirt floor and pressed. A bolt of pain shot up her leg but the wooden pieces serving as a leg brace held firm.

A dim ray of light spilled beneath the door. She studied the glow but didn't spy any movement beneath. Still, she whispered to Argia.

"Honey, if that door opens, I want you to run. It doesn't matter who comes inside. I want you to run as fast as you can to the stairs and get out of this house. Do you understand me? Go get help. Find your daddy."

In the shadows, Argia looked at her. "What if it's Daddy?"

She smoothed the child's hair down her back. The tangled silky locks cried out for a hairbrush.

"If it's your dad, he'll see you and catch you. If it isn't, you have to run as fast as you can. Don't look to see who it is and don't stop until you're outside. Then scream, honey, scream as loud as you can and run to a neighbor's. I know you can do that."

Her small hand touched Noreen's chest. "What about you, Noween? Are you coming too?"

"I can't run, honey. My leg hurts too much. That's why I need you to find your daddy and bring him here to help me. Can you do that for me?"

Saucer-eyed, Argia's head bobbed slowly.

"Good girl."

"What if it's Mother?"

Despite their circumstances, Noreen grinned. The child had a way of cutting to the chase.

"If it's your mother, I'm going to hurt her, Argia. I know that's not nice but what she's done to us isn't nice either. If your mother comes through that door you'll need to run even faster. You don't want her to catch you, no matter what she tells you to do. Don't worry about me. I'll be fine. You find your daddy and bring him back here."

There was a lot riding on this plan. What if Argia couldn't run past whoever entered this dungeon or worse, what if she managed to get by only to find the door locked at the top of the stairs? What if there wasn't enough light out there? How would Argia see which direction to go? Was she brave enough to run through the dark?

What if she didn't run fast enough or managed to make it to the first floor but couldn't leave the house. Blake had explained that he kid-proofed the house once Argia began walking. Surely that included a front door that prevented a young child from escaping.

She couldn't let the uncertainties defeat her. She smiled at Argia's protruding bottom lip.

"Your daddy's out there, honey. Do your best to find him."

The lower lip trembled but Argia nodded her head. Scuffling sounds seeped beneath the wooden portal, as if someone moved furniture, followed by a loud snap. Noreen canted her head to hear better and discern the activity, but she couldn't guess what was happening or who was beyond the door. If it was Blake, did he know about this underground room? Should she take a chance and scream his name?

She eased up into a standing position using the push broom for support and hobbled closer to the entry. She'd fallen into the room and remembered that the door swung inside and to the right. With the cot repositioned the way it was, it impeded the door from opening fully and likely would surprise Lynne if that's who barged in. Noreen tottered on her good leg to the other side so that she'd have a full swing at whoever stepped over the threshold. She was right-handed and this position required a left-handed swing. It wouldn't be her strongest but it would have to be her best.

Her nostrils tingled and she scrunched her nose and sniffed. Smoke? Or more dust? A pungent odor, faint but nonetheless irritating, filtered into the room from the crack between the uneven floor and the bottom of the door. It reminded Noreen of autumn when patio torches fend off the chilly night air. Lamp oil? Was that the smell? Was there a fire beyond this door?

Dear Lord, it wasn't Blake or someone who would rescue them outside the door. It was that monster.

"Get ready, Gia. I'm going to scream and if the door opens, you run. Take the flashlight so you can see. Whatever you do, don't drop it. Don't let it go. Keep it with Mr. Fox and Mr. Dog. Do you understand."

Unquestioningly, Argia nodded and clutched the flashlight with both hands, its dull light shining a straight ray to the ceiling.

Noreen raised the push broom to shoulder level, mimicking her favorite Pittsburgh Pirates batter and his stance at home plate. Well, not quite as professional but she was prepared to swing.

"Help! Help us please! We're locked in here." She screamed as loud as she could. Beside her, Argia jumped up and down. "Daddy! Daddy! It's me! Find me!"

"Help! Help us!"

The latch clicked and the door flew open, banging against the metal rail of the rollaway bed with a loud clang when Lynne stepped inside. The door ricocheted into Lynne's side, startling her.

"What the fuck—"

Noreen swung the filthy bristles of the push broom into Lynne's face and screamed. "Run Argia! Now!"

The effort of her swing and the weight of the movement splintered the rotted sticks tied against her leg and she dropped to the floor like an imploded building. Excruciating pain raged up her leg, crawled into her chest, spread across her shoulders, and grabbed her neck, shoving her to the brink of blackout. She fought to stay conscious, struggling for deep, heavy breaths. The dust choked her.

Lynne shrieked when the broom smashed into her face. In a blurred haze, Noreen watched her crash backward against the doorframe, blood trickling from her mouth and nose, her spine smashing into the wood so forcefully, all the air expelled from her lungs in a loud whoosh. Lynne's eyes bulged to black holes identical to an oversized bug's and her knees buckled. She collapsed to the dirt base, sliding down the doorjamb like a deflated balloon.

Lynne's head swiveled to her right and she reached sideways as a flash bolted past her outstretched hand, those red fingernails at the end of her claw grabbing for its target. She still had the broom in her hand and she threw it like a javelin at Lynne's chest, hitting her target dead center. Lynne yowled and clutched her chest, empty-handed and cursing like a sailor. Beyond her, Noreen noted with satisfaction the yellow blur that scampered away. Argia was out of this prison. That was all that mattered.

"You conniving bitch." It was more hiss than spoken sentence.

Noreen leveled her attention on the grotesque being in front of her. Now it was just the two of them, both of them down on their butts and both injured. Even odds in her mind.

The pounding in her head and buzzing in her ears threatened to drag her into darkness. The room spun, her lungs seized, and her leg burned like a three-alarm fire. She dug her fingers into the compacted dirt and readied a fist full for Lynne's first move.

Blood covered Lynne's face and outlined her teeth when she turned a maniacal grin on her. She rolled over on all fours but instead of advancing on Noreen, she reached her hand beyond the doorway. She began a slow crawl away from the hellhole prison. Once beyond the door, she clung to the frame and drew herself up to a standing position. "That kid can't talk and even if she did, they'll never believe the rantings of a five-year-old, especially when I explain that she's mixed up. It was you who locked her down here and threatened me. It was you who harmed Blake's daughter, the only person in the world he cares about."

She stood at full height but required the doorjamb to steady herself. Blood dribbled from her nose and dripped off her chin, staining her shirt. The corners of Noreen's mouth lifted in a smirk at the sight of Lynne's perfectly applied makeup smeared across her face like a ludicrous Halloween mask. Cast in shadows, her face looked distorted. Or maybe she finally viewed the real person beneath the polished veneer. Whatever the cause, there was no trace of the woman she once felt inferior to.

"Don't feel bad, Noreen. No matter how good you fucked him,

he'd never love you more than that little brat. Believe me, I know. That's why you tried to get rid of her."

She threw her head back and laughed. To Noreen's ears, it was the howl of a banshee. "I have the story all worked out and you'll never get out of here to dispute it. I doubt they'll even find your remains in the ashes."

The monster pivoted and stumbled away toward the steps, hunched over, falling to her knees twice but regaining her footing. Once her form no longer blocked the doorway, Noreen saw the source of the glow that initially spread under the door of their prison. A lighted oil lamp sat on the floor giving off a soft glow. Blake likely kept it around in the event of a power outage.

She scanned the empty, wood-paneled room. No furniture but deep carpet indents where items once sat. In the corner near the stairs, the stub of a votive candle burned, its flame flickering in the draft from the door ajar overhead. No sign of Argia. She must have gotten away. Thank God.

In her peripheral vision, Lynne advanced toward the stairs but she focused on the candle, squinting to clear her vision. From this far away and in semi-darkness, it appeared nested in the middle of a pile of rags and a drop cloth. Paint smears and blotches matching the colors from the walls she'd seen upstairs covered the canvas. Aerosol cans outlined the mound of cloth, encircling it like a decorative border. Other cans lay scattered around the room. More cans than Noreen could count. That must have been the banging sound when Lynne tossed them around the room. Top of the line hairspray cans and designer mousse and styling containers. Spray deodorant cans. Oven cleaner and ant and roach canisters. Products she didn't recognize. Travel containers and cans in all sizes. They fanned out from the cloth and spread around the room. Open magazines and newspaper pages also littered the floor as if tossed in the air like confetti.

Blood or sweat or both rolled off her forehead and trickled into her eyes, burning, and distorting her vision. She swiped her forearm across her face and saw Lynne pause at the bottom of the stairs and glance back at her.

"Imagine how sorry everyone will feel for me when I tell them how my ex-husband's lover kidnapped my only child. And that you held her hostage and I had to fight almost to the death to save her. I'm an incredible mother, don't you think?

"And wait until Blake learns how I defeated your diabolical plan. He'll realize how much we belong together and we'll be reunited. He should've never left me to begin with. The tabloids will love this story. I'll be on all the covers."

Noreen shook her head to clear her fogged brain. The woman was insane. Blake wouldn't believe any of this. She opened her mouth to challenge Lynne and decided against it. If Lynne was leaving her alone down here, she'd need her strength to escape. Plus right now, she wasn't locked inside this black hole. In her desire to escape, Lynne left the door open and the broomstick kept it from closing. She couldn't risk irritating the woman and have her come back and slam the barrier shut.

Lynne climbed the steps shakily, using the handrail to haul herself up each riser. Noreen's eyes darted between her unnervingly slow progress upward and the bright orange flickering flame. From this angle, the fire might touch the rags any second.

Finally, at the top of the stairs, Lynne called out Argia's name and disappeared. At least she hadn't slammed the upstairs door behind her but Noreen knew enough about fires to know they needed oxygen to spread. Lynne had learned well being married to a fireman.

An eerie quiet fell over the room, except for the hiss of the oil lamp. She rose up on her elbows and, much the same as when she crawled into this dungeon, she began a slow belly crawl out. On the second agonizing slide, her elbow squished a soft cushion. Mr. Fox stared up at her, his head at a distorted angle from his body. Argia must have dropped him when she escaped.

She reached for the stuffed animal. "C'mon buddy, we're

getting out of this together." She tucked the animal down the front of her shirt, locking its legs beneath the elastic of her bra.

It had been years since she cried but now, for the second time in as many days, tears streamed down her face with each agonizing drag of her leg against the carpet. The pile resisted her every effort to inch forward. A small waft of smoke began to plume from the corner where the candle burned. The threads must be starting to singe. How long before it caught fire? Burning to death might be less painful than this room filling with smoke and slowly suffocating her.

Each time she came within reach of an aerosol can, she hurled it to the far wall. Her goal now was to reach the steps. They loomed before her like Alaska's Mount St. Elias, one of North American's highest mountain ranges. Seeing it as well as the state's famous glaciers was on her bucket list.

A deep breath. Another strenuous tug toward freedom. She ran her hand beneath her snotty nose. Deep breath. Drag with every ounce of energy she possessed. Think about Alaska. Tow her lifeless leg another inch. Strong breath. Think about Argia. Haul one more time. Inhale, even though it hurt her chest. Think about Blake.

Ignore the loud pop when the top of an aerosol can shot across the room like a bullet. Never mind the increasing spiral of smoke rising from the drop cloth and rolling like a low fog toward her. Disregard a second explosion that scared the hell out of her and ignited the drop cloth into a ball of flames. Fight the sublime escape that unconsciousness offered. She'd saved Argia, that's all that mattered. She was going to die here. Don't think about it.

# 29

They raced toward Blake's Riviera Road home in the ambulance with the fire truck following behind and a convoy of private vehicles to the rear of that. Every man at the station except Shaemus, who stayed as the on-duty man, sped toward the house. Sirens blared and lights flashed to clear the path but Blake pressed his hands against the dashboard as if he could propel the vehicle faster.

"What did we miss? We searched the house. She's not smart enough to outsmart me."

Rob shook his head, equally as stumped. They weren't questions he could answer.

"Is there an attic?"

Blake picked at the wound on his right arm. "No, just a crawl space above the garage and access to it requires a ladder and the strength to raise the lid over your head. It's heavy, even for me. There's only Christmas decorations stored in those rafters because I hated going up there. Even once a year was too much. No floor surface either, just cross beams. Step off the struts and you fall through the ceiling."

"Let's reexamine what we found in Noreen's car. Think about

it, Blake. Her purse and cell phone were there. What situation would present itself that a woman would leave both behind in their trunk? My wife doesn't even go into the bathroom without her cell phone. If the last message from Lynne instructed Noreen to drive to your house, we have to assume that's what she did. She arrives but what makes her jump out of the car without taking either of those items with her?"

He stared at Rob. Talk it through. Rationalize. Reject the implausible. It's what the men of Station Twelve were trained for.

"She's concerned about Gia so she rushes inside." It was the only possible explanation because Rob was right. Noreen wouldn't have stopped to stow either of those items in her trunk. What would be the point? "But that doesn't explain how we found Noreen's car miles away from my house."

Rob agreed. "Let's stay at the house for now. Noreen rushes inside and somehow, Lynne overtakes her. Maybe an injection. Maybe a smack to the back of the head with your Louisville Slugger. Presumably, Argia is already there and now she has Noreen there. Now where does she take them?"

He'd never grasped the way The Captain's mind worked. They were true Venus-Mars opposites. What he thought mattered she trivialized and issues that he deemed important, Lynne failed to understand. "Either she takes them both somewhere, probably in Noreen's car since it disappears from the house, or she hides them. Transporting them doesn't make sense, unless she has help. Maybe there really is a boyfriend in the picture but what kind of man is he who helps abduct a woman and harm a child?" Not someone he'd ever let near his daughter.

"We can't rule out a second person but beyond driving to that shopping mall where we found Noreen's car, Lynne still has to relocate two people, presumably one or both of them unconscious, to a second destination." Rob directed his words at the windshield, thinking out loud. "That's quite a feat. And when did all this occur? You heard from the school that Argia was absent and you were at the house within hours. We can place Noreen at the hospital until seven the next morning. She's at work the day Argia is absent from school. That's a small window to meet someone, overtake them–however Lynne managed to do it–and stow them off premises. And it assumes that you don't learn that Argia is out of school until the end of the day. What guarantee is there that the school doesn't call you at lunchtime or earlier? You sat in that driveway until three in the morning and Joe parked himself there at sunrise. The men have kept that front door and driveway under constant surveillance. Out the back door isn't an option unless she cuts through the backyards on foot. Still, her only egress is a main street. We would have seen her alone or dragging someone.

"Also, if it's a well-planned take down, it's based on the gamble that you don't learn until late in the day that Argia missed school. Could the teacher be in on it?"

"No. No way. Laurie would never hurt Argia. I'd bet my life on that."

Rob agreed, excited by his deductions. "That leaves us back at the house. Lynne has to hide them there. Where didn't we search? The chimney. Hard to believe two people would be in there but we didn't look. A space hidden by a back panel in a closet? Under something? Over something? A forbidden location?"

In response to each query, Blake shook his head.

The radio pinged and Shaemus broadcast into the cab. "Lieutenant? I'm looking at the schematics of your house online. I've been to your place, partied in your man cave and don't remember an anteroom but I'm seeing one on the county plat. Is this an error or is there some sort of hole down there? What am I looking at?"

Blake smashed his hand against his forehead. "Christ, I haven't thought about that space since we bought the house. I walled that off when we renovated the downstairs. It was nothing more than a hole in the ground with plywood for walls and a ceiling underneath the porch. The previous owner left a ratty Army cot and an ancient steel boiler there that was too heavy to haul out. There wasn't even a solid floor. Just dirt. Maybe it was supposed to be a tornado shelter back in the day. I never figured it out. But I closed the door and paneled over it."

"Okay. That's a dead-end. I'll keep checking." Shaemus signed out and, when Rob asked about the chamber, Blake retraced his steps years earlier when he transformed the cinder-block basement to a functional room. "I hung drywall around the area we cordoned off. The door was narrow and the exact distance widthwise that I was placing the studs so I just used that frame for my panel piece. No drywall sheet beneath. I doubt The Captain would remember that room was down there. She wasn't interested in my remodeling project. It'd be hard to find the exact spot from inside except, it made a hollow sound if you pounded on it. Besides, how would she remove the wood panel? She might break a fingernail."

Rob chuckled. "What if a boyfriend opened it for her? Or she hired a handyman? You questioned who installed the lock on the basement door too."

He considered both. But the consequences of such premeditation chilled him to the bone. "I suppose it's possible."

Rob concurred. "I'll check down there as soon as we arrive. You say it's under the front porch? It should be easy to disassemble with our cutters. I'll also—"

The radio crackled and Joe's frantic voice cut through Rob's sentence. "Code three! Code three! Argia sighted. Running into the front yard from the back of the house. I'm going after her."

Blake's jaw dropped. "What'd he just say?" He grabbed the microphone. "Joe. Repeat. Joe. Paramedic Lystle, respond. Come back, Joe."

Radio silence.

They were less than five minutes from Blake's house. The longest five minutes of his life.

~

He'd parked near the corner, backed into the driveway of a vacant house with a 'for sale' sign posted in the front yard. From this vantage point, Joe had a clear view of the lieutenant's home and, more importantly, the garage door and driveway. Lynne Matthews had come and gone twice on his watch, each time oblivious to his presence. Although he took the precaution of slumping down below the steering wheel the second time she passed, she never looked his way. The first time out, she turned in the other direction and failed to notice him following her.

The local cops were friendly with Blake and well aware of Argia's disappearance. It seemed to him they'd increased their patrols along Riviera Road as well, acknowledging him with a nod or a two-finger wave each time they passed. The boys in uniform stuck together, no matter what the patches on their shirtsleeves denoted.

He'd been in place for nearly four hours and already communicated with the man en route to take the next four-hour shift when a flash of color moving along the side of Blake's former home caught his eye. Chestnut strands flapped behind a yellow streak cutting through the eight-inch tall grass. His eyes were weary and might be playing tricks on him but he'd recognize that little face anywhere, no matter how much dirt covered it.

He grabbed the radio mic and screamed the emergency code number. He didn't wait for a response. It was enough to let Blake and the men know he had eyes on Argia. He jumped from his truck and ran toward her, yelling her name. "Argia! Gia! Here!" He pounded his opened hands against his chest. "Run here, Gia. Come to me."

She stopped so abruptly, she fell to her knees and he closed the distance between them in seconds. She looked up wide-eyed and screamed when he loomed over her and he bent and scooped her up. "Gia it's me. It's Joey. You're safe now. Jesus, where'd you come from?"

Snot covered her upper lip and she cried when she recognized him and squeezed his neck in a chokehold, banging a flashlight against the back of his head. Clutching her in his arms he spun in a circle, making sure no one chased the girl. Twice he turned a full three-hundred-and-sixty degrees and then he bolted back toward the street, trying not to jostle his precious, sobbing bundle. Muffled words vibrated against his neck. "Daddy. I want my daddy."

At the end of the driveway he stopped and pivoted to stare at the windows in the house. No sign of Lynne. No evidence that anyone watched his rescue. But Lynne was inside. He was certain of that. She couldn't have left the premises without him seeing. Did she know Argia was outside?

In his arms, Argia trembled and he gently reached under her chin to raise her eyes to his. He summoned up a goofy grin in hopes the terrified look on her face would dissipate.

"It's me, Gia. It's Joey. You know me. Me and Brittni take care of you sometimes. It's okay now. You're okay." He strode toward his truck. "Let's get you far away from here. How about we talk to your daddy on the radio."

The wail of a siren and rumble of the emergency vehicles speeding up the road stopped him in the middle of the street. The passenger door of the ambulance flew open while the truck still traveled and Blake jumped out, falling to his hands and knees on the ground. He jumped to his feet and ran toward Joe, his arms outstretched, yelling for his daughter.

Argia twisted in his embrace and held out her arms. Blake wrenched her from his hold and began smothering his daughter's face with kisses, tears wetting his own cheeks. "Oh my God, Gia. I love you so much. Oh my God, peanut, are you okay?"

He kissed her right cheek, her left cheek, her forehead, and her mouth over and over again, mumbling her name. Argia sobbed in a release of fear and relief, hugging her father, and returning his blanket of kisses. Blake crushed his daughter to his chest. "Gia, I'm never letting you out of my sight again. Never. I love you so much. You're my life."

By now, two police cars arrived as mutual assistance to the emergency vehicles and the cluster of firefighters and police surrounded father and daughter. Rob squeezed Blake's shoulder.

"Blake, ask her what happened. Ask about Noreen."

With everyone's attention on Argia, no one looked at the house until an ear-piercing scream forced them all to turn toward the driveway. Joe narrowed his eyes and studied the structure behind the woman running toward them. It looked exactly the same as when he evaluated it a few minutes earlier. The front door was still closed and the garage door remained down. None of the lower floor windows were opened. Where did Lynne come from? How did she exit? The background looked odd.

She trotted toward the group balanced on high heels and breasts bouncing beneath a low-cut shirt. Her appearance was off, as if she'd tried to repair messy makeup. He'd never seen her without dark eyes and bright red lips, every hair in place yet now, her face appeared lopsided, her hair disheveled. Even stranger than the vista behind her.

"My baby! Oh thank God, my baby." Her arms stretched toward Argia. Impulsively, he stepped in front of Blake and Argia to block Lynne's grasp if she came closer. Mother or not, this woman wasn't getting near Argia again if he could help it.

He needn't have worried. Rob hurried toward the woman, adding speed to each step and when he was in reach, hauled off and punched her in the face. Lynne Matthews fell to the ground like a limp rag doll, her face definitely lopsided now.

# 30

The second Argia heard her mother's screech, she tightened her grip around Blake's neck, knocking the flashlight against his ear, and buried her face in his shoulder. Every muscle in her body tensed and he flattened his hand against her back and pressed her tighter to him.

He watched his ex-wife coming closer and sensed the men standing around him in a semi-circle straighten their backs and brace their stances. The Captain ran straight toward him wailing without shedding real tears, her arms outstretched as if she meant to yank Argia from his arms. That would be a frigid day in hell.

Just as Joe stepped in front of him to provide a human shield, Rob rushed toward Lynne and before anyone could stop him, punched The Captain square in the face. She dropped like an anchor. If his hands weren't full of his baby girl, he would've applauded. A couple of the men chuckled.

In seconds, two uniformed officers were beside Rob, each one grabbing him by an arm to back him away from the crumbled heap in case he intended to inflict more pain on Lynne. He didn't and he stepped back voluntarily, his hands raised in the air in submission, grinning like he'd won the championship belt in a ten-round boxing match. Blood trickled from a small cut on his right knuckle.

Blake offered a silent nod of thanks and felt his own face split into a satisfied grin.

"That'll be worth any charges you file against me." Rob pointed to the cops. "Boys, if you need me to surrender, I'll be right out. I'm going in to check the house." His laughter floated back to them after he turned and jogged away. Blake noted with a degree of pleasure that neither police officer attempted to stop Rob and instead, stood shaking their heads with their hands on their hips. One of the men knelt and examined Lynne and signaled toward him and Joe that she needed assistance. Joe winked. "Relax. I'll get this one." Joe walked toward his patient with the pace of an ancient turtle.

Blake scanned the front of the house, sensing danger still lurked. He ran his hand down his daughter's tangled hair and kissed her ear. "Gia, honey, were you inside the house with mommy?"

She leaned backward, Mr. Dog and the flashlight pressed to her heart, and slowly nodded. "Here, you want me to take this now?" He touched the flashlight, curious why she held it, but she wrapped both hands around it and shook her head vigorously.

"All right, you can keep it." Fresh tears rimmed her eyes. Blake kissed her forehead. "Peanut, you have to talk to me, now. It's important. Was Nurse Noreen in there with you?"

Another nodded confirmation.

"Is Nurse Noreen still inside, honey?"

Rob's yells drew everyone's attention to the house. He ran toward them double-time, signaling with his hands. "There's smoke. And I heard popping. Something's exploding inside. I think the house is on fire or it's gonna blow any minute."

Their training kicked in and each man reached for their turnout gear, stepping into boots, protective pants, and coats, and donning their breathing apparatus. Blake looked into Gia's wide chocolate eyes.

"Gia, where is Noreen. Tell me now, honey. It's important."

She swiped at her runny nose, smearing more dirt across her face. "Down da stairs, Daddy. Her leg is hort weal bad. She hit Mother and she made me wun out of the weally dark woom. Mother closed the door and wouldn't let us out."

He placed Argia on the passenger seat of the ambulance and reached for the radio. Back-up fire trucks already were on their way. He changed the radio channel to the frequency that would allow him to communicate with the firefighters inside the house.

"Lieutenant Matthews here. Noreen Jensen is injured in the basement. Rob, she may be in that anteroom we talked about. It's underground, men, beneath the front porch."

"It's popping like the Fourth of July down there." Rob's words were matter-of-fact. He was in firefighter mode, in control and prepared.

Would Noreen have the sense to stay in that room until she was rescued? If she blocked the bottom of the door, that would keep the smoke out. But the heat would turn the confined space into a furnace. She might literally heat to death. Had she attempted an escape?

He raised Gia's chin so they stared into each other's eyes. Ten silent seconds when they communicated their unique way. But time was a matter of life or death.

"Gia, tell me what you remember. How did Noreen hit mommy? Was she in the really dark room when she did that? Or was she in the bigger room? It's important, peanut. It will help your Uncle Rob find her."

Gia squeezed her eyes shut and buried her face against Mr. Dog's head. Her words were muffled. "Mother scared me. She hollered and said bad words and slammed the door against the bed. Noween hit her with the bwoom weal hard, Daddy. And Mother scweamed. And Noween yelled at me to wun and find you. And I did." Then she started to sob. "I lost Mr. Fox. Mother hurt him weal bad and I dwopped him."

Despite the urgency of the situation, he smiled and kissed the top of his daughter's head. As important as Noreen was to him, Mr. Fox mattered equally as much to Gia. "Uncle Rob might find him, too, honey. Don't worry."

The chatter on the radio indicated flames were evident through the basement window but the firemen were reluctant to ventilate it and feed the fire. Rob commanded the rescue. Blake watched his squad enter the house, only recognizing them from their names imprinted on the backs of their flame-resistant, Kevlar fire jackets. He couldn't stand the silence.

"Rob? Get to the basement. Gia says she's down there."

The radio clicked. "Door to basement ajar. Flames confirmed. Attempting descent. I don't know how far I'll get."

Gia turned enormous round eyes on him. Did she understand what was happening?

Blake retrieved a bottle of water from the rear of the ambulance, ignoring The Captain perched on the back of it and the paramedic tending her. Her nose bled profusely and when she saw him, she moaned as if in excruciating pain. It appeared her eye had started to blacken. Or was her mascara smeared? Neither mattered. He ignored her and returned to the front of the vehicle.

"Here, Gia. Drink some water."

"Daddy, I'm hungwy."

His stomach clutched. How long had it been since his sweet girl ate? "I'll get you something to eat as soon as we know Nurse Noreen is okay. Can you hang on a little longer?"

She reached for the water bottle and agreed.

Static broadcast from the radio. Rob's voice stopped Blake's beating heart. "I've got a possible ten-fifty-four. Stand by."

Dear God, no. That was the emergency code for a dead body. An uncontrolled sob escaped his lungs and he turned away from the ambulance, jamming his hand against his mouth. It couldn't be. If Noreen was dead, she died protecting his daughter. How could he live with that knowledge, knowing he'd drawn Noreen into this mess with The Captain? Sharing his Munchausen's suspicions with her, knowing in his heart she was the kind of woman who wouldn't let it go.

Partial responsibility fell on his shoulders if she was dead. What would he tell her sister and brother-in-law? They'd arrived at the firehouse shortly before Shaemus discovered the recorded phone message on Noreen's phone and every man in that building ran to their private vehicles or the fire apparatus and sped here. Her sister and brother-in-law seemed like nice people in the brief time he'd conversed with them. The sister's mannerisms and attitude mimicked Noreen's. He left them sitting in the kitchen, cups of coffee in front of them, and fear etching their faces. Surely they were listening to all this radio traffic. It broadcast directly into the fire station.

The paramedic who treated Lynne approached him. "Lieutenant? Your wife is insisting she speak to you. She's telling quite a story."

Blake waved him off. "She's not my wife. And I have nothing to say to her." He looked toward Gia, who listened to the exchange and smiled.

By now, two additional ambulances had arrived. "We're transporting her to the hospital. She requested that you accompany her. Says she doesn't feel safe and that she's endured three days of threats against her life and your daughter's life."

Blake's jaw dropped. The Captain had managed to spin this to imply she was the victim. He studied his five-year-old daughter, hungry, dirty, scared and crying. How dare she?

He leveled his gaze on the paramedic. "I don't want anything to do with her. Transport her to hell. That's where she belongs."

## 31

"I have a weak pulse."

Rob's words were like listening to the halleluiah chorus of his favorite church hymn. Hopeful. Uplifting. Energizing.

Blake resisted the urge to snatch the microphone from the dashboard and ask for details. Rob and Joe were the best at what they did. If Noreen teetered on the brink of death, they were the ones who could coax her away from the edge.

He'd turned his back on Gia to stare at his former home. Flames were evident through the windows on the right side of the structure, the spacious great room side that opened into the kitchen. Much more area for a fire to spread on that side but the firefighters had it under control. There was little comfort in that fact. Fire travels skyward, which meant it burned from the basement up.

The back of his shirt tugged. "Daddy?"

Desperately in need of his real-life security blanket, he turned and reached for his daughter, taking her into his arms to hold her close. That was the first time it dawned on him that Gia didn't have her coveted blankey with her. She never went anywhere without it. Likely it and Mr. Fox were destroyed in the flames. Maybe that explained the importance of the flashlight.

"It's okay, Daddy."

He drew back to look into Gia's face. No tears. No trembling lower lip. No fear. Only that soulful stare she summoned up when he needed it most. "Gia?"

She nodded. "It's okay, Daddy."

Joe's voice broadcast behind them. "We're coming out. Request immediate transport to the hospital. Code red."

*Jesus. Hang on Noreen.*

"Gia, honey, stand here beside the ambulance for a minute." He lowered his daughter to the ground and strode to the back of the vehicle to open both doors. He started the engine and radioed the hospital so they'd be prepared for Noreen's arrival, and then he rolled out the gurney so it was ready to accept the patient.

The ambulance carrying The Captain had already departed. He held Gia's hand and stared at the house they used to call home. The fire hadn't caused any visible damage outside. He didn't really care if the interior was gutted. That's how his insides felt.

Three firemen emerged through the front door with a limp figure between them. Her face was so black he didn't recognize her. One man braced her beneath the shoulders and the other two were on either side. A fourth man rushed to them when they appeared and braced Noreen's left leg. Two additional paramedics raced the stretcher to meet them. As soon as they situated Noreen on the ambulance bed and rolled it inside, someone hopped into the driver's seat and Rob and Joe jumped in the back. They immediately began an oxygen feed and started an intravenous line.

The men looked up when he lifted Gia inside and climbed in behind her. "We're coming with you." It wasn't against the rules and he didn't give a damn if it was.

He listened intently to the checklist Rob and Joe recited, all too familiar with the readings they called out, assigning his own assessment to the levels they recorded. Blood pressure. Low. Too low. Pulse. Weak. Barely discernible. Breathing labored. Lung sounds. Cloudy.

His eyes scanned Noreen's body, stopping abruptly when he saw Gia's burgundy blanket tied around her leg, blackened, and smudged.

An alarm sounded and Rob and Joe reacted simultaneously.

"She's in arrest."

"Get the paddles."

Rob grabbed the hem of Noreen's charred hospital shirt and slit it up the middle. "What the hell?"

Mr. Fox stared back at them from his hiding place in Noreen's bra. Blake reached and snatched it out of their way, marveling at the woman unconscious and unresponsive before him. She'd put herself in danger and risked her life for his daughter. And son of a gun if she didn't take a second to remember how much this dirty, torn stuffed animal meant to Gia.

Noreen Jensen couldn't die. She had to survive. He loved this woman.

Blake watched his friends fight to revive Noreen. This must be what the quarterback feels like sitting on the sidelines during the game. Calling the plays in his head but restricted from running out on the field and lobbing the ball. All he could do was squeeze his daughter, sitting on his lap, watching the men's orchestrated movements as intently as he did. Gia pressed her stuffed animals around the flashlight and against her heart. Her chin pulsed in small blips while she fought the urge to cry.

Likely his face contorted from the same emotions. If Noreen

died, he might cry his eyes out right here in this ambulance. He watched the heart monitor and released a breath when an erratic rhythm resumed. The line wavered in strength but it was a sign that Noreen was still with them.

Outside the emergency room entrance at the General Hospital adjacent to Children's Hospital, more doctors and nurses waited than was necessary to receive one patient. But like his brother firefighters, the dozen folks dressed in colorful hospital scrubs waited for family. Blake held back inside the ambulance until Noreen's stretcher was extracted and rolled into the building.

Then he and Gia climbed out and walked hand-in-hand inside. They stood helpless against the wall while the medical staff scurried in and out of the cubicle where Rob and Joe deposited Noreen. He couldn't read their faces, but no one smiled.

Joe emerged from behind the curtains and joined him as a police officer he didn't recognize approached.

"Lieutenant Matthews, I have a lot of questions I'd like answered."

Blake smirked at him. "You and me both." Gia tightened her grip in his hand.

Joe had Gia's blanket balled in his hands. In answer to his questioning gaze, Joe shrugged. "It's touch and go, Lewey. She used this to bind a nasty left tibia break." He passed the blanket to Blake and he lowered it to his daughter's outstretched hands. Wordlessly, she buried her face in it.

He refocused on Joe. "What's your initial assessment?"

"She inhaled quite a bit of smoke and her shirt was burned. I don't know the extent of the damage to her back and shoulders." Blake's eyebrows rose in question. "You couldn't see the burns with her laying on the cot and our first concern was stabilizing her. But I saw charred skin on her side and lower neck when they stripped off what was left of her shirt. I don't know about other injuries, possibly internal ones. The doctors were examining her more thoroughly."

"Is she stable?"

Rob stepped up beside Joe. "Not yet. But don't give up on her. We found her at the bottom of the stairs to the basement. If she was in that underground room as you suspect, that's a hell of a distance she dragged herself. How she planned to get up the steps with that splintered bone and in the middle of a fire is beyond me. But she didn't plan to go down easy." Gia stared up at him, listening intently and he cupped her chin and smiled. "Nurse Noreen wasn't throwing in the towel. Neither should we."

"Daddy, I'm hungwy."

The police officer shifted from one foot to the other. "I need to make out a report, Lieutenant."

Blake cast his eyes toward the curtains that concealed Noreen and the activity going on to save her life. It might be awhile, maybe hours, before anyone knew her fate. He lifted Gia into his arms and nodded to the cop. "Let's go to the cafeteria so I can feed my daughter. I don't know if she can help us connect the dots but I'll do the best I can to answer your questions."

He raised his chin to acknowledge Rob and Joe. "Will you let me know if there's any news?"

Joe shook his head. "I'll let the receiving desk know we're in the cafeteria. We're not leaving the hospital until we know Noreen's condition. I'd like to hear what Gia can tell us." Beside him, Rob agreed.

Blake settled Gia into a booster seat at a cafeteria table in the corner where they had a little privacy. Joe, Rob, and the police officer circled chairs around them. For a while, no one spoke. They watched Gia pick apart a gooey grilled cheese sandwich and alternate bites of it with pieces of fruit from a bowl. She'd begun her meal by emptying a carton of chocolate milk and flashed a grateful smile at Blake when he set a second one beside her plate. Once the sandwich and fruit were gone, Blake suggested a dish of ice cream, which Gia happily agreed to. The joy of watching his daughter spoon the creamy chocolate treat into her mouth was overshadowed by his memory of the last time he bought his daughter a cup of ice cream. The ice cream shop where Noreen met them for the first time. Where The Captain initially saw them together. Was that what started it all? He'd assumed it was the custody papers that pushed Lynne over the edge. But perhaps her insanity was seeded deeper.

"Lieutenant?" The cop blushed as if embarrassed. "I'm not sure where to start."

He understood the officer's dilemma. After a deep breath, he nodded. "I reported my daughter missing three days ago after her school called me. Her teacher chastised me for not letting her know in advance that Gia, ah, Argia, and her mother were planning a trip. Only as far as I knew, there were no such plans."

Four pairs of eyes studied him, including Gia's, two last spoonfuls of ice cream forgotten in the bowl. "It took more than twenty-four hours for me to contact my ex-wife after that phone call."

"Where was she?"

He shrugged. "I've no idea. But she wasn't at home." No need to tell this cop that he'd searched the house without permission. At least not yet. He glanced at Rob, certain his brother wouldn't offer up the information. "I sat in my truck in the driveway until three in the morning waiting on her."

"Is that the Riviera Road address you refer to?"

"Yes, sir. When The Cap, er, when Lynne finally returned my phone call—I lost track of how many times I called her but phone records will bear witness—she claimed she didn't know where Gia was and when I told her what the school told me, she accused Gia's teacher of lying."

"What would make your wife say that?"

"Ex-wife. We're divorced. And I don't know why she would make that false accusation except that she is insecure and possessive and needy. The day before all this happened, she was served with custody papers. I'm taking her to court for full custody of my daughter."

Gia rested her hand on his thigh, reached to slide the flashlight, now wrapped in her blanket, Mr. Fox and Mr. Dog along the table closer to him, and crawled into his lap. He drew the items nearer to them and repositioned Gia's ice cream. But she'd lost interest in the treat.

He kissed the top of her head. "She belongs with me." Bright eyed, Gia grinned at everyone around the table, eliciting a smile from each man who watched her.

"From that point, officer, all I can tell you is that I launched a full-blown search for my daughter. I suspected my ex-wife of something devious. It seems I was right. In the process of looking for Gia, we discovered that Nurse Noreen Jensen was also unaccounted for."

"We?"

Blake motioned with his head toward Rob and Joe. "My friends."

"What is Nurse Jensen's connection to your ex-wife?"

Blake cleared his throat while Rob and Joe each found an abstract point on the ceiling to study. There was no explaining how quickly the woman whom he thought an enemy had endeared herself to him or how, naked in his arms, she'd invaded every pore of his body and made it hers. His heart raced now thinking about how she tasted, how she rode him, and how she slept peacefully in his embrace after they made love. If he had a captain in his life, it was Noreen. She was the captain of his heart.

"Nurse Jensen's connection is to me, Officer." Gia twisted her face upward to see him and he gazed at his daughter. "I believe my daughter and I are both in love with her."

Gia smiled, refocused on the police officer, and nodded, earning a chuckle from the group.

"Do you know how Nurse Jensen came to be at the Riviera Road location?"

He nodded. "I believe I do. My ex-wife called her and asked her to go there. She said Gia was sick and needed attention."

The police officer looked up from the notes he scribbled in a pocket-sized notebook. "Why wouldn't she call a doctor? Or take her to the hospital?"

"I'm afraid you'll have to ask her that, Sir. The last phone call to Nurse Jensen is from my ex-wife, pleading with her to come to the house."

"How do you know that?"

Blake stared at the cop until he got the message that he wasn't answering that question.

"What happened after that?"

His heart ratcheted up a notch. What did happen? "I can't answer that question."

All eyes riveted on Gia. Blake leaned in and whispered loud enough for everyone to hear. "Gia, honey, do you know what happened when Nurse Noreen came to mommy's house?"

An emphatic negative headshake answered his question.

The group remained silent. He tried again. "Gia, can you tell me what happened in mommy's house?"

Tears spilled down her cheeks and she twisted in his lap until she lay against his chest and hugged his neck. Blake shook his head. "I've no idea what she's been through. Hell most likely. I'll talk to her but this obviously isn't the time."

Now he rubbed small circles against her back. "I need to take her home and sink her into a nice bubble bath. Some clean clothes and maybe a little more to eat. Then I'll try talking to her. That will have to do for now."

The officer cleared his throat. "Would you mind if I questioned her?"

Gia's grip around his neck tightened. "With all due respect, that's not going to happen, Officer." He leveled a stare on the man meant to convey menace.

Joe touched the man's arm. "I suggest we locate Lynne Matthews and hear what she has to say. That will give Lieutenant Matthews time to tend to Argia and by then, everyone will be a little calmer."

He stood, drawing the cop up with him. "Let's find out where she was treated and I'll accompany you."

Joe winked and extended his hand to shake Blake's. "I'll contact you as soon as I know something." He was as interested in The Captain's version of events as Blake.

Rob also stood. "I'll stay here and keep tabs on Noreen's condition while you take Gia home. If you want to return to the hospital later, I'll come over and babysit."

It was true, Gia likely needed to rest. But he hated leaving Noreen. Yet, he suspected if Noreen were responsive, she'd instruct him to see to his daughter first. Her patients always came first, no matter what. He learned that the first night they met.

They made their way to the emergency exit and found Noreen's sister and brother-in-law waiting anxiously in the hallway. Tears streaked Noreen's sister's face and Blake's heart stopped.

"Is there a change?" *Please don't let it be the worst news possible.*

The brother-in-law spoke. "They can't stabilize her. She went into arrest again but they brought her back. It's touch and go."

The sister eyed Gia's dirty clothes and disheveled hair. Blake raised his daughter's hand to his lips and kissed the top of it. "This is my daughter, Argia. She was trapped with your sister. I believe your sister saved her life, which I'll be forever grateful for. Gia, this is Nurse Noreen's sister and brother-in-law."

Gia offered a quaking smile.

"I'm going to take her home and get her cleaned up. You're welcome to come with me."

They declined the invitation, which he expected.

"Please take my cell phone number. If anything happens, call me right away. I'll be back as soon as I can."

When he made to leave, Noreen's sister touched his arm. "They haven't told us anything. Why was my sister with your child in a burning house? What is she to Noreen?"

Blake looked from her to Gia and back to Noreen's sister. "It's more a matter of what Noreen is to us, ma'am. We love her."

## 32

Joe's text message to Blake tightened the knots torturing the muscles in his shoulders and amplified the headache he'd battled since this whole ordeal started days ago. He tossed two more painkillers to the back of his throat and swallowed them dry.

Soon, his stomach would protest the invasion of the combination anti-inflammatory and aspirin caplet that likely would float in his belly on a sea of black coffee.

Just as Joe had taken it upon himself to keep Lynne under surveillance at her house, he stood sentry outside the hospital room where doctors treated her facial injury. Likely it was easy for him to get away with that, since the last time Blake saw him, he still wore his paramedic uniform. According to Joe, The Captain screamed loud and long to anyone who would listen, demanding that Rob be arrested for assault, and Noreen and Blake be arrested for kidnapping and attempted murder. She also insisted that her daughter be returned to her immediately. She was adamant that if she didn't get her way, she'd sue the hospital, the police department, the city, county, state, and United States president if she had to.

The punch to her face fractured the bridge of her nose but not hard enough to misalign it and require surgery. Instead, the doctors packed her nose and prescribed pain medication. She launched her tirade after the medical staff informed her she could return home and asked her to sign release papers.

Not only did she demand to be admitted and monitored for a possible concussion and further facial complications from "the attack" she suffered, Joe said she demanded twenty-four-hour police protection until Blake and Noreen were locked up. Never mind that Noreen was fighting for her life in another hospital.

Not wanting Argia to overhear a conversation, Blake opted to text back.

"Are they taking her seriously? I have Gia here. If the police show up on my doorstep, I'm screwed."

"Can't tell. Don't think so. Haven't seen cops yet but news crew on scene. Security keeping them outside. Texting Brittni to head over to your house just in case."

Of course, this would capture media interest. Gia had been the subject of an Amber Alert and the news team monitored the police and fire emergency bands. They'd be aware of the Riviera Road fire and, if neighbors on the street had witnessed all the commotion, may already know that Gia had been located. Caught up in the events, he hadn't paid attention to onlookers.

Rob was still onsite at the hospital waiting for word about Noreen. The police hadn't shown up there either. Maybe that was a positive sign and they weren't taking The Captain's allegations seriously.

At least here at home with his daughter safe again, his heart felt lighter. He watched Gia play in a bubble bath with her tub toys, chattering happily to them about nonsensical topics. She wondered about the smell of the fresh bar of soap, marveled at the feel of the bubbles between her toes, and expressed gratitude over the brightness of the room. She'd asked him to turn on all the lights and leave them on. The sweet sound of her voice brought tears to his eyes. Christ, for a man who never cried he'd sure been emotional in the last eight hours.

Once her fingers and toes were wrinkled and her hair washed, he wrapped her in a fluffy white cotton robe and carried her into her bedroom. Sitting on the bed behind her with Gia between his legs, he began brushing her hair while she settled the flashlight between Mr. Fox and Mr. Dog in her lap. The dull beam had finally burned out and the fox's head dangled from three frayed cords. It was clear that Gia felt safer with these things within reach and he wasn't about to question that. He felt safer with her in his reach.

He eyed the tattered stuffed toys. If they could talk, he'd have answers to the questions everyone was asking. They couldn't. But with a little coaxing, Gia might.

He strived to sound casual while he tended to her. "I'll take a look at Mr. Fox after we get you dressed. I think I can fix him."

"No, Daddy. Noween will make him all better, she pwomised."

His throat closed with emotion. *From your lips to God's ears, honey. Please.*

"Did she promise that?"

Gia's head bobbed.

"How did Mr. Fox get hurt?"

She raised the dirty, partially decapitated animal to her lips and kissed its face. Just when he was certain she wasn't going to answer, she whispered and he leaned in close to catch her words. "Mother twisted him. I told her I wasn't allowed down the steps but she made me, Daddy. She said she'd hort me too. Like she did my arm."

His hands stopped in the middle of a hair braid and his blood pressure spiked, along with his anger. Gia hadn't fallen down the steps. Her mother had manhandled her. He'd better never lay eyes on the bitch again. Despite his fingers trembling with wrath, he resumed braiding her hair. He cleared his throat and coughed to allay his fury.

"You're not in trouble for going downstairs, peanut. Don't worry about that. What did your mom say once you and Mr. Fox and Mr. Dog went downstairs?"

Now she drew the dog to her chest and buried her face between the toys. "Mother hort me. She pinched my neck and shoved me onto a doorty bed. She said I had to wait for you and she made my foot not move. I cwied and Mother yelled at me. Then she slammed the door and it was weally dark."

Gia turned in his lap and he pressed her against his shoulder. "We twied to be bwave, Daddy, but we were ascared."

She began to sob and he peppered the top of her head with kisses, clutching her as tightly as he could without crushing her ribs. "You were brave, Gia. And I'm so proud of you. I love you so much. You should've known Daddy would come for you. I'd crawl to the edge of the earth to find you. But it's okay if you were scared. I understand." He forced a smile. "I was scared too, you know."

Droplets clung to her eyelashes when she raised her eyes to look at him. "Yep, I was afraid if I didn't find you, I'd never have twofers again. How about giving daddy his twofers?"

Her lips quivered but she smiled and kissed him on the left cheek, then the right, then his forehead and finally his mouth. He'd relish that ritual until the day he died. He eased her backward by the shoulders. "Gia, what happened when Nurse Noreen got there?"

Her face paled. "She couldn't walk, Daddy. Her leg was hort weal bad." Then Gia's face exploded in a triumphant smile. "But I helped fix it."

His heart overflowed with love for this child. "You did? How d'you help do that?"

"I got the sticks for Noween. And she wapped my blankey around her leg and tied it and my finger held it tight." She raised her forefinger in the air to show him. "Noween said you would find us, Daddy, and you did. She made me wun out the woom.

Mother twied to gwab me but Noween hit her. I was ascared but I wunned."

"Is that when you dropped Mr. Fox?"

She nodded. "But not the light. Noween said not to let go of the light."

Ah, maybe that explained the attachment to the flashlight. He moved it closer to her side.

"Noween saved Mr. Fox cause she's gonna fix him good as new. She pwomised."

He was starting to piece together the puzzle but so many questions still remained. How did The Captain lure Noreen to the basement and how did she injure her leg? The doorbell rang and Blake scooped Gia up to go answer it.

Brittni smiled at Blake and hugged Gia. "Joe suggested I come over, Lieutenant, just in case."

He hated to leave Gia, but there'd been no word from Rob and he wanted to know about Noreen. Brittni followed them into the living room. "Gia, how about if you take a nap and Miss Brittni stays with you while I go check on Nurse Noreen?"

Gia shook her head. "No, Daddy, I wanna come with you."

"But peanut, you should rest. I don't want you getting sick. You need your sleep." He almost said beauty sleep, the phrase The Captain always used. All those hours she logged asleep hadn't worked. She was ugly to the core.

"If I get sick, Noween will take cawer of me. She's a norse. And she loves me, Daddy, she telled me." Her own mother rarely, if ever, told her that. "I wanna see Noween too."

Brittni read the indecision on his face. "I'll come to the hospital with you, Sir. That way, if I need to watch Argia, I can." Gia eyed her and she added, "Sometimes only grown-ups are allowed in the hospital rooms if the patients are really sick and that means you and I would have to wait outside."

The explanation appeased Gia. And Blake. If the police

decided to follow up on Lynne's accusations and arrest him, Gia would be in capable hands.

The three of them arrived at the hospital and located Noreen's sister and brother-in-law pacing the family waiting area on the intensive care floor.

On the way, Joe sent another text.

Docs releasing your ex. Police taking her to file formal complaint. Doesn't look good. Brittni there yet?

Minutes after Blake responded, Brittni's phone rang and she excused herself to take Joe's phone call.

Dark circles ringed Noreen's sister's eyes. Her clothes, and her husband's, were wrinkled and they both looked haggard. "I thought Rob Yarnell was here."

Noreen's sister shrugged. "He left with a policeman. I think they arrested him."

When he asked, she said Noreen remained unresponsive and the doctors hesitated to offer a prognosis. Since being relocated to the intensive care unit, they'd seen her twice.

"How's she look?"

"Pale. They cleaned her face but her hair is matted with dirt and soot. Her chest, back and arms are burned and they say based on her lung sounds, she inhaled too much smoke." Noreen's sister wrung her hands. "We still don't know what happened. Please, Mr. Matthews, can't you tell us something?"

He settled Gia in a corner chair with a coloring book and crayons. He instructed her to draw a picture to cheer up Noreen. Motioning toward the opposite side of the room, but keeping his eyes on his daughter, he squeezed Noreen's sister's shoulder. "First of all, call me Blake. Please. I only have half the story and a portion of what I think I know comes from my five-year-old so keep that in mind. I'll tell you what I know, or at least suspect."

Where to start? They cared about Noreen, not The Captain's demented ideas about how to be a mother. No sense complicating matters with the Munchausen's concerns.

"Noreen treated Gia for a broken arm several weeks ago. That's how we all met, at the hospital. It seems anyone who meets my daughter immediately takes a liking to her and your sister was no different. She cares about her patients to begin with and when she becomes attached to one, her devotion intensifies. Noreen followed up on Gia's progress after the hospital discharged her and became friendly with my ex-wife. It appears that my ex-wife called Noreen and asked her to go to her house and check on Gia, claiming that she was ill.

"It shouldn't surprise you that Noreen did just that. It's not clear what happened after that but we know that Noreen and my daughter were locked in an underground room in the basement for at least three days. And it appears that Noreen was instrumental in helping my daughter escape, risking her own life in the process."

"Wait a minute." The brother-in-law held out a calloused hand. "Who locked them in the basement? And why?"

Blake felt the weight of the world on his shoulders. He hadn't done the actual deed but he felt responsible.

"I have no proof, but I believe it was my ex-wife. I'm simplifying the story for you because—"

"Why would your ex-wife do something like that?" Noreen's sister couldn't comprehend it. Neither could he. "You said she and my sister became friends."

"Not friends. Friendly. For Gia's sake, Noreen was friendly toward my ex-wife. I'm afraid the catalyst for all that happened is my fault. At least I suspect so. My ex-wife is mentally unstable, in my opinion. I filed custody papers to fight for my daughter the day before this all exploded. And," he hesitated. Were he and Noreen involved? Her family hadn't even known about him.

Noreen's sister pressed for more. "And what?"

"And your sister and I started seeing each other."

In unison, their eyebrows jerked upward and each of them gasped. They both spoke at once, asking different questions, talking over each other. Noreen's sister straightened her back, much like Noreen did when morphing into authoritative mode. He couldn't contain a smile.

"What exactly do you mean by seeing each other? I speak to my sister regularly and she's never mentioned you beyond helping you in the street one day at a car accident. She would've told me if there was a new man in her life."

At the same time, her husband clenched his fists. "You need to give us a hell of a lot more information than that, Blake. When you say this all exploded, what exploded? What the hell happened?"

Brittni returned and Blake inclined his head toward Gia. She grabbed his arm and whispered, "Joe's on his way. So are the police." Brittni settled beside Gia and began praising her artwork.

Blake looked at the brother-in-law. "It seems I don't have much time. Your question is easier to answer, Sir. Noreen and my daughter were locked in a basement and missing for three days. Somehow Noreen managed to open the door and allow my daughter to run for freedom. Somehow, a fire started in that basement and Noreen was caught in it. I believe my ex-wife is behind all of this but she's telling quite a different story. The police are on their way here and I may be arrested."

He turned to Noreen's sister. "I pray that I'm the new man in your sister's life. I'm disappointed that she hadn't shared with you anything about me. Perhaps because allowing me into her world was complicated. That's pretty obvious considering she's fighting for her every breath right now because she did." He flattened his hand against his chest.

"She owns my heart. I haven't had a chance to tell her that and believe me, it's the first thing I'll say when she's conscious. I know she loves my daughter. I only hope that she feels the same about me."

Joe appeared in the doorway and rushed toward them. "Blake. Maybe you should get out of here." His face was flushed and his voice trembled.

Blake shook his head. "Nonsense. I'm not running away. I haven't done anything wrong." He refocused on Noreen's sister. "You know your sister better than anyone. She wouldn't take me into her arms, into her bed, if I was a bad man. You've no reason to trust me but that's what I'm asking. I'll clear this up. I swear."

Two uniformed police officers strode into the room, assessing the occupants, calculating potential threats. Noreen's sister reached out and squeezed his hand when one of the men spoke to him.

"Are you Lieutenant Blake Matthews?"

He nodded.

"We'd like you to voluntarily come down to the station with us for questioning regarding the fire at your home and your daughter's abduction."

He looked at Noreen's sister, curious about her reaction. In her eyes, he saw Noreen. When she smiled up at him, he exhaled with relief. "We'll be here. And we'll look out for your daughter."

He looked over his shoulder and then addressed the cops. "Give me a minute to explain to my daughter why I'm leaving. She's been through a lot. I need to make certain she's cared for. Then I'll gladly accompany you."

# 33

They didn't handcuff him or make him feel like a criminal. And much to his surprise, when he arrived at the police station and was escorted into a small office, Rob sat at the table with a cup of coffee between his hands. An empty fast food bag lay crinkled on the table.

He shrugged when Blake looked at him with an unspoken question on his lips.

"Simple assault charges. They asked me if I hit her and I said yes. It's not a big deal."

His anger torqued again. "The hell it isn't. A criminal charge could ruin your career."

The detective assigned to Gia's disappearance tossed a manila folder on the table and motioned for him to sit down. "Take it easy, Lieutenant. I'm going to try to knock that down for him a little later. But right now, we need to discuss your ex-wife's accusations. Mr. Yarnell spins quite a story about her and concerns about Munchausen's by proxy. I confess, I'd never heard of the syndrome but while we were waiting for you, I did some research. The Internet is a wonderful thing. It's eye opening to read about. And I suspect frightening as hell to live through."

He nodded and stared at Rob. As always, his men had his back.

He gratefully accepted the Styrofoam cup of coffee a uniformed officer handed him and sat beside Rob. The detective tapped the tip of his pen on the top of the folder. "Mrs. Matthews claims you kidnapped your daughter and tried to kill both of them. She alleges that Miss Jensen is your accomplice and that if she hadn't surprised Miss Jensen and overpowered her, she would've been killed." He nodded toward Rob. "Your co-worker here says Mrs. Matthews was running toward you with the intent to attack you when he interceded." The guy nodded and raised his eyebrows.

"When I asked him why your wife would harbor such hostility toward you, he told me one hell of a story. How about if you tell me what's going on?"

It took almost two hours for Blake to recount Gia's medical history, his initial suspicions about The Captain, Noreen's involvement, and the horror of the last three days. He hadn't spent much time alone so an alibi was not in question. For the most part, Rob remained silent while he spoke, only nodding an acknowledgement whenever the detective looked his way for confirmation.

Blake leaned back in the chair, drained of all his energy and tired of talking.

"May I ask where my ex-wife is now? Is she still here at the police station?"

"No. We released her before you arrived. She seemed encouraged that we were bringing you to the station and that we assured her we'd increase patrols wherever she decided to stay. The fire department said the house is uninhabitable. She seemed unsure about temporary lodging."

As far as he knew, she had no friends she could bunk with. He had no idea where she might go.

"The ball's in your court, detective. I don't know how you prove what happened until Miss Jensen is able to corroborate my suspicions. You can be a hard ass and detain me longer. Or you can let me go back to the hospital and to my daughter. I left her with my colleagues and Nurse Jensen's sister but quite frankly, I'm uneasy with my ex-wife roaming around at will and my daughter possibly vulnerable."

The sinking feeling in his stomach was groundless. Gia was with Joe and Brittni and they'd guard her with all they had. Plus, Noreen's sister assured him she'd watch Gia. But he wouldn't relax until he had her in his line of sight.

Forty-five minutes later, with Rob by his side, they exited the police station. He clapped Rob on the back.

"I'll pay that misdemeanor fine for you, buddy. That was a lovely right hook. The finest I've ever seen."

"No thanks. I'll proudly write that check myself. She had it coming. And more, if you ask me."

"I hear ya."

Noreen couldn't discern the sounds. Voices faded in and out. Her chest was weighted down, as if a car parked on top of it. She had no feeling on her left side and couldn't move her leg. She bobbed in and out of consciousness like an ocean buoy. When she opened her eyes, the brightness hurt. But she didn't want to be in the dark anymore.

Shadowy figures circulated around her. Looming forms standing close, tugging on the lines taped to her arms, and then vanishing. Replaced by different sized shapes. Taller. Broader. A soft, constant rhythm of blips repeated somewhere behind her head.

Taking a deep breath hurt. Moving was painful. Focusing her thoughts fell just out of reach. Still, she reached.

*Think, Noreen. What do you remember?*

Flames. Smog blanketing her, suffocating her. Argia running. Lynne Matthews screaming like a banshee, her teeth outlined in blood. Dirt clogging her mouth. Noreen gagged in reflex. Agonizing leg pain. Mr. Fox pressed to her breasts. Mr. Fox!

The motion took forever but Noreen raised her right hand and pressed it to her chest. *Where was Mr. Fox?*

"Noreen? Can you hear me?"

Shuffling sounds and commotion from the doorway. Multiple shadows on her right side.

"Noreen? Open your eyes." *That was her sister's voice. What was she doing here?*

"Miss Jensen? Squeeze my hand if you can hear me." A man's voice she didn't recognize, but she did as she was told. His hand was strong and warm. Blake?

Now a blinding beam of light shined directly in her right eye. She jerked her head away.

"I think she's coming around." *No, that wasn't Blake's voice.*

"Noreen." *Her sister again.* "Noreen, open your eyes for me. Right now!"

And she did. She blinked to clear her vision. Was there gauze across her face? Everything looked hazy.

Her sister sobbed. Her brother-in-law beamed and made the sign of the cross. Their faces slowly came into focus. Her eyes jerked to either side of them. She recognized the nurse and the floor doctor but she saw no one else. Blake. Where was Blake? And Argia?

She tried to wet her parched lips but her mouth was as dry as a stale piece of toast.

"Here. Take an ice chip."

Cold and wet, she pressed her tongue to the roof of her

mouth until cool water teased her tongue. Then she licked her lips.

She eyed her spectators, each one smiling broadly. Her sister's cheeks wet.

"Blake?"

It was barely a whisper and she repeated it, straining for volume. "Blake. Where's Blake?"

Her sister's eyes widened but she touched and clasped her hand. "We're calling him now."

Her brother-in-law punched the screen on his phone and raised it to his ear. *Why would he have Blake's phone number?* She scanned the room a second time.

"Argia? Where's Argia? Is she okay?"

The adults whispered to each other and nodded in agreement before her sister moved out of sight. In seconds, she returned carrying Argia.

The little girl's face burst into a broad smile and Argia cried out. "Noween." Before her sister knew what happened, Argia wiggled out of her arms and fell to the bed with a thud. Every inch of pain that coursed through Noreen's body was worth it when Argia spread her arms across her shoulders and dropped her head onto her chest.

"Noween. They said you were sleeping but I was ascared you wouldn't wake up. Do you feel bettor now?"

She stroked Argia's hair, inhaling deeply to fill her damaged lungs with the smell of baby shampoo. Her lips edged up. Yes. She felt better now.

"I'm fine, honey." She didn't recognize her voice. So raspy. "What about you? Are you okay?"

Argia pushed herself up using Noreen's chest for leverage and she grunted.

"Careful, Argia. You can't press on Noreen like that. Her insides are hurt." Her sister was in mother mode.

"Sowwy, Noween. I wunned when the door opened just like

you told me." She held up the flashlight, no longer emitting a shine. "I keeped the flashlight. Just like you said. And I found Daddy." Now, she proudly displayed the dirty stuffed animals. "And Mr. Dog and Mr. Fox are safe now. But you still have to make Mr. Fox all better. You pwomised."

Noreen laughed at the absurd distortion of the stuffed toy, immediately regretting the reaction when a jolt of pain shot through her chest. "I'll make him better, I promise."

Blake. Where was Blake?

If Argia was here, Blake couldn't be too far away. But why wasn't he here? If he didn't care about her, he at least should keep Argia in sight considering all she'd been through. Had he come to rescue them and been hurt in the fire? Was he in his own hospital bed in another room? Did the police believe Lynne Matthews' outrageous story and arrest him? If that was the case, she should speak to someone right away.

She groaned and lifted herself up, attempting a sitting position. In minutes, two pillows supported her back and she relaxed against them. Argia settled in against her side and Noreen stroked her arm, aware that her sister, brother-in-law, Joe and Brittni watched.

"Where's your daddy, Gia?"

Joe stepped toward the bag of fluids dripping steadily into her arm and studied the settings. He spoke softly. "The police asked him to go to the station and, ah, make a statement. We expect him back soon."

She narrowed her eyes. "Really?"

Joe's eye movements glided from her face to Argia and back to her. "That's our expectation."

The sinking feeling in her stomach disturbed her. Like a foreboding of impending evil. "Was he okay?"

Joe nodded but her sister spoke up.

"He seemed fine, Noreen. Relieved that his daughter was safe but rather anxious about you. I think you've been holding out on me, little sister. Why didn't I know about Blake Matthews?"

"Daddy likes Noween." Argia announced her news with a toothy grin and the bystanders chuckled.

Noreen smiled at her sister. "Now you know."

From behind them, Sheila, the intensive care monitor clapped her hands to gain their attention. "What are all of you doing in here? This isn't a visitor's window."

Her gaze fell on Noreen and she smiled broadly. "Oh Noreen, honey, it's so good to see you alert." Sheila squeezed her colleague's shoulder. "But you can't over exert and you know rules are rules." She checked her watch. Visiting hours in this unit were on the hour in fifteen-minute blocks. "I'll let your family back in as soon as it's allowed."

Noreen couldn't argue. On her floor, she adhered to the rules too.

Joe reached for Brittni's hand and gestured. "We're not relatives but that's all right, nurse. Now that we know Noreen will be fine, we don't need to come back in. We'll wait until Blake returns and then we'll rustle up some food for everyone. Something more than the cafeteria has to offer."

Looking toward Noreen he nodded. "I'm glad you're going to be okay, Noreen. Welcome to the family."

Her heart leapt. She understood his meaning and the words meant the world to her. Brittni kissed her lightly on the cheek and they left the room.

Her sister likewise leaned in to kiss her. "We'll be back in when we're allowed, hon. Unless that man of yours shows up and wants you all to himself. I'll give him five minutes and then I'm coming in."

Sheila eyed Argia, fast asleep against Noreen's side.

"She's been through an ordeal, Sheila. Don't disturb her. She's not bothering me and, quite frankly, I'll rest easier if she stays by my side. At least until her father gets here."

Sheila nodded. "How's your pain? Do you want something to take the edge off?"

She did. Every inch of her ached. But she wasn't about to take drugs while Argia was in her care. And not until she saw Blake. She wanted to be coherent when she confessed that she'd fallen in love with him and hoped that he'd make room in his life for her. In his and Argia's lives because he'd described them once as a package deal. And she very much wanted the whole bundle.

"I'm fine. I'll rest, don't worry."

Sheila removed the extra pillows and dimmed the lights. Noreen kissed the top of Argia's head and closed her eyes. She needed sleep. And maybe when she woke up, Blake would be here.

## 34

Blake and Rob made their way to the intensive care floor. His step was lighter in part because Joe texted that Noreen was alert, responsive, and asking for him, and also due to the voice message the brother-in-law left, requesting that Blake return to the hospital as soon as possible because Noreen wanted to see him.

Considering the guy hadn't known Blake existed until several hours ago, it was a small sign of acceptance. At this point, it didn't matter if Noreen's sister and brother-in-law approved of him or not. As long as Noreen did.

That was a matter he wanted to discuss with her. To make clear that, if she'd have him and Gia, he wanted to spend time with her. A giant block of time. Like the rest of his life. That new horizon he planned to set sail for? He wanted Noreen Jensen by his side at the helm.

They encountered Joe when the elevator doors opened.

Joe's head bobbed. "She looks good. A little beat up but coherent. She was asking for you."

Out of the corner of his eye, Blake noticed a nurse in dark blue hospital scrubs move through the swinging double doors that separated the patient area from the public. 'Medical personnel only' was stenciled on the front. He squinted to watch her movements. Something seemed familiar about her posture. And the wavy ponytail down her back.

"They kicked us out of her room." He returned his attention to Joe. "Visiting hours are on the hour. I'm making a food run." He held up a list and Blake smiled at his familiar scrawl. "Either of you want something? There's a burger joint around the corner."

Blake couldn't remember the last time he ate but the idea didn't appeal to him. Rob requested a burger and fries. Before they departed, he grasped Joe's hand and shook it warmly. Through the windowpane, he watched the nurse slow her pace, peering into each cubicle. Her uniform was blue. Everyone else on this floor wore green scrubs.

Joe sensed his preoccupation. "Lieutenant? You okay?"

Blake focused on him. "Yeah, yeah Joey. I'm fine." He pumped Joe's hand. "I'll never be able to thank you or Brittni. Is she still with Gia?"

Joe inclined his head. "Britt's in the waiting room with the others. Argia fell asleep beside Noreen in the bed and the nurses allowed her to stay there."

He smiled. There was something comforting about the mental picture of Noreen and Gia resting safely together. "Speaking of sleep, you look exhausted. You should head home."

Joe laughed. "No way. I'll be right back. Everyone is in the waiting area." He pointed down the hallway. "Text me if you change your mind and want something to eat."

That nurse still distracted him. There was something about her manner that he recognized. He hadn't met any of Noreen's coworkers. That wasn't it.

Joe stepped into the elevator.

"Joey, which bed is Noreen in?"

"Last one on the right."

The nurse was halfway down the corridor, still looking in each room. Was she simply checking each patient? A head count, perhaps? Or was it something else? Rob nudged him. "There's the sister."

Noreen's sister and brother-in-law greeted him and Rob with wide smiles. When they entered the room, Brittni also rose and hugged him. "Argia's asleep with Noreen, Lieutenant. She's doing fine."

Blake rubbed the hairs on the back of his neck. They stood on edge.

"Thanks, Britt. I'm going to go check on her."

Noreen's sister grabbed his forearm. "It's not visiting hours yet but..."

He shrugged out of her grasp and hurried out of the room. He glanced down the hall when the elevator chimed to see Joe emerge from the separating doors. He must've forgotten something but he didn't wait to ask. Instead, he peered through the windowpane in search of that nurse. When he didn't see her, he pushed through the double doors and trotted toward the end of the hall.

A high-pitched scream from that direction shattered the silence on the floor. Loud. Wild. Incoherent. And then a crash followed by another scream. And a young child's terrified yelp. Gia. He'd hear her cries even if he was deaf.

He sped the remaining distance and burst into the hospital room. In a scene much like when he barged into Gia's room weeks ago, his eyes fell on a woman leaning over the bed. Same woman. Lynne. Only this time, the occupant under the covers was fighting back.

He grabbed Lynne by the shoulders and thrust her to the side. Her hands flailed in the air and latched onto Noreen's intravenous line, yanking it from her arm. Blood spurted from the vein like an uncontrolled fire hose. Noreen's face was flushed and she wielded Gia's flashlight in her hand, leaning toward the stretching tube until she fell out of bed. Gia. Where was Gia?

Lynne hadn't gone down, only stumbled backward and now she launched herself at him and screeched. "I'll kill you. You son of a bitch. She's my daughter. You can't have her." Her fingernails clawed his face and she kicked his shins.

Noreen screamed. "Somebody help us! Code red! Code red!"

Gia screamed. "Daddy! Daddy!"

And he screamed. "You're done. Do you hear me? It's over."

He wrapped his hands around Lynne's neck and shoved her backward. Her breath assaulted him in the face when he slammed her against the wall. He tightened his grip around her throat. "No more, bitch. Never again." The Captain's eyes bulged and the veins on either side of her head pulsed. Slobber rolled out of her gaping mouth and snot oozed from her nose.

Noreen screamed.

Gia screamed.

Rob and Joe screamed, each of them clutching his biceps, trying to wrench his grip free. Lynne's eyes rolled to the back of her head and her body went limp. It wasn't enough. He wouldn't let go. Not until she was dead.

Large hands from behind wrapped around his chest and tried to jerk him back. The force dragged Rob and Joe with it, both still yanking on his arms. And then smaller fists pelted his thighs. "Daddy! Daddy! No, Daddy!"

In that second, he opened both of his hands and splayed his fingers wide. Lynne's lifeless body sagged to the floor at the same time the men exerted their energy in tandem and wrestled him away. The room was jammed with people but he heard only two sounds. Noreen yelling his name and his daughter's cries, "No, Daddy."

Blake dropped to his knees and Gia flew into his embrace, her wet cheeks sliding against his damp face. He buried his face in her curls, inhaling deeply, calling on the familiar scent of her soap to bring him back to sanity. Rob and Joe rushed to Lynne and her hand fluttered between them, those red fingernails waving like signal flags. She wasn't dead.

With Gia clasped to his chest he pivoted on his knees to see behind him. Noreen lay on the floor in a tangle of bed covers slowly turning blood red, propped up on one elbow, tears spilling down her cheeks, her hand stretching toward him. He crawled closer and reached out to grasp it. His lifeline.

# 35

There was so much uproar in the room Noreen couldn't make out what was happening. All she saw was Blake crawling toward her, Argia clutched to his chest sobbing and him mouthing her name.

He closed the distance between them and she wrapped her arm around him, crushing Argia between them. "Oh my God, Blake, are you all right? Where'd you come from? I thought she was going to kill me." She babbled. And cried. And didn't care.

He breathed heavily and shuddered as if controlled by his own sobs. "I'm sorry," he whispered. "I'm so sorry." And then he kissed her. On her lips. On her nose. On each cheek. He peppered her face with kisses between words. "Are you hurt? How did you save Gia? I'd die if I lost you." And the words that caught her breath. "I love you, Noreen. We both love you."

Argia giggled and kissed first her father and then her, a sloppy wet kiss that sealed the deal for Noreen.

She drew back to see Blake's face and cringed at the bloody scratches over his ear and across his cheek. "I love you too. Both of you."

And then a crowd surrounded them. Hands reached to lift her

off the floor while someone applied pressure to her bleeding arm. Blood still sprayed and everyone within close proximity looked as if they'd been in a paintball battle. And lost.

Hospital security rushed into the room, hollering for everyone to stand down, rushing to Lynne Matthews prone on the floor. Joe knelt beside her.

Her brother-in-law and Rob lifted Blake to his feet while Brittni reached for Argia. It seemed everyone was crying. Blake shrugged off the men and helped settle Noreen back in bed. The pain arcing up her leg was unbearable, driving her to nausea. She dug her fingers into Blake's arm to gain his attention. "Sick."

He read her dilemma immediately and positioned a tray beneath her chin. In the corner, Lynne groaned when Joe and two orderlies lifted her onto a gurney. Noreen breathed a sigh of relief once they rolled her out of the room.

Blake laid a damp cloth across her forehead. Her sister hovered behind him, flanked by her brother-in-law and one of the police officers she recognized from the ice cream shop. Quentin. On the other side of her bed, two nurses fussed over her. She hated being a spectacle like this.

"Please, I'm fine. Enough."

"Miss Jensen?" Quentin likely had a million questions for her.

Noreen immediately raised her free hand. "It was self-defense. She tried to kill me. I'll make a full statement."

Rob stepped to his side. "Give them a minute, Quentin. She's not going anywhere."

Blake leaned into her ear. "I never want to lose you, Noreen."

No need for pain medication now, not with so much love surging through her. "Where's Argia?"

Joe spoke up. "Brittni took her out. I'll get them."

Blake turned. "Joey, what made you come back?"

He shrugged. "I know how you get when you sense something's wrong. It was that look on your face. I didn't feel right leaving when you were that distracted."

Now the female officer who questioned her at the ice cream store stepped into the room followed by a handful of firefighters, some whose faces she recognized. Blake acknowledged each one by name and they encircled her bed, all staring at her expectantly. She must look a sight.

Blake caressed her cheek. "These are the men from Deep Creek Station Twelve, Noreen. This is my squad, my family. In case you haven't figured it out yet, every man in Station Twelve is our back-up. If you decide to take us, me and Gia, I'm afraid you inherit all of us."

The blue wall of men smiled.

"Noween!" Argia stretched her arms out and Blake drew her out of Brittni's arms and settled her in his lap on the bed. One soft hand slid into hers while the other clung to Mr. Dog and Mr. Fox. Noreen gazed around the room nodding to the uniforms.

"I'll have to learn your names. I look forward to getting to know all of you better." She squeezed Argia's hand and leveled loving eyes on Blake. "First let me tell my family how much I love them."

The End

If you enjoyed reading *Loving Gia To Death*, please leave a review on Amazon.

For more about the author, visit renakoontz.com

## SNEAK PEEK

THE DEVIL SHE KNEW

## CHAPTER 1

Black rivulets swirled in the white porcelain sink, gurgling in the drain as it swallowed her old identity. Her head under the faucet, Cassidy Hoake watched the waves of dark liquid fade while she continued to massage her scalp under the warm water. The box said to rinse until the water ran clear. Just a few more minutes.

She grabbed a towel, draped her head, and stood, rubbing vigorously with her eyes closed. Ready or not, she looked at her reflection in the mirror behind the sink.

The new look surprised even her. Gone was the thick, auburn mane her mother had often bragged about. She'd replaced the shoulder-length locks she'd worn since high school with a lustrous black, short haircut that she planned to spike up and out and fringe to frame her face. She stared wide-eyed at herself, then walked barefoot into the bedroom and retrieved a pair of burgundy-framed eyeglasses from the bureau. Thank goodness she'd discovered that year-round costume store. Buying items for a disguise was easy.

Standing in front of the mirror again, she took a deep breath and carefully edged the eyeglasses up her nose. Her eyebrows raised in surprise at the result. She barely recognized herself. Surely, he wouldn't.

Clay Cestra gently laid his nephew in the crib and switched on the overhead mobile. Four stuffed bears in football jerseys and helmets began to circle slowly around a plush football in the center. Softly, the Ohio State fight song played, making him smile. He checked to make sure the baby monitor was switched on, then quietly walked out of the nursery, leaving the door halfway open. Carrying his sister's cell phone, he walked to the bathroom.

He knocked on the open bathroom door. "I'm going in to work early, Sis, and relieve Dan. Are you sure you're okay? Do you want Dan to bring you anything?"

Maggie Armstrong sat beside the toilet, her back against the wall and a white washcloth molded to her forehead. She opened her eyes and inhaled tentatively. "I think it's stopped. Remind me to never order bleu cheese dressing again. Just ask Dan to come straight home. I'll be fine, go." A weak hand wave punctuated her words.

Clay stepped into the bathroom and leaned over to kiss his younger sister on the forehead. "Jack's asleep." He handed her the phone. "I'll call and check on you when I get to the station."

He retrieved his gun from the top of the china hutch and tucked it into its holster as he walked to the car. Opening the car door, Clay smiled. Who would've ever thought when he introduced his partner to his sister they would end up together? Maggie said the minute she looked into Dan's eyes, her heart lit up with stars. He turned his gaze to the sky. It glowed tonight with a thousand different lights. That must be how she felt.

He drove to the Stakron police station, the full moon casting everything below in a hazy shadow. The midnight shift was his favorite. The city looked softer in the dark and usually, by mid-shift, would be quiet except for the stray drunk, burglar, or speed demon.

Hopefully, tonight would be no exception.

~

Cassidy loved the chimes on her mantel clock, one of the few treasures she had left of her mother. It chimed in the other room and she counted twelve bells. Midnight and she was wide awake. Tomorrow, she started her new life, or at least would try again to forget her old one. The gold clock under its glass dome stuck out in the dowdy room like a rose in the desert. She had no furniture in there except for a folding card table and two chairs she bought at a garage sale. The room was a combination kitchen and living area squished into one square space. Her bedroom was just as sparse, with only a recycled full-size mattress and box spring on the floor in the corner and a scratched and worn nightstand and lamp. She'd cleaned the two rooms as best she could, but the carpet still looked filthy and the windows seemed permanently stained.

A dozen second-hand throw rugs she'd laundered twice protected her bare feet from the dirt-packed carpet and marked a path through the apartment, like the yellow brick road leading the way for Dorothy. She tiptoed along the rugs to the apartment door, knowing it was latched, but needing reassurance. She checked the deadbolt, patted the door chain, and then made sure the two windows in the front room and the one in the bedroom were locked. She'd rented here for two weeks now and still the noises of the other tenants unnerved her. How long would it take to get used to that?

Fully clothed, Cassidy pulled the blankets back and slipped into her makeshift bed, longing for the soft cotton comforter on the four-poster she used to own. That was another thing she would have to get past, sleeping with her clothes on. Always ready to run.

She dozed fitfully, ready to wake the second the radio alarm filled the room with soft jazz. She bathed, applied her makeup, fussed with her new hairstyle until it was just right and stepped into The Packing Place's uniform—black pants and a brown pullover shirt. Yesterday, she rode a test run on the bus to familiarize herself with the route. The seven-ten bus would get her to the store about twenty minutes early. A good way to start her first day on the job.

Cassidy walked in the front door of the store with her shoulders straight and her head high. She remembered an old commercial slogan that suggested, "never let them see you sweat" and decided it would be her new mantra. She could do this. She had no other choice. Her funds were low and she'd been on the run long enough to be tired, really tired. She needed to fly under the radar for a while.

The first handshake with her new boss felt wrong. Warm, slightly clammy, yet forceful, almost clutching, sending a sensation up her arm like a band of tiny ants in a convoy. Wayne Keaseling released her hand and she raised it to the back of her neck, thinking to smooth her hair and shake away the uneasiness. His lopsided smile didn't help.

"You observed what we do here yesterday afternoon, so you know a little of what to expect. I wanted Rosie to train you. She's my assistant manager. But she's not back from vacation yet, so we'll start you with someone else. Any questions you have, any concerns, you come to me." He placed his hand over his heart. "I want you to be happy here."

He turned toward the front of the store and called out to his other employee. "Amber?"

Amber Malone appeared in the doorway flashing a bright white, even-teethed smile that said at one time she wore braces. She inspected Cassidy from her sneakered feet to her oversized glasses.

Cassidy likewise eyed her new co-worker. Amber had a pierced right eyebrow, a pierced tongue, and a microdot in the left side of her nose. A two-inch wide magenta streak highlighted her shoulder-length midnight black hair. Straight cut bangs hung into her eyes, which were outlined in heavy black, as if she used a charcoal briquette to make herself up.

Amber raised the pierced eyebrow and a tiny shudder jolted Cassidy's spine under the intense scrutiny, the second time in her first ten minutes on the job. It was as if Amber saw right through her disguise. Had Cassidy been more like the thug she was running from, she could have changed her name along with her looks and paid for forged documents to authenticate her new persona. But who knew how to do that? Besides, she'd had to show identification to rent her dingy apartment, so a fake name was out of the question. Did Amber recognize her? It was unlikely.

Standing with a hand on one hip, Amber shifted the wad of pink bubble gum in her mouth, cracking it three times in the process. "Sure, Boss, I'll train her."

"Get rid of the nose doo-dad and the gum first. I'm going to the bank and then to the other store. I'll be back later."

He walked out the rear employees' door and Amber stuck out her tongue at his back, giggled, and offered Cassidy a conspiratorial grin. "Welcome." She extended her hand and widened her smile until it reached her eyes, immediately easing Cassidy's anxiety. Unlike the boss' handshake, Amber's was warm and firm, but not dominating.

"I heard you just moved into town. Where'd you come from? No ring on your finger. Have a boyfriend? If you don't, make one up or he'll be all over you. Come over here. I'll show you how to clock in."

Cassidy stood dumbfounded. "What? Who?"

Amber strolled to the computer keyboard and began punching keys. "Don't worry. It will take a while. He'll be on his good behavior at first. Use your name to sign in and you'll need a password. What do you want to use?"

The entry bell chimed and both women looked toward the front door at the day's first customer. Amber smiled and leaned forward onto the counter, using her arms to squeeze her breasts into the opening of her collared shirt.

"Good morning, Officer Good Body. I was a very bad girl last night." She swiveled her hips. "Don't you think you should handcuff me and take me away?"

Mouth agape, Cassidy watched her ball her fists, lock her wrists together, and extend her arms to the police officer standing at the counter.

He chuckled, the movement crinkling his eyes. "Good morning, Amber. You're in rare form this morning."

Amber winked, straightened, and began typing on the computer screen. Cassidy stepped up behind her in time to see a shipping label appear on the screen.

"This is the new girl, Cassidy." Turning to Cassidy, she raised her hand toward the cop. "We have a lot of regular customers. You'll get to know them pretty quick. C.C. is my favorite."

Cassidy turned to the police officer. His dark blue uniform fit snugly, stretching over a broad chest and trim waist. He blushed at Amber's words and extended his hand.

"Clay Cestra. Nice to meet you."

Handshake number three. This one strong, confident and quick. Almost enticing. Much nicer than the boss's.

Amber stepped to the counter with a printed label and handed Clay a pen. Cassidy watched him scrawl his initials on the bottom line and slide a small shipping bag to Amber.

"See?" She showed Cassidy the label. "C.C. That's the way he always signs."

"Good luck with the new job." He spoke over his shoulder as he strode to the door. "I'll see you tomorrow, Amber."

The door chimed again when he exited.

"The police drop off these packages every morning to go to the lab. Some poor drunk got busted last night. These are the swabs. All we have to do is generate this label," she pointed to the button on the computer screen, "and have them initial it. It's usually C.C. coming off the midnight shift or on daylight and he knows the drill. It's only when he's off or on the afternoon shift that someone else comes in."

Amber pointed her forefinger at Cassidy. "Make sure you get this label initialed or it fucks up their chain of evidence. Your initials will show up in this corner. I'll show you where this goes."

Through the course of the morning, Amber explained how to work the computers, how to pack and ship items, and how to operate most of the office equipment designed to provide printing and copying services for customers. She had an easy way with the regulars, calling most of them by their first names and openly flirting with the men.

Cassidy gasped when Amber offered to cook spaghetti for an elderly man and promised a special dessert. He left the store chuckling.

"You wouldn't really go out with him, would you?"

"Nah, he knows I don't mean it. But it makes him feel good to think I might give him a tumble. And I love men. Who knows? If I were drunk enough I might."

The look on Cassidy's face made her laugh.

"You might as well know right up front. I drink. I smoke weed. I like to party and have a good time. Life is too short not to. Most of the girls who work here call me a slut behind my back. I don't give a damn what they think."

"How long have you worked here?"

"Four years. The boss keeps threatening to fire me, but he won't. I always get to work on time and I'm good at my job. I do what he asks me to do. Everything he asks."

The day passed quickly. By the end of her shift, Cassidy felt comfortable processing the basic shipments, called drop-offs because they had preprinted labels on them. Under Amber's guidance she also managed ground, air, and high value shipments and performed multiple copying tasks. Amber proved to be a good teacher, letting Cassidy think through the process and correct her own mistakes while sweet-talking the customers, since the task took a little longer than usual. Everyone was patient. They clocked out together. Amber waved cheerfully and said she'd see Cassidy the next morning.

Cassidy flopped into the back seat of the bus for the ride home. Her feet hurt, her back ached, and she'd broken two fingernails. Each time she bent to pick up a heavy package Amber reminded her to use her legs, but the throb in her lower back screamed she'd have to do a better job tomorrow.

# LEARN MORE ABOUT RENA KOONTZ

Find more of Rena Koontz's books on Amazon
and other online retailers.